Predator to Prey

B.M.K.

ISBN: 979-8-9921172-3-3

Table of Contents

Trigger Warning

This book contains graphic and mature content that may not be suitable for all readers. It is intended for an adult audience and includes themes and depictions that some readers may find distressing or triggering. Please be advised that the story explores and describes:

- Graphic Violence: Including detailed scenes of torture, mutilation, and physical harm.
- Sexual Violence and Assault: Explicit depictions of non-consensual acts and their aftermath.
- Sexual Content: Including explicit consensual and non-consensual sexual acts, BDSM dynamics, and power imbalances.
- Psychological Abuse: Manipulation, degradation, and acts of humiliation.
- Mature Themes: Racism, trafficking, corruption, and power abuse.
- Strong Language: Profanity and explicit dialogue.
- Death and Gore: Graphic descriptions of death, murder, and body mutilation.

This story is a work of fiction and does not condone or glorify the actions depicted within its pages. It is intended to provoke thought, explore complex moral questions, and immerse the reader in a dark and challenging narrative.

Readers are strongly encouraged to assess their comfort levels with such content before proceeding. Your mental and emotional well-being are important—please prioritize them as needed.

If you or someone you know needs help, please reach out to one of these resources:

United States

National Suicide Prevention Lifeline: 988 (or 1-800-273-TALK)

www.suicidepreventionlifeline.org

RAINN (Rape, Abuse & Incest National Network): 1-800-656-HOPE (4673)

www.rainn.org

The National Domestic Violence Hotline: 1-800-799-SAFE (7233) www.thehotline.org

United Kingdom

Samaritans: 116 123 (free 24/7 helpline) www.samaritans.org

National Domestic Abuse Helpline: 0808 2000 247

www.nationaldahelpline.org.uk

Canada

Talk Suicide Canada: 1-833-456-4566

www.talksuicide.ca

ShelterSafe (Domestic Abuse Resources):

www.sheltersafe.ca

Australia

Lifeline: 13 11 14

www.lifeline.org.au

1800RESPECT (National Sexual Assault, Domestic and Family Violence Counselling Service): 1800 737 732

www.1800respect.org.au

Global

Befrienders Worldwide:
www.befrienders.org (For a list of helplines in different countries)

For Trafficking Victims and Survivors

National Human Trafficking Hotline (US): 1-888-373-7888
www.humantraffickinghotline.org

For Mental Health Support

Crisis Text Line: Text HOME to 741741 (US and Canada)
Text SHOUT to 85258
(UK) Text HELLO to 50808
(Ireland) www.crisistextline.org

I was asked to write something dark, twisted, yet undeniably creative and captivating. Predator to Prey is my answer—a story crafted to push my own moral limits. Written by someone with A.D.H.D., for people with A.D.H.D.

To the A'nnas, Michelles, and Katies of the world—stay dark dolls. This one's for y'all!

B.M.K.

Predator to Prey

CHAPTER 1

SIX YEARS

The large auditorium buzzed with warm laughter and the clinking of glasses as family and friends gathered around a long banquet table with silver and gold accents. The centerpiece—a towering cake adorned with intricate lace designs—stood as a testament to the six-year marriage that seemed to defy the odds. The room's ambient lighting cast a soft glow on the couple standing at the center of attention.

Grip Williams, a tall, broad-shouldered man with piercing eyes and a demeanor that hinted at his military past, raised his glass high in a toast. His sharp suit was tailored perfectly to his athletic frame and did little to soften his edge—a reminder of the years he spent as an elite sniper, trained to track and recover assets most people never knew existed.

Beside him stood his wife, Veronica,. Barely reaching his chest in height, she looked like a porcelain doll—delicate and radiant. Her petite frame, flowing champagne-colored dress, and youthful features made her look younger than her twenty-seven years. Her smile exuded a confidence and charm that made it impossible for anyone to mistake her for anything but a woman fully in control.

Grip's deep, commanding voice broke through the hum of chatter. "Family, friends, thank you all for being here tonight. Six years ago, I married this incredible woman beside me, and I can say without hesitation, it was the best mission I've ever taken." His words drew a ripple of laughter.

Veronica smiled up at him, her small hand resting on his arm. "You've been my rock," she said, her voice sweet but steady. "I couldn't imagine navigating life without you."

"Here's to many more milestones," Grip added, raising his glass. "To love, loyalty, and the strength that keeps us moving."

The crowd erupted into cheers and applause, and glasses clinked across the room. Veronica leaned closer to Grip, her voice just audible over the noise. "Did I mention how good you look in that suit tonight?" she teased, her innocent features betrayed by a playful glint in her eyes.

Grip smirked, leaning down to whisper, "Careful, doll. This suit comes off faster than you think."

Their moment was interrupted by a shout from the crowd. "Speech! Speech!" called an older man from the back, prompting laughter and nods of agreement.

Grip waved them down, but his smile stayed. "Maybe later. Right now, I just want to enjoy this moment with all of you. Let's eat, drink, and celebrate."

The couple moved through the crowd, greeting friends and family, unaware that the night would soon take a turn none of them could have anticipated.

The last guests filtered out of the auditorium, their laughter and congratulations fading into the quiet hum of the late night. Grip stood near the entrance, his arm around Veronica as she leaned against his side, a warm, satisfied smile playing on her lips as she looked up at him with eyes full of gratitude. The night had been perfect so far.

"You really outdid yourself," she said softly. "I can't imagine a better way to celebrate six years."

Grip smiled down at her, his hand gently tracing along her back. "Oh, it's not over yet, doll. The best part's still to come."

Before she could respond, a man in a black tuxedo with an air of quiet sophistication approached them. He moved with the precision of someone accustomed to serving the elite, but his presence felt more calculated than ordinary waitstaff.

"Mr. and Mrs. Williams," the man said with a polite bow. "Your car is ready. If you'll follow me, the next part of your evening awaits."

Veronica blinked, turning to Grip with a questioning look. "What's this about?"

Grip smirked, his expression betraying nothing but confidence. "Just trust me."

She let him lead her outside where a sleek, black limousine waited under the soft glow of the streetlights. The driver held the door open, bowing slightly as they approached. Veronica slid into the plush interior first, her dress shimmering in the dim light.

She froze, her breath catching as her eyes took in the scene. The seats were lined with a display of masks—some simple, others ornate with glittering jewels and elegant designs. Beside them lay neatly arranged clothing options, gowns and suits that seemed tailor-made for an exclusive masquerade ball.

"Grip," she said slowly, turning back to him as he climbed into the limo and settled beside her. "What is this?"

He leaned back casually, a knowing grin on his face. "Happy anniversary, doll. I thought it was time we did something ... different."

Her fingers hovered over a delicate mask adorned with black lace and feathers, her eyes wide with curiosity. "You planned all this?"

"Of course," he said, his tone steady. "You think I'd let you handle everything tonight? This is our night, and I wanted to give you a little surprise."

A spark of excitement flickered in her eyes as she picked up the mask, holding it to her face. "A masquerade?"

"Not just any masquerade," he replied, reaching for a sleek, understated black mask for himself. "This one's exclusive. High-end. The kind of place where no one knows who's behind the mask."

Her lips parted slightly as the realization hit her. "You've been planning this for a while, haven't you?"

Grip chuckled, leaning in close, his voice low and warm. "Let's just say I had a hunch you'd be up for an adventure."

The limo purred smoothly through the streets of downtown Houston, the city lights casting fleeting shadows inside the car. Veronica's anticipation grew with each passing block, her fingers brushing over the luxurious fabric of the gowns.

"You always know how to keep things interesting," she said, her voice playful yet sincere.

"That's the idea," Grip replied, his eyes gleaming behind the mask. "You ready to see what's next?"

Veronica smiled, her curiosity and excitement bubbling over. "Let's go, Mr. Williams. Lead the way."

As the limo neared its destination, the energy between them buzzed with the thrill of the unknown. Tonight wasn't just an anniversary, it was an adventure, a celebration, and a testament to the spark that had kept them together for six unforgettable years.

Since returning from the military, Grip Williams had parlayed his elite skills into building a private tactical operations company specializing in high-stakes, covert missions for governments and private clients alike. With contracts spanning the globe and a reputation for delivering results no one else could, the company quickly soared to astronomical success. Today, their wealth rivals that of the world's richest families, granting them a lifestyle of unparalleled luxury and freedom.

Veronica was no stranger to privilege. Born into an immensely wealthy family, her parents had pioneered and later sold a groundbreaking software empire specializing in medical imaging and diagnostics. The sale of the company had secured her family's legacy and afforded Veronica a life of ease. Together, she and Grip formed a power couple, seamlessly blending her old-money sophistication with his hard-earned success.

Their days weren't spent punching clocks or managing mundane tasks; instead, a team of highly capable assistants handled the day-to-day operations of their respective empires. Grip and Veronica only stepped in when their expertise or decisions were truly needed, leaving them free to pursue the finer things in life—and each other.

Their relationship was anything but conventional. Living a non-monogamous lifestyle, Veronica was free to explore her desires with other men, a freedom that Grip not only allowed but encouraged. Watching her find pleasure in the arms of others thrilled him in ways most couldn't understand, deepening their connection and trust. It was this openness, combined with their shared hunger for adventure, that made their bond uniquely unshakable.

CHAPTER 2

THE PARTY

The limo maneuvering through the dimly lit outskirts of Houston, leaving the bustling city behind. As the urban sprawl gave way to quieter roads and sprawling estates, Veronica noticed the walls growing taller, the gates more imposing. Finally, they approached a massive compound surrounded by walls higher than most privacy fences she'd seen, topped with sleek, unobtrusive security cameras that tracked every movement.

At the entrance, after a quick inspection, two armed guards waved the vehicle through, their sharp eyes portraying a no-nonsense demeanor. Beyond the gate, the driveway wound through manicured lawns and lush gardens that framed the sprawling estate at its center. But rather than pulling up to the front, the driver veered toward a side entrance, disappearing into an underground passage.

The parking substation beneath the estate was massive, its ceilings high and floor gleaming under fluorescent lights. Veronica couldn't help but glance out the window at the collection of vehicles parked neatly in rows. From high-end supercars with sleek, angular designs to rugged, unassuming pickup trucks, the eclectic mix suggested the owners here came from all walks of life—or they wanted to remain unseen.

The car rolled to a smooth stop at the far end of the garage, where two figures stood by a heavy metal door. One was a broad-shouldered guard, armed and dressed in tactical black, his stance rigid and his gaze sharp. Beside him stood a sharply dressed man in a tailored suit, clipboard in hand, exuding an air of quiet authority.

Grip exited the limo first, his movements confident and deliberate, and then turned to help Veronica out. Her heels clicked softly against the concrete as she emerged, her provocative red dress hugging her petite frame in all the right places. The mask she wore—a delicate combination of lace and glittering gemstones—concealed just enough of her features to heighten the mystery. Grip, in contrast, was dressed in a sleek black suit, his open collar and matching black mask giving him a commanding, almost predatory edge.

They paused for a moment, Veronica adjusting her mask and running her hands over her dress, while Grip offered her his arm. She accepted it with a sly smile, leaning close enough to whisper, "What happens now?"

"You'll see," Grip said, his voice low, his gaze fixed ahead on the well-dressed man by the door.

They walked toward the entrance, their polished shoes echoing softly in the vast parking garage. As they approached, the man with the clipboard looked up, his sharp eyes assessing them behind wire-rimmed glasses. The armed guard beside him straightened slightly, his hand resting on the weapon at his side.

Veronica felt her heartbeat quicken. Not from fear, but from the intoxicating blend of curiosity and excitement. The door, the guards, the underground setting—it was all so secretive, so forbidden. And with Grip by her side, his confidence unshaken, she felt utterly safe and ready for whatever lay beyond that door.

The limo driver stepped forward, striding confidently toward the men with the precision of someone familiar with such introductions. "Mr. and Mrs. Predator," he announced, his voice echoing slightly in the cavernous parking garage. With a flourish, he produced an intricate card from his pocket and handed it to the well-dressed man with the clipboard.

Veronica's eyes widened as the card caught the light, revealing a futuristic design. The sleek metallic surface shimmered, and as the man with the clipboard turned it, a holographic projection emerged from its center. The glowing emblem with an intricate design seemed to pulse faintly. She tilted her head slightly, intrigued.

"Fancy," she murmured to Grip, who smirked beneath his mask.

Charles studied the hologram briefly before nodding, his sharp features unreadable. "Everything seems in order," he said, his tone brisk but polite. He scanned the card with a small device at his side, which beeped approvingly. "Welcome, Mr. and Mrs. Predator. My name is Charles. Please follow me."

Without another word, Charles turned on his heel, motioning for them to follow. Grip placed a reassuring hand on Veronica's lower back, guiding her as they trailed after their host. The heavy metal door slid open with a hiss, revealing a hallway bathed in dim, sultry lighting. The sound of bass-heavy music and soft, mingling voices drifted toward them, growing louder with every step.

As they walked into the party, Veronica couldn't help but pause for a moment, taking it all in. The room was vast, its ceiling draped with black and crimson fabric, creating a dark, intimate atmosphere. Small chandeliers cast soft, flickering light across the scene, illuminating the lavish gathering. People filled the space—some elegantly dressed, others nude or in provocative outfits, their laughter and conversation blending with the pulsing rhythm of the music.

One corner of the room housed an elaborate buffet where attendees helped themselves to decadent dishes, their plates laden with colorful delicacies. A sleek, polished bar stretched along the wall, manned by bartenders mixing cocktails with effortless precision. On the far side of the room, a dance floor throbbed with energy of bodies swaying to the beat, while others lounged in plush chairs, sipping drinks and watching the scene unfold.

Charles stopped at the bar and turned to face them. "Your room is the fourth door down the lounge hallway on the right," he said, producing a sleek black keycard and handing it to Grip. "This will grant you access. Enjoy your evening. If you need anything, the attendants are available to assist."

"Thank you," Grip said with a curt nod, pocketing the keycard. Veronica stayed silent, her eyes flickering around the room as her mind tried to keep pace with the sheer decadence of it all.

Charles disappeared into the crowd, leaving the couple alone at the bar.

Grip leaned in, his voice low and teasing. "You're staring, doll."

Veronica turned to him, her lips curving into a mischievous smile. "Can you blame me? This is … a lot."

Grip chuckled, signaling the bartender for two drinks. "We've only just begun."

The bartender slid two glasses across the counter—something dark and smooth for Grip and a shimmering cocktail for Veronica.

She raised her glass, her eyes sparkling behind the

mask. "To surprises," she said softly, her voice laced with excitement.

"To adventure," Grip replied, clinking his glass against hers.

They stood there for a moment, savoring the anticipation of what lay ahead. With the keycard in Grip's pocket and the night still young, the possibilities were endless.

The atmosphere grew heavier as Grip and Veronica left the bar, their hands brushing as they wandered deeper into the party. The sultry music pulsed in their ears, reverberating in time with the heat and energy of the room. Each turn revealed something new—something tantalizing, forbidden, and utterly mesmerizing.

The first door they passed stood slightly ajar, revealing a dimly lit chamber outfitted with sleek, black leather furniture and gleaming steel contraptions. Inside, a woman was strapped to a cross-shaped apparatus, her body arching as she gasped under the steady rhythm of a flogger wielded by a masked man. The sound of leather meeting skin mixed with her cries of pleasure, drawing Veronica's attention.

Grip noticed her lingering glance and leaned down to whisper, "Curious?"

She tilted her head up at him, her lips curling into a coy smile. "Maybe."

They continued down the hallway, passing another room where a man crawled on all fours, a leash clipped to the collar around his neck. His handler, a tall, commanding woman in thigh-high boots and a fitted corset, led him confidently around, occasionally tugging on the leash and whispering something that sent him into an obedient bow.

"I guess some people take loyalty to a whole new

level," Grip remarked, his voice rich with amusement.

Veronica giggled, her fingers tightening around his arm as they turned another corner. The next door was wide open, giving them an unfiltered view of a sprawling, oversized bed that looked like something out of a royal fantasy, draped with silk sheets and soft pillows. But what caught their attention was the tangle of bodies. A dozen people at least were entwined in a sensuous, uninhibited display. Hands, mouths, and limbs moved together in a rhythmic dance, their moans blending into a chorus of pleasure.

Veronica's breath hitched, her cheeks flushing as she glanced at Grip. He met her gaze, his expression unreadable behind the mask, though the way his hand rested possessively on her lower back spoke volumes.

"Quite the sight," he murmured, his voice low and intimate.

"I've never seen anything like this," Veronica admitted, her voice barely audible over the hum of activity around them.

They moved on, leaving the enticing spectacle behind as they continued to explore. The energy of the party seemed to shift with every step, alternating between indulgence and mystery. As they rounded another corner, Veronica's gaze lingered on a figure standing alone in the far corner of the room.

The woman was striking. Her confidence radiated even as she stood apart from the crowd. She wore a floor-length blue skirt encrusted with glittering gemstones that shimmered under the low lights, catching Veronica's attention like a beacon. Her top, while elegant, dipped dangerously low, leaving little to the imagination. A delicate mask framed her features, enhancing her piercing green eyes that seemed to glow as they met Veronica's.

Grip felt Veronica pause and followed her gaze, his lips twitching into a small smirk. "See something you like?"

Veronica didn't answer immediately, her focus locked on the woman in the corner. The stranger tilted her head slightly, a knowing smile playing on her lips as if she'd been waiting for this exact moment.

"I think she's looking at me," Veronica whispered, her voice tinged with curiosity and something else she couldn't quite name.

"Oh, she's definitely looking at you," Grip said, his tone teasing but approving. "Go on, doll. Let's see where this takes us."

As Veronica took a hesitant step forward, her pulse quickened. The woman's gaze never left hers. The room seemed to fade around them, leaving only the promise of what might happen next.

The mysterious woman didn't keep Veronica waiting long. As if drawn by an invisible thread between them, she gracefully moved across the room, the glittering gems on her blue skirt reflecting the light with every step. Her presence commanded attention, and the faintest scent of jasmine lingered in her wake. She stopped just short of the couple, her emerald eyes flicking between them with an amused smile.

"Mr. and Mrs. Predator," she said, her voice smooth as silk. "I've heard whispers about you tonight."

Grip tilted his head slightly, his grin playful. "Whispers, huh? I hope they're flattering."

"Always," the woman replied, her lips curving into a mischievous smile. "You may call me Mistress Blue."

Veronica's curiosity flared at the title. "Mistress Blue,"

she repeated. "What brings you to us?"

Mistress Blue's gaze settled on Veronica, her eyes sparkling with a hint of mischief. "I couldn't help but notice you," she said. "Something about you radiates … intrigue."

Before Veronica could respond, Mistress Blue gestured toward the far side of the room where a peculiar setup had gone unnoticed. A man was encased in a black latex vacuum wall, his body immobilized in an unmistakable outline. A narrow breathing tube protruded from the surface, the only connection to the outside world. Nearby, a petite woman with a pixie haircut stood poised, a golf club in hand. She swung with precision, sending a golf ball careening into the latex wall with a loud thwack! that echoed through the room.

Veronica's jaw dropped, and Grip let out a sharp laugh, shaking his head in disbelief. "What in the Hell did he do to deserve that?"

Mistress Blue's smile deepened, her demeanor cool and unbothered. "My pet is being disciplined for a lapse in obedience," she said matter-of-factly. "Lessons must be memorable to be effective."

Veronica tried to stifle a laugh, but it bubbled out anyway, her hand covering her mouth. "I'll say … that's definitely memorable."

Grip's eyes sparkled with amusement as he glanced between the scene and Mistress Blue. "Do you think he's learned his lesson, yet?"

"Not nearly," Mistress Blue replied, her tone light but unwavering. "Though my dear friend over there seems to be enjoying her role as instructor."

The couple couldn't help but laugh again, their mirth

mixing with the surreal energy. Mistress Blue's calm confidence in the face of such absurdity only made the situation more entertaining.

"Well," Grip said, tipping an invisible hat, "to each their own, I suppose."

Mistress Blue nodded, her eyes lingering on Veronica for just a moment longer before returning to Grip. "Indeed. Discipline, like pleasure, comes in many forms."

Another thwack! resounded from across the room, the scene seemed to freeze in time, hanging in the air between them like an unspoken promise of more to come.

Mistress Blue's smile lingered as she regarded Grip and Veronica, her voice low but clear enough to cut through the ambient noise. "When the reservation came through the Network, I must admit, I was intrigued to see 'Mr. and Mrs. Predator' on the list," she said. "It's not often we host guests with such … intriguing reputations."

Grip's expression didn't shift, but there was a subtle glint of amusement in his eyes. "We like to keep things interesting," he replied smoothly, resting his hand lightly on Veronica's back.

Mistress Blue inclined her head, acknowledging his comment with a knowing smile. "I can see that. It's always refreshing to welcome such discerning guests to my events."

Veronica blinked, her lips parting slightly. "Your events?"

"Indeed," Mistress Blue confirmed, her voice silky and composed. "Every detail here, every room, every encounter, is under my direction." Her eyes narrowed slightly, though her smile remained. "And speaking of details, your room has been organized specifically to your specifications, Mr. Predator."

Grip gave a slight nod, his expression unreadable beneath the mask. "I expected nothing less."

Mistress Blue's gaze softened as she turned her attention to Veronica. Without a word, she took a step closer, her hand brushing lightly against Veronica's cheek. Before Veronica could fully process what was happening, Mistress Blue leaned in and pressed a soft, deliberate kiss to her lips. It wasn't hurried, nor was it overly intimate, but it sent a shiver through Veronica's body and left an indelible impression.

As she pulled away, Mistress Blue's emerald eyes sparkled with a hint of mischief. "Enjoy your evening," she said, her voice like velvet, before turning and gliding back toward her post.

Veronica touched her lips absently, her cheeks flushed as she turned to Grip. His grin was subtle, but unmistakable.

"Still curious, doll?" he asked, his tone teasing but approving.

"Oh," Veronica said softly, her voice tinged with a mixture of excitement and disbelief. "You have no idea."

CHAPTER 3

THE ROOM

Grip held Veronica's hand firmly as they strolled down the dimly lit hallway. The low hum of music and faint murmurs of activity from the main party hall echoed behind them, growing quieter with every step. When they stopped in front of the fourth door on the right, Grip pulled the sleek, black keycard from his pocket.

He turned to Veronica, his intense gaze meeting hers through their masks. His voice was calm, with a note of anticipation. "Doll, we're experimenting tonight," he said. "So, keep an open mind, alright?"

Veronica's eyes flicked between his and the door, her curiosity flaring once more. "Grip, what did you plan?" she asked, her voice a mix of excitement and nervous energy.

"You'll see," he replied with a small, reassuring smile. After sliding the keycard through the reader, the door unlocked with a soft click. He pushed it open to reveal a massive, elegantly designed room.

Veronica's breath hitched as she stepped inside. The space was unlike anything she'd imagined. The lighting was low, casting soft shadows along the walls, and the air was warm, humming with quiet energy. Circling the perimeter of the room, masked men and women stood completely nude, their expressions unreadable but their postures relaxed and inviting. The centerpiece of the room was a small stage, elevated just slightly above the floor.

On the stage sat a queen-sized bed, draped in luxurious black and crimson silk. To the side of the bed was a table covered with an array of items that immediately drew Veronica's attention. Tools of the BDSM lifestyle were laid out with meticulous care: floggers in varying sizes and materials, leather paddles, clamps glinting under the soft light, and neatly arranged needles in sterile packaging. The table was a showcase of possibilities, each item carefully placed to entice and provoke curiosity.

Grip gently guided Veronica toward the stage, leading her up the steps. She followed in silence, her wide eyes fixed on the table as they stopped in front of it.

Her lips parted slightly as she took it all in, her fingers twitching as though she wanted to reach out and touch the items but didn't dare. The array of tools, combined with the surreal atmosphere, left her momentarily speechless.

Grip leaned in close, his voice low and steady. "Everything here is for us tonight. Take your time, doll. This is just the beginning."

Veronica turned to him, her eyes sparkling with awe. Before she could respond, the scene held still, charged with a sense of expectation, as though the room itself was waiting for what would come next.

Grip's commanding voice cut through the low hum of the room, drawing every eye to him. "Number one, step forward."

The air seemed to thicken as a young black man, tall and lean with an air of quiet confidence, emerged from the circle. Veronica watched his long but rather thin cock sway between his thighs as he moved with purpose, climbing onto the stage without hesitation. He approached the table and, after a moment's consideration, selected a long wooden paddle. The polished surface gleamed under the soft light as he turned and presented it to Veronica with both hands, his head slightly bowed in submission.

Veronica blinked, her lips parting in confusion as she instinctively took the paddle. Its weight felt foreign in her hands, the smooth wood cool against her skin. Her heart quickened as the man moved to the edge of the stage, bending over at the waist, his hands gripping the sides of the platform for support. His posture was submissive, and expectant.

She turned to Grip, confusion and unease settling over her. "What am I supposed to do?" she asked softly, her voice barely audible over the pulse of the music.

Grip stepped closer, his imposing presence grounding her as his deep voice rumbled with authority. "Each of these individuals," he began, gesturing to the circle surrounding the stage, "has volunteered to experience a certain aspect of tonight. And you," he brushed his hand along her arm, guiding her to hold the paddle correctly, "are going to administer those aspects."

Her eyes widened, her grip tightening on the paddle. "Me?"

"Yes, doll," Grip said, his voice commanding. "Tonight, you're going to get a taste of power. I may be in control, but this will show you what it feels like to command someone else's experience."

Veronica hesitated, looking between the paddle in her hands and the man bent over in front of her. She could feel the eyes of the room on her, expectant yet patient.

Grip leaned in, his voice low but firm. "Now, take the paddle and give him a deliberate, powerful swing to his ass. He's waiting for you, doll. Show him what you've got."

Her breath caught in her throat, but she nodded slowly, gripping the paddle with both hands as she stepped closer to the man. She felt a rush of adrenaline from fear and exhilaration as she raised the paddle, her muscles tensing. The moment stretched out, every sound fading except for the thrum of her heartbeat.

And then she swung.

The paddle connected with a resounding crack, echoing through the room like a shot. The man flinched slightly, a sharp intake of breath confirming the impact, but he stayed in position, his body steady.

Veronica froze for a moment, stunned by what she'd just done. She turned to Grip, who smiled approvingly, his eyes gleaming behind his mask.

"Good," he said simply. "Now again."

The power in his words sent a thrill down her spine as she turned back to the man, the paddle steady in her hands. Veronica felt something new—a burgeoning confidence.

The second swing cut through the air with precision, the paddle landing with a sharp crack that reverberated through the room. The edge of the paddle caught the man's cleanly shaven balls. The man's reaction was immediate—his head tilted back slightly, and a low, audible groan of pleasure escaped his lips.

"Please, Mrs. Predator," he said, his voice raw with desire. "Harder!"

Veronica froze for a moment as the man's cock becoming erect, and throbbing at every heartbeat. Her eyes darted to Grip in astonishment. He nodded slightly, his expression calm, giving her permission to continue.

Her grip on the paddle tightened, and with a newfound determination, she raised it again. This time, she swung with all the force she could muster, the paddle connecting with a thunderous crack that echoed louder than the last. The man let out a deep, guttural moan as he sank to his knees, trembling with visible pleasure.

The room seemed to pause, the energy shifting as Veronica stepped back, her heart pounding. She looked down at the paddle in her hands, her breathing quick and shallow as the realization of her actions settled over her.

Grip stepped closer, his voice low and steady as he addressed her. "How do you feel, doll?"

Veronica's eyes met his, wide with a mix of emotions—shock, exhilaration, and something else she couldn't quite name. "I … I don't know," she admitted, her voice shaky. "It's … powerful. Thrilling, even." She could feel the heat brewing between her thighs.

Grip nodded, a small smile playing on his lips. "Good," he said, his voice full of approval. "That's what tonight is about. Learning what it means to take control—to hold that power in your hands and see the effect it has."

Veronica glanced back at the man still kneeling before her, his body relaxed, his breathing steady, his cock dangled still erect between his thighs, and his expression one of pure satisfaction. She swallowed hard, her pulse still racing, as she turned back to Grip.

"I think I understand," she said softly, her voice steadier.

Grip reached out and took the paddle from her hands, setting it gently back on the table. "That was just the beginning," he said, his tone low and promising. "There's more, don't worry."

Grip's voice rang out with calm authority, cutting

through the charged atmosphere. "Number two, step forward."

The young black man stood up, erect cock pointing forward with a slight curve to the left, which Veronica couldn't miss, as he exited the stage and took his spot back observing. From the circle around the stage, an older woman emerged. She moved with a deliberate, quiet confidence, her presence commanding attention despite her unremarkable appearance. Her body bore the marks of time. Her breasts sagged slightly, with dark erect nipples and a soft fold of skin at her stomach hinted at motherhood. There was no shame in her posture, no hesitation in her movements.

She approached the table and scanned its offerings with a practiced eye before selecting a small flogger. Its leather straps gleamed under the low light, but the sharp metal tips at the ends glittered like tiny fangs. The woman turned to face Veronica, holding the flogger with both hands, presenting it with quiet reverence.

Veronica hesitated, her gaze flicking from the woman's face to the unusual instrument. The sharp edges glinted ominously, and her pulse quickened as she reached out to take the flogger. It was lighter than she'd expected, the leather straps cool and smooth against her skin.

The older woman stepped back, her expression serene as she moved to the center of the stage. With deliberate care, she lowered herself to her knees, her arms resting behind her back, leaving her body exposed and vulnerable. Her head tilted forward slightly in a gesture of submission, her breathing calm and even.

Grip leaned close to Veronica, his voice low and reassuring. "Don't worry. Trust me, each of these people are

experienced and willing."
Veronica's fingers tightened around the handle of the flogger as she looked down at the woman kneeling before her. The room seemed to grow quieter, the expectant tension thick in the air as Veronica prepared to take her next step into this unfamiliar world. She raised the flogger hesitantly, the leather straps dangling ominously in her hand. Her gaze flickered to Grip, who stood silently beside her, his imposing presence both grounding and expectant. With a steadying breath, she turned her attention back to the older woman kneeling before her, her back exposed and awaiting the touch of the flogger.

Summoning her nerve, Veronica swung lightly, the flogger barely brushing across the woman's back. The metal tips dragged across her skin, leaving a series of thin, vivid scratches that bloomed in stark contrast against her pale complexion.

The woman gasped, her body tensing briefly before she let out a scream—not of pain, but of pure, unfiltered ecstasy. Her head tilted back slightly, and she exhaled a shuddering breath, her voice trembling with exhilaration.

"Please, Mrs. Predator," the woman pleaded, her tone desperate but laced with gratitude. "Faster. Harder. I want more!"

Veronica froze, the flogger still clutched tightly in her hand, her heart pounding against her ribs. She looked back at Grip, her expression a mix of uncertainty and disbelief.

Grip gave her a subtle nod. "She's asking for it, doll. Trust yourself. Give her what she wants."

Veronica turned back to the woman, adrenaline coursing through her veins, making her movements steadier. She raised the flogger again, the leather straps swaying slightly, catching the light. Her grip tightened as she swung, this time with more force.

The flogger sliced through the air, landing across the woman's back with a sharper crack. The metal tips left deeper, more pronounced marks, and the woman let out another piercing scream of ecstasy, her body shuddering in pure delight.

"Yes!" she cried, her voice raw and trembling. "Thank you, Mrs. Predator. More!"

Veronica's breath quickened, a strange blend of power and apprehension coursing through her. She could feel the passion between her thighs as her pussy began to throb with anticipation. She lowered the flogger slightly, her mind racing. She couldn't deny the exhilaration surging through her.

Grip leaned in close, his voice a low murmur in her ear. "You're doing perfectly, doll. Look at her. You've given her exactly what she wanted."

Veronica glanced down at the woman, who remained on her knees, her posture relaxed despite the visible marks adorning her back. Her expression was blissful, her eyes half-lidded as she basked in the sensations coursing through her.

The room felt charged, the tension palpable as Veronica stood there, the flogger still in her hand, realizing just how much control she truly held. Their pain and pleasure was hers to give.

Veronica steadied herself, her grip tightening on the flogger as she looked down at the older woman still kneeling before her. Something had shifted within her—a flicker of confidence, a realization of the control she now held. She straightened her shoulders and took a step forward, her voice firm and clear.

"Stand," she commanded, her tone leaving no room for hesitation.

The woman obeyed instantly, rising to her feet with a calm grace that belied the fresh scratches on her back. Her gaze remained lowered, submissive, as she awaited further instruction.

"Face me," Veronica continued, her voice steady but laced with an edge of authority that surprised even herself.

The woman turned to face her, her bare chest exposed and unguarded. Her breathing was steady, her body completely still, awaiting whatever came next.

"Now," Veronica said, her eyes locking onto the woman's, "lace your hands behind your back and look up at the ceiling."

The woman complied. Her arms moved gracefully behind her, her fingers interlocking as her head tilted back, her neck exposed. The light above caught the faint sheen of perspiration on her skin, emphasizing her vulnerability.

Veronica stepped closer, the flogger dangling from her hand. Her pulse raced, but her movements were deliberate. She traced the flogger lightly across the woman's chest, letting the cold metal tips brush against her skin, teasing but not yet striking. The older woman shivered slightly, and her nipples became more erect, a quiet gasp escaping her lips.

With a sudden movement, Veronica swung the flogger, the leather straps lashing across the woman's bare chest with a sharp crack. The metal tips left faint red lines in their wake, the force of the strike causing the woman to inhale sharply, her body momentarily tensing.

But instead of retreating or crying out in pain, the

woman moaned, her voice trembling with raw ecstasy. "Yes, Mrs. Predator," she whispered, her voice barely audible but filled with unmistakable pleasure.

Veronica didn't hesitate. She raised the flogger again, delivering another aggressive lash, the straps striking across the woman's chest with precision. The sound of the impact echoed in the room, drawing the attention of the silent audience encircling the stage.

The woman trembled, her chest rising and falling with deep breaths as she absorbed the sensations. Her eyes remained fixed on the ceiling, her lips parted slightly, her expression one of complete surrender.

Veronica stepped back slightly, her chest heaving as she lowered the flogger. Her gaze lingered on the older woman, noting the way her marks began to bloom across her skin blood trailing from the small scratches leading up to the woman's dark nipples. For the first time, Veronica felt the weight and the thrill of her power, the realization settling over her like a wave, the wetness in her pussy unavoidably noticeable.

Grip's voice broke the silence, low and approving. "You're learning, doll," he said with pride.

Veronica glanced at him, her lips curving into a small, determined smile before turning her attention back to the woman. "You may lower your hands," she said softly, the authority in her voice undeniable.

Grip's commanding voice rang out once more, "Number three!"

The older woman, her chest adorned with the marks of Veronica's work, turned to her with a respectful nod. "Thank you, Mrs. Predator," she said, her voice filled with gratitude and a subtle undertone of satisfaction. With graceful composure, she descended from the stage and disappeared into the circle of onlookers.

From that same circle emerged an older man, his presence commanding. His body was covered in thick gray hair, matching the impressive beard that framed his weathered face. Despite his age, he moved with a surprising and captivating confidence.

He approached the table and selected a large set of anal beads that increased in size along the strand and a bottle of lube. The beads gleamed under the soft light, each sphere polished to perfection. The man turned toward Veronica, his sharp eyes briefly meeting hers before he handed her the items with a deliberate, respectful motion.

Veronica accepted them instinctively, her fingers curling around the cool beads and the bottle of lubricant. Her heart raced as she processed what was about to unfold, her gaze following the man as he walked past her. He made his way to the edge of the bed, and bent over. He rested his hands on the silky sheets, his posture leaving no question about his intent. His body was completely exposed, his submission stark, offering Veronica easy access to his rear.

The room fell silent once more, the air thick with anticipation as Veronica stood there, the tools of control now in her hands. She glanced at Grip, seeking his approval, but his face betrayed no hint of emotion beyond calm authority.

"This is your moment, doll," he said simply, his voice steady.

Veronica turned back to the man before her, the weight of the moment settling over her as she took a steadying breath. The circle of onlookers seemed to fade away, leaving only the task at hand and the growing realization of her newfound power.

CHAPTER 4

PROGRESSION

The room fell silent once more, the air thick with anticipation as Veronica stood there, the tools of control now in her hands. She glanced at Grip, seeking his approval, but his face betrayed no hint of emotion beyond calm authority.

"This is your moment, doll," he said simply, his voice steady.

Veronica turned back to the man before her, the weight of the moment settling over her as she took a steadying breath. The circle of onlookers seemed to fade away, leaving only the task at hand.

Veronica stepped forward, the items in her hands feeling heavier than before as she positioned herself behind the man. Her pulse quickened, her mind racing with both nervous anticipation and the undeniable thrill of control. She uncapped the bottle of lubricant and the faint sound of the click seemed to echo in the charged silence of the room.

She tilted the bottle, liberally applying the cool, slippery gel to the beads. The smooth surface gleamed under the light as she worked, ensuring they were well-prepared. Her voice, steady but firm, broke the quiet.

"Spread your cheeks more," she instructed, surprising herself with the command's firmness.

The man obeyed immediately, his hands reaching back to widen the access for her. His submission was absolute, and Veronica couldn't help but feel a strange rush of power in the face of his vulnerability.

With a deep breath, she pressed the smallest bead against his entrance, pausing for a moment to gauge his reaction. To her surprise, it slipped inside effortlessly with only the slightest pressure. The man released a low groan of pleasure, his body visibly relaxing under her touch.

Encouraged, Veronica continued, guiding the next bead into him, then the third and fourth, each one sliding in with increasing ease. The man's moans grew louder with each addition, his voice trembling with pure, unfiltered delight. "Please, Mrs. Predator," he murmured between breaths. "More."

The fifth bead disappeared inside him, leaving only the final, largest bead. Veronica paused briefly, her eyes flicking to the exposed handle and the taut stretch of his body. With deliberate care, she pressed the last bead forward, feeling the resistance before it finally settled into place with a satisfying motion. The man let out a deep, guttural moan, his head tilting forward as he shuddered in pleasure.

Veronica stood back, her breathing shallow as she surveyed her work. The beads rested inside him, the handle the only part left visible, a stark contrast against the man's exposed form. For a moment, she simply stared, her lips curving into a subtle, amused smile. The sight before her—a man, powerful in stature yet so completely under her control—was nothing short of fascinating.

Grip's voice broke through the haze, calm and approving. "Enjoying yourself, doll?"

Veronica glanced at him, her amusement evident in her eyes. "More than I expected," she replied softly, her gaze shifting back to the man who knelt before her, utterly lost in the experience she had created for him.

Veronica turned away from the man, her heart still pounding from the rush of control she'd felt. Her eyes scanned the table once more, drawn unexpectedly to the wooden paddle she'd used earlier. Without hesitation, she picked it up, the smooth weight familiar in her hands. Her lips curved into a mischievous smile as she turned back to the man, still bent over the edge of the bed, his breaths ragged and uneven.

"Beg for it," she commanded, her voice sharp and deliberate, echoing through the charged silence of the room.

The man tilted his head slightly, his voice trembling with desperation as he obeyed. "Please, Mrs. Predator," he gasped, his words laced with both anticipation and submission. "Please strike me. I need it."

Veronica stepped closer, positioning herself behind him once more. She raised the paddle and measured her aim. With a sudden, forceful swing, the paddle connected with a resounding crack, striking both his rear and the exposed handle of the beads still inside him. The impact sent a jolt through his body, causing him to cry out in what could only be described as pure ecstasy.

His moans filled the room, raw and unrestrained, as his body trembled under the dual sensations. Veronica's eyes were drawn downward, and she noticed something that caught her off guard—his sack visibly pulsing, the unmistakable drip of semen trailing from his small manhood onto the sheets below. The sight was both shocking and arousing, a visceral display of the power she now wielded.

"Thank you, Mrs. Predator … please, again," he begged, his voice quivering with need.

Veronica stood still for a moment, the paddle resting lightly in her hand as she processed the scene before her. The audience around the stage remained silent, their collective attention fixed on her, their anticipation palpable. For the first time, she felt not just in control but entirely liberated, a strange sense of exhilaration coursing through her veins.

Grip's voice cut through the tension, low and approving. "You're a natural, doll."

Veronica glanced back at him, her lips curving into a small, knowing smile. "Maybe I am," she whispered, turning her gaze back to the man as she contemplated her next move.

Veronica stepped closer to the man, her lips curling into a sly, commanding smile. She leaned in, her voice low and deliberate. "Good boy," she whispered.

Before he could respond, she gripped the handle of the beads firmly and yanked them out in one swift motion, like starting a lawnmower. The sudden, intense sensation caused the man to lose all composure. He let out a guttural scream of pleasure, his body convulsing as his manhood erupted, sending a thick stream of semen onto the silky black sheets beneath him.

Veronica stepped back, watching with a mix of satisfaction and amusement as the man's body trembled, his breathing uneven as he began to settle. "Now," she said sharply, her tone leaving no room for hesitation, "clean up your mess."

Without a word, the man dropped to his knees and eagerly began licking the sheets, his submission complete and unquestioning. Veronica turned her gaze back to Grip, who watched with an approving smirk.

"Four, five, six!" Grip shouted, his commanding voice

cutting through the lingering tension in the room.

From the circle, three individuals emerged. First was a young white man in his early 30s, tall and athletic, his manhood very thick, his mask revealing piercing blue eyes. Beside him walked a petite black woman, also in her 30s, her frame delicate, almost flat chested. Finally, an older black man—nearing his 70s with a body softened by age but a presence that still held dignity, slowly stepped forward. His manhood was thick and long and already semi erect, clearly not needing any medication to help.

The three of them ignored the table entirely, moving directly to the bed where they stood side by side, waiting silently for further instruction.

Veronica observed them carefully, her mind racing with curiosity and possibilities. She turned back to Grip, raising an eyebrow as she spoke. "I assume I'm the puppeteer here, meant to direct this scene?"

Grip's smirk deepened, his voice low but firm. "Exactly, doll. You're in control now."

Veronica glanced back at the trio, her lips curving into a thoughtful smile as she took in the expectant faces before her. The air crackled with anticipation as the stage was set for her next move.

Veronica's heels clicked softly against the stage as she strode toward the older black man, her presence commanding attention. His posture remained straight and respectful, but her keen eyes didn't miss the obvious.

She stopped in front of him, tilting her head as she studied him with a calculated, almost teasing expression. Reaching out, she lightly trailed her fingers along his chest before moving lower, heightening the tension in the room, drawing the attention of the silent onlookers.

"Well, well," Veronica said, her tone a mix of amusement and control. "It seems someone is eager." Her hand briefly stroked his massive throbbing cock, but then she stopped, her voice sharpening. "Did I tell you to be ready?"

The man's eyes widened slightly behind his mask, his voice low and apologetic. "No, Mrs. Predator. I'm sorry."

Her lips curved into a knowing smile as she straightened, her posture exuding authority. "Apologies won't fix this," she replied. Her hand moved with deliberate intent as she delivered a firm, controlled slap to the thick cock, just enough to send the message. The sharp sound of the impact echoed faintly, and the man flinched slightly but kept his composure.

"Everything happens when I say it does. Understood?"

"Yes, Mrs. Predator," he replied, his tone filled with respect and submission.

Satisfied, Veronica turned her attention to the younger white man, standing silently nearby. She gestured toward the bed with a subtle nod. "Lie down," she instructed, her voice steady and unwavering.

He moved quickly and obediently as he positioned himself on the luxurious silk sheets. Veronica's gaze then shifted to the petite black woman, who stood quietly at his side.

"You," Veronica said, pointing at the woman. "Prepare him. I want his tool at its highest potential."

The woman nodded, stepping closer to the bed with confidence. Her hands moved with care, following Veronica's silent expectations as she began her task. Stroking the man's dick as it began to swell in her tiny hands.

Veronica stepped back slightly, observing the scene before her with satisfaction as her own confidence swelled.

The room hummed with anticipation.

Veronica watched with a calm, confident gaze as the young woman diligently prepared the man on the bed. His body responded to her touch, and the anticipation in the room became almost tangible. Veronica took a step closer, her heels clicking softly against the stage as she surveyed the scene.

Satisfied, she addressed the petite black woman with an authoritative tone. "Now, mount him," she commanded, her voice smooth and deliberate.

The woman nodded, moving with a graceful ease as she climbed onto the bed and positioned herself atop the man. A soft gasp escaped her lips as she lowered her pussy around his thick, white shaft. She began to move, her rhythm slow, her moans of pleasure punctuating the sultry air in the room.

Veronica's eyes flickered with satisfaction as she turned her attention to the older man standing nearby. She gestured for him to step forward. "Don't waste this moment," she said, her voice laced with quiet authority. "Stand beside me. Observe."

The man obeyed immediately, moving to her side with a respectful bow of his head. Together, they observed the couple on the bed, their movements growing in intensity as the woman's moans harmonized with the deep groans of her partner.

Veronica stood tall beside the older man, her commanding presence unmistakable as they watched the couple on the bed. The young woman's movements grew more confident. The air in the room felt charged, a mix of tension and satisfaction radiating from the stage.

Veronica glanced at the older man beside her, his posture respectful and attentive. With a sly smile, she leaned slightly toward him, her voice low but laced with playful authority. "Tell me," she began, her tone teasing, "is this scene pleasing enough for your aged eyes?"

The man's cheeks flushed slightly, but he didn't hesitate to respond. "Yes, Mrs. Predator," he said, his voice steady but filled with reverence. "It's more than pleasing."

Veronica let out a quiet hum of approval, her eyes returning to the bed where the couple's movements had grown more intense.

"Good," she said softly, the corners of her lips curling upward. "Then enjoy the view."

The older man nodded, his gaze fixed on the bed as Veronica's commanding presence anchored him, a subtle reminder of who controlled the room. Veronica reached down and began to stroke the man's long, black shaft.

Veronica pulled her hand back, a deliberate and commanding motion that signaled a shift in focus. She turned to the older man beside her, her voice sharp yet composed. "Go to the table and grab the lube. Return to me quickly."

The older man nodded obediently, turning on his heel and moving as swiftly as his aged body would allow. His steps were steady, though his eagerness was evident in the way he reached for the bottle on the table. The lube glistened under the dim light as he held it securely, returning to Veronica's side.

When he stood before her, he extended the bottle with both hands, his head slightly bowed. Veronica took it from him with a small, approving smile, her gaze shifting momentarily to the couple still entwined on the bed. The woman's movements had grown more fluid and confident, her moans of pleasure blending seamlessly with the heat in the room.

"Good," Veronica said, her tone smooth and authoritative. She gestured toward the bed with a tilt of her chin. "Now, take position behind her. Make yourself useful."

The older man's posture straightened as he processed her command. "Yes, Mrs. Predator," he replied, his voice steady despite the anticipation radiating from him. He moved toward the bed, his steps careful yet purposeful as he approached the young woman.

Her back arched slightly as she continued her rhythmic motions, her focus entirely on the man beneath her.

The older man positioned himself behind her as instructed, waiting for further guidance, his respect for Veronica's authority evident in his every action. She stood back, observing the scene with a satisfied expression, her hands clasping the bottle of lube as she prepared to orchestrate the next step.

Veronica stepped closer to the bed, her commanding presence drawing the attention of everyone in the room. Her gaze fixed on the older man, who stood behind the young woman as instructed, waiting silently for her next command.

"Prepare yourself," Veronica said, her tone calm but firm, holding the bottle of lube out to him. "You're going to join them."

The older man's hands trembled slightly as he took the bottle from her. He worked quickly, applying the lubricant with care as he readied himself for the task she had assigned him.

Veronica watched with a small, approving smile, her eyes flickering between the participants on the bed. The young woman continued her rhythmic movements atop the man beneath her, her moans growing louder as the intensity of the scene built. The energy in the room grew charged, each passing moment a testament to the control Veronica wielded over the unfolding tableau.

When the older man finished preparing himself, he turned his gaze to Veronica, silently awaiting her next instruction.

"Good," she said, her voice low and authoritative. "Now take your position and fuck her tight little asshole."

He nodded, his posture straightening as he moved closer to the young woman, positioning himself behind her with careful precision. Veronica stepped back slightly, her gaze sharp as she surveyed the scene before her, the anticipation thick in the air. The older man placed his hands on the small of the woman's back as his thick member entered her unsuspecting anus with ease. The woman let out a shriek of pleasure and pain, but she didn't miss a lick in the rhythm riding the cock pulsing inside her wet pussy and the newly placed cock in her ass.

The rhythm between the three participants intensified, their synchronized movements creating a palpable energy. The soft sounds of pleasure and the hum of tension mingled with the ambient music playing faintly in the background, heightening the charged atmosphere.

Veronica stepped back slightly, her eyes narrowing with satisfaction as she watched the scene unfold before her. Her control, her orchestration, was evident in every detail, from the way their motions aligned to the soft gasps and murmurs that punctuated the air.

The onlookers around the stage remained silent, their gazes fixed intently on the scene. Some shifted slightly, caught up in the moment, while others remained still, their expressions masked yet revealing subtle hints of intrigue and arousal.

Veronica tilted her head as the young woman suddenly let out a cry, her voice rising above the other sounds in the room. Her body trembled, her cries turning into soft whimpers as she collapsed forward onto the man beneath her, her energy seemingly spent.

A satisfied grin crept over Veronica's face as she stepped forward, glancing between the participants. The man beneath her sped up his pace slamming into her worn cunt as he let out a guttural moan, his cock throbbing for each stream of the man filling the girl with his cum. She observed their flushed faces and their slowing movements with a calm, as suddenly the older man straightened, stroking his cock vigorously before shooting four thick, long shots of cum over the woman's collapsed body nearly hitting the man.

"Well done," Veronica said softly, her voice cutting through the thick silence that followed.

As the participants began to settle, Veronica glanced over her shoulder at Grip, who stood watching from the edge of the room. His approving nod met her gaze, silently affirming her control of the moment.

CHAPTER 5

THE PARTY'S END

Grip's voice rang out boldly, cutting through the quiet hum that followed the conclusion of the scene. "Bedding change, please."

From the corner of the room, three women dressed impeccably in black server attire moved with speed and precision. Their actions were quick, yet efficient, stripping the bed of its silken sheets and replacing them with fresh, pristine linens. They worked silently, wiping down every surface and cleaning the items that had been used with careful attention to detail.

Veronica watched them, still catching her breath, as the women seamlessly restored the space to its original immaculate condition. Within moments, the stage was spotless, and the three servers had returned to their corner, standing silently with their hands clasped in front of them, awaiting further instruction.

Grip approached Veronica, his imposing figure towering slightly over her as he placed a hand lightly on her back. His gaze was steady, his tone calm yet firm. "Tell me, doll," he said, his voice low, "how is your body feeling right now?"

Veronica paused, her lips parting slightly as she let the question settle. A faint smile played on her lips as she turned to meet his gaze. "It's electric," she said softly, her voice carrying a hint of breathless excitement. "Every part of me feels alive, like a fire spreading through my veins. My heart is racing. Every inch of my skin feels like it's humming with anticipation."

Grip's smirk deepened, his approving expression making it clear he was pleased with her answer.

"Good," he murmured, his voice almost a growl. "That's exactly what I wanted to hear."

The moment lingered between them, charged with unspoken tension.

Grip's voice cut through the room with a commanding authority, sharper and more deliberate than before. "Now," he commanded, "it's time for a twist."

The energy in the room shifted as he gestured to the circle of naked participants surrounding the stage. "Gather closer," he instructed.

The onlookers obeyed without hesitation, stepping forward until they formed an intimate semicircle around the stage. Their eyes remained fixed on Grip and Veronica at the center of the room, the anticipation thick in the air.

Grip turned to Veronica, his eyes glinting behind his mask as he produced a small, sharp knife from his pocket. She blinked, her lips parting slightly in surprise as he stepped toward her.

"Trust me," he said softly, his voice meant only for her.

Before she could respond, he lowered the blade to the strap of her dress, slicing through it with a single fluid motion. The fabric slipped from her shoulders, pooling at her feet in a cascade of silk. Veronica gasped softly, her arms instinctively moving to cover herself before she hesitated, realizing the intensity of the moment.

The power dynamic had shifted. Where she had commanded the room moments ago, now she stood as its centerpiece, exposed and vulnerable under the watchful gaze of fifteen naked individuals. The soft hum of their breathing and the flicker of emotions on their faces—curiosity, admiration, and anticipation—only heightened the intensity of the moment.

Veronica's heart raced as she became acutely aware of every eye on her naked body. Her pink nipples erect, her pussy throbbing and the wetness dripping down her thigh, Grip stepped back slightly, his expression calm and confident as he allowed the silence to stretch.

"Perfect," he said softly.

The room remained still, the gathered crowd watching with rapt attention as they waited for Grip's next move, the suspense building with every passing second.

Grip's voice rang out, bold and demanding, cutting through the thick anticipation in the room. "Everyone, pay homage to this goddess before you."

Veronica's breath caught in her throat, her cheeks flushing deeply. She stood still, her bare form illuminated by the soft lighting of the room, the heat of the moment making her acutely aware of her vulnerability and power all at once. The sounds in the room began to shift, soft murmurs giving way to something more physical, more visceral as every person before her started to pleasure themselves. Men stroking their cocks with vigorous intent, women rubbing their breast and stimulating their mounds between their thighs as they stare up at Veronica's naked body.

Grip, standing beside her, moved with purpose. With deliberate motions, he began to remove his clothes, piece by piece, until he stood beside her, his presence even more commanding without the barriers of fabric. The energy in the room charged as all attention remained fixed on Veronica.

She turned her head slightly, her gaze meeting Grip's as he stood tall at her side. His eyes gleamed with satisfaction, a subtle reassurance that he was still in control of the scene. Veronica's chest rose and fell with each deep breath as she let the moment wash over her, the sheer audacity of it igniting something raw within her. She couldn't help but notice the throbbing hard cock bouncing to his every heartbeat in front of her.

Her breath hitched as she noticed the readiness in his posture, the intensity in his eyes behind the mask. He exuded power, an unrelenting force that seemed to make the air around them heavier.

Without a word, Grip reached out, his large hand wrapping around her neck—not tightly, but firmly enough to assert his dominance. Veronica's body instinctively relaxed under his grip, her breath steady as she surrendered to his control. With seemingly no effort, Grip lifted her off the ground by her throat, her petite frame feeling weightless in his grasp.

The onlookers around the stage gasped softly, their murmurs blending with the escalating sounds of pleasure in the room. Veronica's limbs dangled as she allowed herself to be held, her body completely under his control. Then, with a swift motion, Grip threw her onto the bed, her body landing on the soft surface with a graceful yet unceremonious flop. Her tits rocked with the momentum nearly hitting her in the face. The silk sheets absorbed her impact, and she sprawled there, wide-eyed and breathless.

She stared up at him, her heart pounding as she tried to process what had just happened. The sheer display of strength and dominance left her both exhilarated and uncertain, her mind racing with anticipation as she awaited his next move. Around her, the sounds of the onlookers grew louder, their pleasure peaking as they took in the scene unfolding before them.

Grip stepped forward slowly, his presence looming larger than ever as Veronica lay motionless, her body still recovering from the sudden toss. The room seemed to vibrate with energy, the onlookers' sounds of pleasure creating a symphony of primal emotion that filled every corner of the space.

Grip let out a deep, guttural grunt, his voice reverberating through the room like a thunderclap. "On all fours," he commanded.

Veronica reacted instinctively, her breathing quick as she scrambled to comply. She positioned herself on her hands and knees, her movements deliberate yet filled with anticipation.

The silk sheets shifted beneath her as she took her place at the center of the bed, her head lifting slightly to meet the gaze of the crowd before her.

Grip moved with purpose, his footsteps slow and measured as he circled her like a predator sizing up his prey. His presence was magnetic, every step amplifying the tension. When he came to a stop behind her, the dynamic shifted once again.

He placed a firm hand on her lower back, his touch both grounding and commanding. Veronica's chest rose and fell as she steadied herself, acutely aware of the crowd's eyes on her. The onlookers' sounds of pleasure grew louder, their rhythmic motions creating a palpable energy.

Facing the crowd, Grip's towering form behind her, Veronica felt a strange mix of vulnerability and power. The attention, the tension, and the intensity left her charged and buzzing with anticipation.

Grip's hands moved to Veronica's hips, his grip firm and commanding as he steadied her. His presence behind her radiated dominance.

The faces of the onlookers were masked, yet their intent was unmistakable. Their rhythmic movements and soft sounds of pleasure filled the room, a symphony of indulgence echoing in her ears.

Veronica's breath hitched as Grip's dick slammed into her awaiting pussy, parting her wet lips with ease, his control over her evident. She never broke eye contact with the crowd, their attention fueling the passion coursing through her. She was being taken in front of them.

Around the room, the sounds of pleasure grew louder, the collective energy feeding into the scene. Veronica's flushed face and steady breaths mirrored the crowd's. Her tits swung with every stroke of Grips massive cock slamming into her cervix. She could feel the unmistakable pulse of Grips manhood as he climaxes. Grip let out a sigh as his cock pulsed and filled his wife with thick cum.

Grip stood tall behind Veronica, his commanding presence dominating the room as the attention of every onlooker remained fixed on the scene. Veronica began to shift, tensing as she prepared to rise from the bed, dripping with cum, but Grip's hand pressed firmly against her lower back, keeping her in place.

"You're not done," he said.

Veronica froze, her breath catching as she glanced back at him.

He turned his gaze to the group of men surrounding the stage, his voice sharp as he addressed them. "Line up," he instructed, motioning toward Veronica with a subtle gesture.

The men obeyed without hesitation, their movements swift and deliberate as they formed an orderly line behind her. The energy in the room shifted again, anticipation building with each passing moment as all eyes remained focused on Veronica, still positioned on all fours in the center of the bed.

Grip leaned down slightly, his hand still resting on her back as he spoke low and steady. "You'll take them, one by one," he said, his tone calm yet commanding.

Veronica's breathing quickened, but she remained still, her vulnerability on full display for the crowd. Around them, the onlookers murmured softly, their movements halting as they waited for the next step.

The first of the males was the older black male in his seventies from before, cock throbbing with anticipation. Was it revenge for Veronica slapping his dick or lust for her 0perfect body before him? Veronica couldn't tell as the head of his dick spread her lips and entered her. She could feel it stretching her, filling every inch of her. She winced as she thought to herself, "this has to be all of him. There can't be any more," but she was quickly corrected, and he pushed even deeper, further back than she's ever had. The pain was so intense she wasn't sure she could take anymore. Suddenly he withdrew nearly all the way out.

"Oh fuck," Veronica murmured. She knew what was coming.

The man slammed all the way back into her, and the pain nearly caused her to crawl off the bed. She looked up to see Grips cock at her face. She couldn't go anywhere if she wanted to.

"Open your mouth, doll," Grip commanded, stroking his hands through her hair.

Veronica could barely focus enough to make coherent thoughts as the dick slammed into her over and over, but she instinctually obeyed, opening her mouth for Grip to ram his cock as far down her throat as it would go.

A once powerful, in control woman was now being taken from both ends in front of the onlookers.

Isn't this a turn of events. Veronica thought to herself as they pounded into her.

Suddenly the man's pace sped up, she felt his cock growing thicker, the head of his dick stretching her inner walls as it pulsed and the warm sensation of his cum filled her void. "Oh my god," he cried out as he withdrew his long, thick dick and his cum literally poured out of her used hole and down her bare thighs.

Veronica couldn't say a word as her mouth was still filled with Grips dick, sliding in and out of her, but she didn't have a moment to think before the next man took his position behind her dripping cunt. The older hairy white man with the small dick took the first man's place.

Veronica moaned as Grip slipped out of her mouth and slapped her face with his dick.

"Good girl. You enjoy being used in every way don't you, doll?"

As she eagerly responded, "Yes sir!" she didn't even notice the man behind her had already entered her and had been stroking as deep as his dick would go. "Wrong hole" Grip commanded, as he tossed the lube to the older man.

Veronica's eyes narrowed in confusion before her ass cheeks were spread open and the man slid his little manhood into her tight hole. "FUCK," Veronica moaned as the man began to slam into her like a rabbit. His pace increased with every stroke. She thought he may end up passing out. Then out of nowhere, he reached up and grabbed a hand full of her hair, ripping it backward as he thrust one last time into her tight ass, moaning. Veronica let out an intense but pleasurable yelp as she felt him unload inside her.

As the man withdrew, her tight hole was quickly filled with another man's thicker cock. She felt as if her asshole was being ripped open from the inside. The sensation of pain quickly turned to pleasure as the man's pace met her body's needs. She felt the pleasure building.

"Fuck me harder!" Veronica screamed, and the man took hold of her hips and began to slam into her cheeks with everything he had.

Veronica could feel the pressure building, the tingling in her clit. She was about to climax. She needed it. But the man, as most men do, messed up the rhythm and pulled out, shooting rope after rope of warm semen over her ass.

"I was so close!" Veronica cried, looking up at Grip who was stroking his cock in front of her.

He laughed. "Well good thing there seems to be another participant already in position."

Suddenly, she felt her pussy spread open, she looked back, and it wasn't a man at all. The older woman with small welts across her chest was thrusting a thick strap-on deep into Veronica's needing pussy.

"Please make me cum," Veronica begged.

The woman's pace was perfect. Veronica could feel her pussy pulsing, energy rising and building. SIt wouldn't be much longer. Out of nowhere a sudden warmth covered her face and she looked forward to see Grip shooting cum right into her forehead.

The feeling of warm cum dripping off her ass, and the newly warm stream dripping off her face pushed her over the edge. As the strap on hit her cervix in the most perfect timing, her body started to shudder and she screamed in pleasure. Veronica's pussy throbbed, squirting the previous loads of cum and her own juices as she squirted out as the woman pulled the dildo out of her.

Veronica collapsed on the bed, her body completely spent, trembling slightly from the aftershock of pleasure. The once-vibrant room had grown quieter as the participants began to leave, their hushed murmurs and retreating footsteps fading into the background. The only constant was Grip, standing tall beside her, his commanding presence grounding her as she basked in the overwhelming sensations coursing through her.

The silence between them was comfortable, charged with a sense of completion. Grip reached out, brushing a hand gently along her shoulder before straightening. His voice broke the stillness, calm yet authoritative. "Ladies, assist her," he commanded, addressing the three women who had remained in the corner of the room throughout the evening.

The women moved with quiet efficiency, gathering supplies from a nearby cabinet. Each carried a warm, damp washcloth, their movements graceful and respectful as they approached the bed. Veronica felt the soft warmth of the cloth against her skin, the gentle touch soothing and unintrusive as they carefully cleaned her. The sensation was almost meditative, a stark contrast to the intensity of what had unfolded moments ago.

The three women worked in silence, their focus entirely on Veronica as they attended to her with meticulous care. Grip watched from the side, his arms crossed, his expression unreadable. He gave a small nod of approval as the women finished their task, folding the used cloths, and stepping back into the shadows of the room.

Veronica's breathing steadied, her body relaxed as she

turned her head slightly to look at Grip. He met her gaze, his lips curving into a subtle, satisfied smile. Without saying a word, he reached down and lightly traced a finger along her jawline, a quiet acknowledgment of everything they had shared.

The room felt different now—quieter, softer, and intimate. It was just the two of them. The hum of the evening faded into the background.

As the room settled into complete stillness, Grip lowered himself onto the bed beside Veronica. His presence, normally commanding and intense, softened as he rested on the silk sheets next to her. He reached out, pulling her closer until her head rested against his chest, his hand lazily tracing small circles on her back.

"You did a great job tonight, doll," Grip said, his voice low and warm, so difference from the authority it had carried earlier. "I'm proud of you."

Veronica tilted her head up slightly, her eyes meeting his as a small, tired smile spread across her face. "I had no idea what to expect," she admitted, her voice soft, "but I think this might just go down as one for the history books."

Grip let out a deep chuckle, his chest rumbling beneath her. "One for the history books, huh?" he teased, his fingers brushing a stray strand of hair from her face. "That's what I was going for."

Veronica laughed softly, the sound light and genuine. She nestled closer to him, her body completely relaxed in his embrace. The weight of the evening seemed to fade, replaced by a warm, comforting intimacy that wrapped around them like a blanket.

"You always know how to surprise me," she murmured, her eyes closing as she let herself sink into the moment.

Grip kissed the top of her head, his lips lingering for a moment. "That's the point, doll," he said. "Here's to six years, and to making every one better than the last."

The two lay in the quiet of the now-empty room, the soft hum of the ambient music fading into the background. In each other's arms, they felt a sense of completion, their connection as strong as ever, even after everything the night had held.

#

The sound of hurried footsteps echoed through the quiet corridors as Veronica and Grip made their way back toward the entrance. She clutched his arm, their shared laughter breaking the tension of the evening's intensity. Despite her exhaustion, a playful smile lingered on her lips, mirrored by Grip's own satisfied expression.

Waiting by the door was Mistress Blue, her enigmatic presence as commanding as ever. The glint of her jeweled skirt sparkled under the dim lights as she regarded the couple with a knowing smile.

"Mr. and Mrs. Predator," she said. "I trust the evening met your expectations?"

Grip nodded, his hand resting on Veronica's back. "Exceeded them," he replied. "Thank you, Mistress Blue. Truly, an unforgettable anniversary."

Veronica chimed in, her voice warm. "Yes, thank you. It was extraordinary."

Mistress Blue gave a small bow of her head, the faintest hint of amusement tugging at her lips. "I look forward to seeing you both again. Safe travels."

The couple stepped outside, the crisp night air brushing against their skin. The city skyline glowed in the distance, a stunning contrast to the dark, shadowed walls of the estate. Their driver was already waiting, standing beside the open limo door with a professional, neutral expression.

"Mr. and Mrs. Predator," he greeted them with a polite nod, "your car is ready."

Grip motioned for Veronica to enter first, and she slid into the plush leather seats, her body sinking into the comfort of the vehicle. Grip followed, closing the door behind them as the driver took his place and the engine purred to life. The driver looked in the mirror into the cabin and asked, "Shall we depart?" and suddenly Veronica noticed he was one of the men who, just mere moments ago, filled her body. She grinned and looked at Grip. "Yes, tonight was a success." She laughed, "for all of us".

The limo pulled away from the grand estate, gliding smoothly down the private drive and through the tall, guarded gates. As they merged onto the city streets, the vibrant lights of Houston danced across the windows, reflecting in Veronica's tired but contented eyes.

Grip leaned back in his seat, his hand finding hers and giving it a gentle squeeze. Veronica turned to him, her smile soft. The city lights illuminated the path ahead, a symbolic reminder of the world they were returning to—together.

The limo rolled on through the bustling streets, the hum of the engine blending with the faint sounds of the city, carrying them back toward their condo and the promise of a new day.

CHAPTER 6

THE AWAKENING

The morning sunbathed the city in a golden glow, the light reflecting off the high-rise buildings that stretched toward the sky. From the rooftop of their condo, the sprawling urban expanse below seemed almost serene, a far cry from the hustle and noise of life on the ground. It had been a few weeks since their unforgettable anniversary, but the memory still lingered between them like an unspoken thread.

Grip leaned against the railing, a steaming cup of coffee in his hand as he took in the view. The warm breeze ruffled his hair slightly, and the faint sound of water splashing behind him drew his attention. He turned his head to see Veronica slipping effortlessly through the water of their rooftop pool, her bare form shimmering beneath the morning light.

Her movements were languid, almost hypnotic, as she floated on her back, her arms drifting lazily at her sides. She seemed completely at ease, her face tilted toward the sun with her eyes closed, a contented smile gracing her lips.

Grip smirked, taking a sip of his coffee before speaking. "So, doll," he began, his deep voice cutting through the peaceful silence, "what's on your agenda today?"

Veronica cracked one eye open, turning her head slightly toward him. She let out a soft, amused laugh, her voice light and carefree. "You're looking at it," she replied, her tone playful as she gestured lazily to the pool around her. "This is all I've got planned. Nothing but relaxing."

Grip chuckled, shaking his head as he set his coffee mug down on a nearby table. "Living the dream, huh?" he teased, walking closer to the edge of the pool.

Veronica tilted her head back, floating as she looked up at him. "Why not? I think I've earned it."

Grip crouched down by the pool, his hand trailing lightly through the water as he watched her. "Fair enough," he said, his voice softening. "You deserve it."

Veronica closed her eyes again as she continued to float, the sun warming her skin as the morning unfolded, peaceful and unrushed.

Grip watched her float effortlessly in the pool, the morning light reflecting off the rippling water. A sly smile tugged at his lips as he tilted his head, his deep voice breaking the comfortable silence.

"So, doll," he began, his tone playful yet suggestive, "are you feeling up to a little ... spice today? Just to keep things interesting."

Veronica opened her eyes, meeting his gaze with a knowing grin. "Sure," she said, her voice laced with excitement. "I was wondering when you were going to come around to more fun."

She flipped gracefully onto her stomach, paddling closer to the edge of the pool where Grip crouched. Resting her arms on the pool's edge, she looked up at him, water dripping from her hair as her curiosity sparkled in her eyes. "So," she asked, her tone teasing but eager, "what did you have in mind?"

Grip leaned closer, his grin deepening as he placed a hand lightly on her wet shoulder. "Oh, I've got a few ideas," he said, his voice low and deliberate, carrying a promise that sent a shiver through her.

Veronica's smile widened, anticipation building as she waited for him to elaborate. "Well," she said, resting her chin on her arms, "don't keep me waiting."

Grip's hand lingered on Veronica's shoulder, his thumb tracing small circles on her damp skin. His gaze softened slightly. "Actually, doll," he began, "Mistress Blue reached out."

Veronica raised an eyebrow, her curiosity piqued. "Mistress Blue?" she echoed, tilting her head slightly. "What does she need?"

Grip smirked, his fingers trailing briefly down her arm before resting on the edge of the pool. "Apparently, someone very important to the Network, a dignitary from Kenya, has expressed interest in experiencing the company of a beautiful, young American woman."

Veronica blinked, her lips curving into a sly smile as she processed his words. "And by 'beautiful, young American woman,' I assume you mean me?"

Grip chuckled, nodding. "Mistress Blue seems to think highly of you," he said. "This dignitary funds a substantial portion of the Network's operations, and she wants to show her appreciation. She thought we might be the perfect pair to entertain him."

Veronica leaned against the pool's edge, her wet hair clinging to her shoulders as she considered the proposal. "Entertain, huh?" she said, her playful demeanor never faltering. "And what exactly does that entail?"

Grip's grin widened as he leaned closer. "Whatever we decide, doll. The ball's in our court," he replied. "But knowing Mistress Blue, she'll want it to be unforgettable."

Veronica pushed herself up slightly out of the water,

her body glistening in the sunlight. "Well," she said, tilting her head thoughtfully, "if Mistress Blue needs us to step up, who am I to say no?"

Grip sent a direct message to Mistress Blue, confirming their participation and the details of the dignitary's visit. It didn't take long for preparations to swing into motion.

By mid-morning, a team of staff arrived, bustling in and out of the condo with precision. They meticulously arranged an assortment of elegant finger foods and fine drinks in the dining area, carefully selected to impress their esteemed guest. The deck was attended to, adorned with soft ambient lighting and comfortable seating, perfect for an intimate evening with the glow of the city skyline as the backdrop.

As the sun began to dip toward the horizon, painting the sky in hues of orange and gold, everything was in place. The staff had departed, leaving the condo immaculate and ready. Grip stood by the front entrance as a sleek black car pulled up. The dignitary, a tall, imposing man in his mid-forties, stepped out. His name was Mwangi Ochieng, a prominent Kenyan businessman with deep tribal roots and connections that made him both influential and enigmatic.

Mwangi's demeanor was confident, yet his sharp eyes betrayed a sense of curiosity as Grip greeted him. "Mr. Ochieng," Grip said warmly, extending his hand. "Welcome to our home. I hope your journey was pleasant."

Mwangi shook Grip's hand firmly, a small smile tugging at the corners of his mouth. "It was," he replied in a deep, resonant voice. "Thank you for hosting me. Mistress Blue spoke very highly of you."

Grip nodded, his smirk returning. "The pleasure is

ours. Let me show you around."

He led Mwangi through the condo, pointing out the prepared food and drinks, though Mwangi's sharp gaze seemed to take in more than just the decor. It wasn't long before Grip guided him toward the deck, where the warm evening breeze carried the faint sound of the city below.

As they stepped onto the deck, Mwangi's footsteps faltered slightly. His gaze locked onto Veronica, who was lounging casually on a chaise near the edge of the pool. She wore a tiny black thong and no top, her toned, sun-kissed body glistening in the fading sunlight. Her arms rested lazily behind her head as she soaked in the last rays of the day.

Mwangi's expression shifted to one of disbelief, his composure momentarily slipping as he took in the sight. He turned to Grip, his voice low but incredulous. "You didn't mention … this."

Grip chuckled, stepping forward and leaning casually against the railing. "I figured some surprises were in order," he replied smoothly, his tone light. "Veronica has a way of making an impression."

Veronica glanced up, her lips curling into a slow, knowing smile as her eyes met Mwangi's. She didn't move to cover herself, her confidence and ease only adding to the allure of the moment. "Good evening," she said softly, her voice warm and inviting. "I hope you're enjoying the view."

Mwangi let out a quiet laugh, shaking his head as if to compose himself. "It's … extraordinary," he said, his voice thick with awe.

Grip's smirk deepened as he gestured toward a nearby seat. "Why don't we relax and enjoy the sunset? There's plenty of time for more surprises."

Mwangi nodded, still slightly stunned as he took his seat, his eyes darting back to Veronica, who stretched languidly, completely at ease under their watchful gaze.

The conversation on the deck began with casual pleasantries, Mwangi's deep voice blending seamlessly with Grip's as they discussed the city skyline and its vibrant energy. Veronica remained relaxed, her body language confident and inviting as she reclined, the golden light of the setting sun highlighting every curve of her nearly naked body.

As the small talk continued, Veronica's keen eyes drifted toward Mwangi, catching the faint but unmistakable outline of a growing bulge in his tailored trousers. A knowing smile crept onto her lips as she turned to Grip, her voice light yet teasing.

"It looks like we may need to be a little more welcoming, don't you think, darling?"

Grip chuckled softly, his gaze flicking to Mwangi, who shifted slightly in his seat, his composure faltering for just a moment. "The night is yours, my dear," Grip replied, leaning back in his chair with a relaxed smirk.

Veronica stood gracefully, every movement deliberate as she rose from her seat and stepped toward Mwangi. Her confidence radiated as she came to a stop just in front of him, her body fully on display under the fading light. She tilted her head slightly, her eyes meeting Mwangi's, the air between them thick with anticipation.

Mwangi's breath hitched, his usually composed demeanor replaced by a visible mix of intrigue and desire as he looked up at her. Veronica's posture remained effortless, her hands resting lightly on her hips as she gave him a moment to take in the full view.

"Well," she said softly, her voice carrying a playful

edge. "What do you think so far?"

Mwangi swallowed hard, a low chuckle escaping his lips. "I think ... I couldn't have imagined a warmer welcome."

Grip remained seated, watching the exchange with an amused expression as the atmosphere on the deck shifted from casual to charged. Veronica took a step closer, her presence filling the space between them, setting the stage for what was to come.

Veronica's confident smile deepened as she took another step closer to Mwangi, her tone suddenly shifting to one of playful authority. "Stand up," she commanded, her voice low yet firm.

Mwangi blinked, momentarily caught off guard by the sudden shift, but he rose from his seat. As he did, Veronica's gaze dropped, her eyes zeroing in on the undeniable strain of his bulge against the fabric of his tailored trousers. The outline was prominent, nearly threatening to tear the seams.

She met his eyes again, her expression both teasing and inviting. "No need for clothes here," she said, her voice silky and smooth. "Let us both enjoy a good view, shall we?"

Mwangi hesitated for only a moment before nodding, his hands moving to his jacket first, sliding it off and draping it neatly over the chair. With deliberate motions, he began unbuttoning his shirt, his eyes never leaving Veronica's as he revealed his broad chest and toned torso beneath. The shirt joined the jacket, followed by his belt and pants, which he stepped out of with surprising ease for someone so composed.

Now standing completely bare, his powerful frame was on full display, his confidence growing as Veronica's approving gaze lingered.

Not to be outdone, Veronica reached for the small string at her hips, her fingers teasing the delicate fabric before slipping it down her legs in one smooth motion. She stepped out of the thong and playfully tossed it toward Grip, who caught it effortlessly, his smirk widening as he twirled it casually around one finger.

"Well, doll," Grip said with a chuckle, leaning back in his chair. "You certainly know how to set the tone."

Veronica turned her attention back to Mwangi, her movements slow as she stepped closer, her bare form glowing in the soft light of the setting sun. "Now," she said with a playful edge, "let's see just how welcoming we can be."

Mwangi's eyes glimmered with a mix of anticipation and admiration, the tension between them growing as the moment stretched, full of unspoken possibilities.

Veronica's gaze flickered with mischief as she stepped even closer to Mwangi, her movements deliberate and confident. Slowly, she sank to her knees before him, her head tilting back as she looked up, her eyes meeting his with a glimmer of playful defiance.

From her position, she took in the sheer presence of him. The golden hues of the sunset cast a soft glow across her features, accentuating the commanding yet inviting air she exuded. Mwangi stood perfectly still, his breathing deep and steady as he watched her, his once composed demeanor now softened by the sexual tension.

Behind them, Grip leaned back in his chair, the faintest smirk on his lips as he observed Veronica's boldness. "Well, doll," he said casually, his voice carrying a note of amusement, "you've certainly got his full attention."

Veronica didn't respond immediately, her focus entirely on Mwangi as the charged energy between them thickened. Her hands rested lightly on her thighs as she remained poised, completely in control despite the suggestive nature of the moment.

Veronica's movements were deliberate as she leaned closer. Mwangi's breath hitched, his composure faltering slightly as her mouth wrapped around the large head of his thick member. Veronica bobbed her head, sliding his dick in and out of her mouth, wrapping her tongue around the shaft and flicking the tip teasingly before taking all of him as far as she could, holding her breath. She shoved his cock down her throat and thrust him into her over and over, a deep, hollow sound resonated, paired with a rhythmic, almost choking vibration that never crossed into full gagging as she pleasured his cock.

Grip sat back, his gaze unwavering as he watched Veronica. His expression softened, a mixture of admiration and amusement playing across his face. "You always know how to captivate, doll," he murmured, his voice low but audible in the quiet tension of the rooftop.

Mwangi's low moan broke the stillness, his head tilting back slightly, caught in the sensations Veronica so expertly evoked. The sounds of the city below faded into the background, leaving only the intimate moment shared among them.

Grip's eyes gleamed as he watched, his arms resting casually on the chair's armrests. "Looks like you're making an impression," he remarked with quiet pride, the dynamic between them perfectly balanced.

Veronica slowly pulled back, her movements deliberate as she rose to her feet. She met Mwangi's gaze with a knowing smile, her confidence radiating as she turned away from him. The light of the setting sun played across her skin as she took a few steps toward one of the chairs overlooking the pool.

Without a word, she bent forward, her hands resting on the chair's backrest as she positioned herself. The pose was deliberate, her body perfectly framed by the shimmering water below.

She glanced back over her shoulder, her expression both inviting and commanding as she caught Mwangi's eye. Her voice, low and teasing, broke the tension. "Well?" she asked, the single word heavy with meaning.

Mwangi stepped forward, his breathing deep and steady as he moved behind her, his gaze fixed on the sight before him. Veronica's posture exuded both power and submission, a delicate balance that left them both charged with anticipation.

Grip, still seated nearby, watched, his arms now folded casually across his chest. The flicker of pride in his eyes was unmistakable as he observed Veronica's control of the scene.

Mwangi stepped forward, his presence towering over Veronica as she held her position, her body perfectly aligned to accommodate him. The anticipation was palpable as he placed his hands firmly on her hips, steadying himself as he moved closer.

Veronica's breath quickened, her gaze lifting to meet Grip's across the pool deck, a subtle smile playing at her lips.

Grip's eyes never left Veronica's.

As Mwangi moved behind her, his powerful presence added to the weight of the moment. Veronica's expression shifted to one of blissful focus, her connection to both men evident as her gaze flicked between Mwangi and

Grip as Mwangis large cock pressed against her entrance. Her wet hole was opening to accommodate the thick round head as best as it could, and with enough pressure from Mwangi's thrust, the tip popped in.

Veronica let out a blissful moan, "Yes please, deeper," she begged. As Mwangi grabbed her hips and rammed all of him into her. she screeched in pain and bliss.

Mwangi began to move, his powerful thrusts creating a steady, deliberate rhythm. The sound of their bodies meeting filled the air, a symphony of wet smacks and deep moans that blended with the distant hum of the city below. Veronica's fingers gripped the edge of the chair, her knuckles whitening as her body rocked in time with Mwangi's motions.

Her moans grew louder with each thrust, mixing with Mwangi's guttural grunts as he maintained his relentless pace. The chair beneath Veronica creaked, a testament to the intensity of their movements. Each impact sent waves of pleasure coursing through her, her blissful expressions never breaking as she occasionally locked eyes with Grip, who watched with a lustful gaze.

Grip remained seated, his posture relaxed. His eyes stayed fixed on Veronica, admiration and amusement playing across his face as he observed the raw passion. The corner of his mouth curled into a small, knowing smile, clearly enjoying the passionate moment between his wife and their guest.

The pace quickened, Mwangi's thrusts growing more forceful and rhythmic. The sound of skin meeting skin echoed across the deck, accompanied by Veronica's gasps and Mwangi's deep, throaty moans. Veronica arched her back slightly, pushing herself into him as the sensations overwhelmed her, her cries reaching a crescendo of pleasure.

The city lights began to sparkle as the sun dipped below the horizon, the warm hues of the day fading into the cool, electric glow of night. The rooftop became their own private world, filled with sounds of ecstasy and undeniable energy.

Mwangi's pace grew erratic, his powerful thrusts becoming uneven as he neared his climax. Veronica's body moved in perfect rhythm with his, her gasps and moans intensifying. The energy between them reached its peak, an undeniable charge that filled the air.

Then, in one final, deep thrust, Mwangi suddenly froze. His grip on Veronica's hips tightened momentarily. His body stiffened, and a sharp, guttural gasp escaped his lips, completely out of rhythm with the pleasure-filled sounds that had dominated moments before.

"Ah—" Mwangi started, his voice strained and weak.

Veronica turned her head slightly, confusion flashing across her face as she felt his dick convulse with such power she has never felt before, so thick and large filling her every inch, so much pressure on her walls as she felt his semen shoot to the back of her cervix so hard it felt as if someone flicked her insides.

"OH FUCK YES!" Veronica screamed in pure bliss as her body trembled with her orgasm. Her knees shook, her body covered in goosebumps. It was one of the most exhilarating orgasms she had ever had. Mwangi slipped out of her body's grip on his member and fell to the floor.

Grip rushed over only to find that Mwangi had no pulse. He instructed Veronica to call for an ambulance as he started CPR.

Veronica's hands trembled as she grabbed her phone,

her breaths coming in short, panicked bursts. She quickly dialed for emergency services, her voice shaking as the operator picked up.

"911, what's your emergency?" the calm voice on the other end asked.

"My—my guest!" Veronica stammered, glancing over at Grip, who was already performing chest compressions on Mwangi. "He … he collapsed. He's not breathing! We're at the penthouse—uh, rooftop—of 412 Skyline Tower in downtown. Please, hurry!"

"Ma'am, stay calm," the operator replied, their tone steady. "You said he's not breathing. Is anyone performing CPR?"

"Yes, my—my husband is," Veronica said, her voice cracking as she watched Grip methodically push down on Mwangi's chest. His movements were precise, his military training evident in this moment of chaos.

"Good. Keep it going until help arrives," the operator instructed. "Is the patient responding at all? Any movement?"

Veronica's eyes darted to Mwangi's face, his expression eerily still. "No, nothing," she said, her heart pounding as adrenaline coursed through her veins.

Grip glanced up briefly, his face calm but focused. "Tell them to bring a defibrillator," he said firmly.

"They'll need a defibrillator," Veronica relayed to the operator.

"Understood, ma'am. Paramedics are en-route," the operator reassured her. "They should arrive in under five minutes. Just stay on the line and keep updating me."

Veronica nodded, even though the operator couldn't see her. Her gaze shifted between Grip and Mwangi, the surreal nature of the moment hitting her all at once. Moments ago, this man had been towering over her, full of life and energy. Now, he lay motionless on the deck, his fate uncertain.

Grip's voice broke through her spiraling thoughts. "Stay with me, Mwangi," he muttered, his movements unrelenting as he kept the rhythm steady.

The faint sound of sirens in the distance began to grow louder, a small sliver of hope cutting through the tense atmosphere.

"They're almost here," Veronica said into the phone, her voice barely above a whisper.

"Good," the operator replied. "Keep the CPR going until they take over."

The rooftop was a flurry of controlled chaos as EMS arrived, their equipment in tow. The team barely glanced at Grip and Veronica, who was still naked, and began quickly assessed Mwangi's condition, their faces serious and focused. Grip stepped back, pulling Veronica gently with him to give the medics space as they took over CPR and attached a defibrillator.

"Charging," one of the paramedics called, placing the paddles on Mwangi's chest.

"Clear!" another said, and Mwangi's body jolted slightly from the electric shock. His cock still stiff from the lustful events before shook from the efforts.

Veronica clutched Grip's arm, her breath hitching with every attempt to resuscitate him. Despite their best efforts—multiple shocks and continued chest compressions—there was no visible sign of response.

"Let's get him to the hospital," one of the paramedics finally said. "We'll continue en-route."

The team carefully loaded Mwangi onto the stretcher,

securing him and covering his naked body with a blanket, then wheeled him to the elevator.

Veronica stood motionless, her hands trembling as she watched them leave. The sound of their departing footsteps and the faint whir of the elevator doors closing echoed through the now-silent rooftop.

#

Later That Evening

Veronica and Grip stood at the kitchen bar, a heavy silence between them. The events of the night replayed in Veronica's mind as she gripped a glass of water, her knuckles white against the clear surface. Grip leaned against the counter across from her, his arms crossed and his expression unreadable.

The sharp buzz of Grip's phone broke the silence. He glanced at the screen and sighed before answering. "Mistress Blue," he said, his voice low.

Veronica watched as he listened intently. Though she couldn't hear Mistress Blue's words, the gravity of the conversation was clear in Grip's demeanor.

When he hung up, he placed the phone on the counter, exhaling deeply. "She wanted us to know…" he began, pausing to meet Veronica's gaze, "he didn't make it."

Veronica felt a cold wave rush over her. "Heart attack?" she asked softly, her voice trembling.

Grip nodded. "Yes. She said he passed shortly after arrival. But …" he hesitated, then added, "She wanted to thank us. For giving him an unforgettable evening. It meant a lot to her, and, she suspects, to him."

Veronica stared down at her glass, the weight of the night pressing heavily on her chest. "I don't even know what to say," she whispered, her voice barely audible.

Grip moved around the counter, placing a reassuring

hand on her shoulder. "Neither do I," he admitted, his voice softer. "But we'll process this together, doll. Like we always do."

The two stood in silence, the soft glow of the city lights casting faint patterns across the walls, as they tried to come to terms with the surreal and somber turn their evening had taken.

The bedroom was dark, illuminated only by the faint glow of the city lights filtering through the curtains. Veronica and Grip lay side by side in their spacious bed, the weight of the evening still heavy between them. The silence was comfortable but thick with unspoken thoughts.

Veronica shifted slightly, her head turning to face Grip. Her voice broke the stillness, hesitant and quiet. "Can I tell you something, and you promise not to judge me?"

Grip turned his head toward her, his gaze soft and reassuring. "Of course, doll. Always."

She hesitated, her fingers nervously twisting the edge of the blanket as she searched for the right words. Finally, she spoke, her voice trembling slightly. "When he … when he passed, inside me … it was the most pleasure I've ever felt."

Grip's expression didn't change, his eyes remaining steady on her as she continued, her cheeks flushed with a mix of guilt and vulnerability.

"I don't know how to explain it," she admitted, her words spilling out in a rush. "It was like… the blood rushing, the tension, everything. It all built into something I've never experienced before. The moment his dick exploded inside me, it caused this overwhelming release. I've never felt anything like it."

Grip reached out, placing a hand gently on her cheek.

"You don't need to explain, doll," he said softly, his voice calm. "Your body reacted in the moment. It doesn't mean anything more than that."

Veronica exhaled a shaky breath, her eyes searching his for any hint of judgment but finding only understanding. "I was scared to tell you," she admitted, her voice barely above a whisper.

Grip leaned in to press a gentle kiss to her forehead. "You never have to be scared to tell me anything," he murmured. "We're in this together, no matter what."

She nodded, her body relaxing slightly as she nestled closer to him, her head resting on his chest. The steady rhythm of his heartbeat was a comforting reminder of their connection, grounding her after a night filled with chaos and intensity.

As the city outside fell quiet, the two drifted into an uneasy sleep, their thoughts still lingering on the strange and unforgettable events of the evening.

CHAPTER 7

CHASING THE FEELING

The morning sun crept over the horizon, casting soft golden light across the sprawling city skyline. On the rooftop of their luxurious condo, the air was still, save for the faint hum of activity from the streets below. Veronica lay on one of the loungers near the pool, her expression distant, while Grip stood leaning against the railing, sipping his coffee.

The sharp ring of the phone cut through the peaceful silence. Grip glanced at it and picked it up, his tone casual as he answered. "Hello?"

"Grip," Mistress Blue's smooth, familiar voice purred on the other end. "I trust you've had some time to rest after recent events. I wanted to extend an invitation to another gathering tonight. Something intimate."

Grip listened, a faint smile tugging at his lips. "Appreciate the offer," he said, glancing over at Veronica. "Give me a moment to check."

Walking over to where Veronica reclined, he crouched down beside her, his voice soft and measured. "Doll, that was Mistress Blue. She's inviting us to another party tonight. Something smaller, more private."

Veronica turned her head to look at him, her eyes half-lidded. She paused, then shrugged nonchalantly. "Maybe next time," she said softly, her tone lacking its usual spark. Grip frowned slightly, his sharp eyes studying her. "You sure?"

Veronica nodded, letting her gaze drift back to the skyline. "Yeah, I'm sure."

Grip stood, returning to the phone. "We'll have to pass this time," he told Mistress Blue, his voice polite but firm. After a brief exchange of goodbyes, he hung up and set the phone on the bar.

Walking back to Veronica, he sat on the edge of the lounger, his hand brushing gently over her arm.

"What's going on, doll?" he asked, his voice filled with quiet concern. "Something bothering you?" The morning light bathed them both. Veronica remained silent, her lips pressing into a thin line as she avoided his gaze. Grip waited patiently, his hand still resting lightly on her arm, as the unspoken tension lingered between them.

Veronica sat up slightly, pulling her legs beneath her and wrapping her arms around them. She let out a long sigh, her gaze fixed on the city skyline but her thoughts clearly elsewhere. Grip waited patiently, his hand resting on her arm as he watched her wrestle with whatever was on her mind.

"Grip ..." she began softly, her voice barely audible over the faint hum of the city below. "I don't even know how to explain this."

He tilted his head slightly, his voice calm and encouraging. "Take your time, doll. You can tell me anything, you know that."

She hesitated for a moment before turning to meet his eyes. "Ever since ... that night with Mwangi, I've felt ... off." Her voice trembled slightly, but she pressed on. "Everything we've done since has just felt ... empty. Nothing's been enough."

Grip's brow furrowed as he listened, his gaze steady and attentive. "Empty how?" he asked carefully.

"It's like ... I can't stop thinking about how intense it was," she admitted, her cheeks flushing slightly. "Not just the physical part, but the ... the thrill. The danger. It was so raw, so uncontrollable." She looked down at her hands, twisting them nervously. "And now, I can't seem to feel anything close to that."

Grip stayed quiet for a moment, his hand moving to gently squeeze hers. "You're chasing that feeling," he said simply, his tone understanding rather than judgmental.

Veronica nodded. "I know it sounds insane, but I need that intensity again. I need something more, something ... uncommon." She glanced up at him, her eyes searching his. "But I can't do this without you. I need to know you're okay with me experimenting. Pushing boundaries."

Grip leaned back slightly, his expression thoughtful. "Doll, you know I've always been open to whatever makes you happy," he said after a pause. "But experimenting further... that's not something you take lightly."

"I'm not taking it lightly," she said quickly. "I just ... I need to feel alive again. And I think the only way I can do that is to try something different. Something darker."

Grip studied her for a long moment, his face unreadable. Then he nodded. "If that's what you need," he said finally, "we'll figure it out. Together."

Relief washed over Veronica's face as she let out a breath. She leaned forward, wrapping her arms around him tightly. "Thank you," she whispered.

Grip pulled back slightly from their embrace, his hands resting on Veronica's shoulders as he studied her face. "Have you put any thought into anything specific?" he asked, his voice calm but deliberate. "What exactly do you think would get you closer to that feeling you're chasing?"

Veronica hesitated, chewing her bottom lip as her gaze darted to the skyline, then back to Grip. "Well," she began tentatively, "there's this book my sister mentioned once. In it, there's this scene where a woman is being chased through the woods by a man. She doesn't know when or where he'll catch her, but when he does… he takes her against her will."

Grip raised an eyebrow, his expression neutral as he listened carefully.

"It's not just the … act," Veronica continued, her cheeks flushing. "It's the idea of being hunted. The unpredictability of it. Not knowing when or how it'll happen." She paused, taking a deep breath. "The closest thing to that is consensual non-consent, but even that feels … fake. There's no real danger. You still have control because you know it's just a game."

Her words hung in the air, the weight of them settling between them as she searched Grip's face for a reaction. He remained quiet, his sharp eyes locked on hers, absorbing every word.

"It's thrilling to think about," she admitted, her voice softer now. "But I know it's… extreme."

Grip leaned back slightly, his arms crossing over his chest as he processed what she'd said. The faintest flicker of something crossed his face—curiosity, perhaps—but he didn't speak right away. Instead, he nodded, his gaze drifting out to the city skyline as if mulling over her words.

Veronica stayed quiet, unsure of what to say next, as the silence between them stretched. Grip's thoughtful expression gave nothing away, leaving her wondering what he might be thinking.

Grip opened his mouth to respond, his brow furrowing as he considered her words, but the soft chime of the elevator door interrupted him. He turned his head sharply to see his assistant, Ethan, rushing in, his face flushed and his breathing uneven.

"Sir," Ethan began, his voice urgent. "There's been a mission posted just now. Prepayment has already been received. It's four times our normal rate." He paused, glancing between Grip and Veronica. "The only note included was: Will contact soon."

Grip's eyes narrowed as he absorbed the information, the tension in his shoulders immediately noticeable. Before he could ask for further details, his phone vibrated on the countertop, the caller ID flashing Mistress Blue across the screen.

He picked up the phone quickly, holding it to his ear. "Mistress Blue, I'm in the middle of something. I'll call you—"

"Sorry, Grip," she interjected, her voice firm but laced with urgency. "I've hired your company. This is serious. I have a major issue, and I need your personal touch on it."

Grip's expression hardened as he straightened. "You've hired us? What kind of issue are we talking about, Blue?"

"Not over the phone," Mistress Blue replied curtly. "This needs to be handled delicately. Can you meet me within the hour?"

Grip glanced at Veronica, who was watching him with a mix of curiosity and concern. He nodded slowly, his voice calm. "Where?"

"I'll send the details," Mistress Blue said, her tone softening slightly. "Grip, I wouldn't call if it wasn't urgent."

The line disconnected, leaving Grip standing there with the phone still in his hand, his mind already shifting gears. He looked at Ethan, who was waiting silently. "Get the team prepped and ready," he instructed. "We're moving on this as soon as I get the details."

"Yes, sir," Ethan said, turning and hurrying back to the elevator.

Grip turned his attention back to Veronica, his expression unreadable. "Looks like things just got interesting," he said quietly.

Veronica tilted her head, a faint smile playing on her lips despite the tension. "When don't they?"

Grip's phone vibrated again on the countertop, the screen lighting up with a set of coordinates. His sharp eyes scanned the message as another notification followed—a picture. He opened it to see the image of a young Russian woman, her face lovely but etched with fear, along with a single line of text: Needs immediate extraction.

Grip exhaled deeply, his expression hardening as he placed the phone back down. He turned to Veronica, his tone calm but firm. "I have to go. This one's urgent. It'll take me to Russia, but I should be back within five or six days."

Veronica stood, her brow furrowing with concern as she watched him grab his go-bag from a nearby cabinet. She approached him, her hand lightly resting on his arm. "Be careful, okay?" she said softly, her voice laced with worry.

Grip gave her a small, reassuring smile, leaning down to kiss her forehead. "You know I always am, doll. I'll call if I can, but don't worry if you don't hear from me. Sometimes these things get complicated."

She nodded, stepping back as he slung the bag over his shoulder and headed toward the elevator. "I'll be waiting," she said, her voice quieter now.

He turned just before stepping inside, his gaze lingering on her for a moment. "I'll see you soon," he said simply, and with that, the elevator doors closed.

#Veronica's days passed uneventfully, though Grip's absence left a strange emptiness in the condo. She went about her routine, filling her time with small errands and distractions, but her thoughts often drifted to him and the dangerous mission he'd undertaken.

By the fifth day, anticipation began to bubble beneath her calm exterior. She found herself glancing at the clock more often, wondering when he might walk through the door. The thought of his return brought a mix of relief and excitement as she moved through her morning, readying herself for the possibility of seeing him again.

Steam billowed softly from the bathroom as Veronica stepped out of the shower, her skin glistening and her damp hair cascading over her bare shoulders. Wrapping a towel around her, she padded across the bedroom, feeling a familiar spark of excitement as she imagined Grip walking through the door at any moment.

The sound of the elevator chime echoed through the condo, and her heart leapt. A wide grin spread across her face as she quickly let the towel fall to the floor, revealing her flawless form. Her bare feet moved quickly across the hardwood as she rushed toward the door, anticipation and unspoken longing radiating through her every step.

As the elevator doors slid open, she froze mid-step. Instead of Grip, a man dressed in white overalls, carrying a toolbox, stepped into view. His shirt bore the logo SunnyDays Pool

Maintenance. His eyes widened slightly at the sight of her before he quickly averted his gaze.

"Oh," Veronica said flatly, her excitement deflating as disappointment washed over her. She stood there for a moment, letting out a soft sigh before turning on her heel.

"Well," she said, her tone light but laced with teasing as she turned back toward her bedroom, deliberately swaying her hips. "Enjoy the view while you can."

The maintenance man chuckled awkwardly, his eyes flickering back for a split second before returning to the toolbox in his hands. "Wish I was whoever you were expecting," he said with a grin as he moved past her, toward the pool area.

Veronica smirked faintly, bending to pick up her towel and draping it loosely over her shoulder. She made her way to the closet, slipping into a soft robe before returning to her vanity to dry her hair.

Out by the pool, she could hear the faint clatter of tools and the maintenance man's occasional hum as he worked near the pumps. The moment was an amusing interruption to her morning, but her mind quickly drifted back to Grip and the hope that he would return soon.

Veronica stepped out onto the pool deck, the warm sun kissing her skin as she adjusted the straps of her skimpy swimsuit that barely covered her. With a sigh of contentment, she reclined on one of the plush loungers, tilting her head back and closing her eyes, letting the sunlight warm her.

Nearby, the maintenance man tinkered with the pool pumps, the faint sound of tools clinking against metal breaking the otherwise serene quiet. After a few moments, he wiped his brow with the back of his hand and glanced over at her.

"Hey, hope you don't mind me asking," he started, his voice friendly, "but would it be okay if I helped myself to your bar? I'm parched out here."

Veronica opened one eye, looking over at him with a faint smile. "Not at all," she replied. "Go ahead."

The man set down his tools and made his way over to the sleek bar setup. He scanned the bottles and mixers with a practiced eye, then called back to her, "You know, I used to be a hell of a bartender in my younger days."

Veronica raised an eyebrow, intrigued by the sudden claim. "Oh yeah?" she said, her tone teasing. "Prove it."

He laughed, grabbing a few bottles and starting to mix with practiced precision. "You got it," he said confidently. "I'll whip you up something killer. Trust me, you'll love it."

A few moments later, he walked over to her with a chilled glass in hand, the liquid inside was a perfect blend of vibrant colors. "One special drink, made just for you," he said with a grin, handing it to her.

Veronica took a sip, her lips curling into a genuine smile as the flavors danced on her tongue.

"Wow," she said, nodding approvingly. "You weren't kidding. This is amazing."

"Glad you like it," he replied, his grin widening as he turned to head back to the pumps.

Veronica reclined again, the cool drink in her hand and the warm sun on her skin, momentarily forgetting her anticipation for Grip's return as she enjoyed the relaxing afternoon.

Veronica took another sip of the drink, savoring the refreshing taste. But as she set the glass down on the small table beside her, her fingers fumbled, and the glass slipped, tumbling to the ground with a soft clink.

She blinked, her vision suddenly swimming, and a wave of exhaustion washed over her. Her body felt unusually heavy, her limbs refusing to cooperate as she tried to sit up.

"What ... the hell?" she murmured, her words slurring as her head lolled back against the lounger.

The edges of her vision blurred, and an intense drowsiness settled over her, pulling her into its grip. She struggled to keep her eyes open, her breaths shallow and uneven.

The last thing she saw was the pool maintenance man standing over her, his face twisted into a wicked, shit-eating grin. His eyes glinted with malice, his presence looming over her like a dark shadow.

Then, everything went black.

CHAPTER 8

CHASING VERONICA

Veronica groaned softly as her senses slowly returned. Her head was pounding, her body sluggish, and an unfamiliar damp, earthy smell filled her nose. As she blinked her eyes open, the world around her came into focus—or rather, the overwhelming expanse of trees, stretching endlessly in every direction.

Confusion quickly turned to panic as she shifted, realizing her hands were tightly bound behind her, secured around the rough trunk of a tree. The bark pressed uncomfortably against her back, and she could feel the unrelenting pressure of the ropes cutting into her wrists.

"What the—" she muttered, her voice hoarse, before stopping as her gaze landed on the pool maintenance man standing just a few feet in front of her, a malicious grin plastered across his face.

He tilted his head slightly, watching her struggle with an unsettling calmness. "Ah, sleeping beauty finally wakes," he said, his voice smug and casual.

Veronica's breathing quickened as she looked around, her heart pounding. "Where the Hell am I? What's going on?"

The man chuckled, taking a step closer to her. "Oh, don't worry. We're in the middle of nowhere. Just you, me, and all these trees." He spread his arms as if to emphasize the isolation.

Veronica's mind raced as she pulled at her bindings, her voice rising. "What the fuck are you doing!"

The man's grin widened, his eyes glinting with twisted amusement. "Oh, when those elevator doors opened, and I saw you standing there with nothing at all on, looking like that, I knew I had to have a taste."

Veronica's stomach turned, fear mixing with rage as she glared at him.

"So," he continued nonchalantly, "I found my opportunity. That drink? Just a little something to help you sleep. After you passed out, it was easy. I stuffed your limp body into one of those big boxes I used for the old saltwater pump. No one even batted an eye as I wheeled you right out of your condo and into my van."

Veronica's blood ran cold as she listened, her eyes darting around the clearing, searching for any sign of help. But there was nothing—just dense trees and the sound of rustling leaves.

"And now," he said, his voice dropping slightly as he stepped closer, "we're out here, where we can have some peace and quiet."

Veronica's stomach churned as her gaze dropped, noticing the bulge in his pants. Her heart raced, anger and panic surging through her as she tried to steady her voice. "You're making a huge mistake," she hissed, her mind frantically trying to come up with a plan.

The man tilted his head, clearly amused by her defiance. "Oh, I don't think so," he said softly, his grin never wavering.

Veronica's fear bubbled over, and she let out a piercing scream, her voice echoing through the dense forest. "HELP! SOMEBODY HELP ME!"

The man laughed, a dark, guttural sound that sent shivers down her spine. "Scream all you want," he said, stepping closer. "There's no one out here but us. Just trees, birds, and ... well, me."

Her heart pounded as she thrashed against her bindings, her wrists raw from the rough rope. She glared at him, her defiance flaring even through her fear. "You're insane," she spat, her voice trembling but firm.

He grinned, his hands moving to his waistband as he began to slide his pants down. "Maybe I am," he said with a chuckle, "but you're going to wish you hadn't been so loud."

As he stood before her, fully exposed, Veronica's eyes flicked down and quickly back up, her lip curling in disgust. "That's it?" she said, her voice laced with derision. "You're going to pull all this, and that's what you're working with?"

His smug grin disappeared instantly, replaced by a scowl. "What did you just say?" he growled, his tone dropping.

"Average at best," she snapped, leaning into her bravado despite the panic rising inside her. "You're pathetic. All of this just to feel like a man?"

The man's face twisted in fury. He took a menacing step closer, his breathing growing heavier. "You think you're so tough, don't you?" he hissed. "Let's see how tough you are now."

Veronica's heart raced as she struggled to maintain her composure, refusing to let him see the fear bubbling beneath the surface. She knew she was playing a dangerous game, but she clung to her defiance like a lifeline, desperate to keep some semblance of control in the situation.

The man's scowl twisted into a sinister grin as he crouched down in front of Veronica. His rough, calloused hands worked quickly, tying her ankles together with a thick rope, leaving just enough slack to hobble her movements.

"There," he muttered, satisfied with his work. He stood, brushing dirt from his hands, and walked around behind the tree where she was bound.

"I want you to fight, you little bitch," he sneered as he began untying her wrists with surprising efficiency. Before Veronica could react, his powerful hands gripped her arms and yanked her roughly away from the tree.

She landed hard on her face, the impact sending a jolt of pain through her body. The coarse dirt scraped against her skin, and as she shifted, her swimsuit top slipped down, exposing her breasts.

The man let out a low, mocking laugh. "There they are," he said with a sickening glee. "That's what I want to see."

Veronica's heart pounded as she tried to push herself up, her arms shaking with effort. Desperation surged through her as she began crawling forward, the rope around her ankles making her movements slow and awkward.

The man loomed behind her, his heavy boots crunching against the forest floor with each step as he closed the distance between them. "Where do you think you're going, sweetheart?" he taunted, his voice dripping with malice.

Veronica's breath hitched as she scrambled forward, her mind racing for a plan, any way to get out of this nightmare.

Veronica's hands worked furiously as she clawed at the knot binding her ankles. Somehow, in the chaos of her struggling and his mocking taunts, the rope loosened. With a sudden snap, her legs came free.

The man let out a startled, "Oh shit!" as Veronica scrambled to her feet, adrenaline surging through her veins. Barefoot and barely covered in her disheveled swimsuit, she bolted into the woods, her breaths coming in panicked gasps.

"Get back here, you little bitch!" he roared behind her, the sound of his boots pounding against the forest floor growing closer.

Branches tore at her skin, whipping across her arms and legs as she ran. Each sharp sting only pushed her faster, her instincts screaming for her to survive. Her feet struck the uneven ground, sharp twigs and stones slicing into her soles, but the pain was drowned out by the sheer terror of his pursuit.

"Stop running!" his voice bellowed, closer than she wanted it to be.

Veronica dared to glance over her shoulder and saw him closing the gap. His outstretched hand grazed her shoulder, and with a forceful tug, he yanked at her top. The fragile fabric gave way, and she stumbled forward, tearing it completely free from her body.

"Gotcha!" he growled triumphantly, holding the flimsy piece of fabric in his hand, but Veronica pushed forward, the thought of capture fueling her desperate sprint.

She darted through the dense trees, her bare chest heaving with each ragged breath. Her heart thundered in her chest as she zigzagged, trying to throw him off her trail. Behind her, his grunts and curses told her he wasn't giving up.

The forest seemed to close in around her, the trees growing denser as she ran. Her legs burned with exertion and her lungs screamed for air, but she couldn't stop. Not now.

Suddenly, the terrain dipped, and she stumbled down a small incline, her arms flailing as she fought to keep her balance. A stream glistened ahead, its water rushing over jagged rocks. Veronica pushed herself toward it, the sound of the water masking the relentless pounding of his footsteps.

But as she reached the edge of the stream, she skidded to a halt, her heart sinking. A massive downed tree lay sprawled across the bank, its gnarled branches creating an impenetrable barrier on one side. The stream on the other side was too deep and fast-moving to safely cross.

She spun around, her chest heaving as she searched for another way out, but it was too late.

The man emerged from the trees, his face twisted with anger. "End of the line, sweetheart," he sneered, tossing her torn swimsuit top aside.

Veronica backed up against the downed tree, her breath catching in her throat as she realized there was nowhere left to run.

As Veronica pressed herself against the downed tree, her heart hammering in her chest, a faint buzzing sound caught her attention. She glanced up and froze. A small drone hovered above the clearing, its camera fixed on them.

Hope surged through her, igniting a spark of adrenaline. *Someone's watching! I'm not alone!* she thought desperately. She bolted from the tree, darting past the man, her arms flailing in the air as she screamed. "Help! Please, help me!"

But before she could get far, his rough hands clasped firmly around her waist. She let out a cry as he hoisted her off the ground, her legs kicking frantically.

"Oh no, you don't," he growled, slinging her over his shoulder like a sack of flour. "We're not done here."

Veronica struggled, pounding her fists against his back, but his grip was unyielding. As he started walking back into the woods, she felt a sharp sting on her bare backside.

SMACK.

She yelped as his hand came down on one cheek, followed by another stinging slap on the other.

SMACK.

"That's for thinking you could outrun me," he sneered, his voice dripping with condescension.

Veronica's face burned with humiliation as the blows continued. Her body bounced with each step he took, her position over his shoulder leaving her powerless to stop him.

"Look at you," he taunted, his tone mocking. "All that running, and for what? Back to square one. Should've just stayed put like a good little girl." SMACK. "Maybe I'll teach you some manners this time," he added with a chuckle, his hand striking her again.

Every step he took back to their original clearing was punctuated by another demeaning comment or sharp smack, the sound of his hand meeting her skin echoing through the trees. Veronica bit her lip, trying to suppress her tears as the helplessness of her situation set in.

Finally, they emerged back into the clearing where it had all started. "Now," he said, cracking his knuckles, "let's pick up where we left off, shall we?"

He dropped Veronica roughly onto the ground, and she scrambled to sit up, her heart racing as she watched him pull out another length of rope from his bag. His movements were efficient, his focus sharp as he grabbed her wrists and bound them tightly in front of her.

"Stop—please," she begged, her voice trembling as she tried to pull away, but his grip was like iron.

He ignored her, his rough hands working quickly as he tied her ankles again, this time with a tighter knot that bit into her skin. Her body trembled as she realized there was no escape this time.

As he stood over her, Veronica's eyes darted down, and she couldn't help but notice the unmistakable throbbing in his dick. Blood vessels straining against the skin, his arousal painfully obvious.

"Please," she stammered, her voice breaking. "Let me go. I-I have money—I can pay you. Whatever you want, just let me go!"

The man let out a harsh laugh, crouching down so his face was level with hers. "I don't want your fucking money, slut," he sneered, his eyes dark and wild. "I want your body."

Veronica's stomach churned as his words sank in, the malicious intent in his voice sending a cold wave of fear through her. Her breath came in shallow gasps as she tried to back away, but the ropes and his imposing presence left her trapped.

He stood again, his gaze raking over her with twisted satisfaction as he began to stroke his cock.

Veronica's chest heaved as tears welled up in her eyes, the weight of the moment pressing down on her. She felt utterly powerless, her usual confidence stripped away. The man's voice, low and commanding, broke through her panicked thoughts.

"Bend over," he ordered, his tone sharp and unwavering.

Her tears spilled over as she hesitated. But there was no room for defiance. With tear-filled eyes and a shaky breath, she slowly turned and followed the instruction, her movements stiff and reluctant.

"There you go," he said with a twisted glee. "Now that's a good slut."

Veronica flinched at the word, but she bit her lip, holding back a sob as she tried to steady herself.

"Let's make something clear," he continued, his voice dripping with condescension. "When I give you a command, you respond with 'Yes, sir.' Got it?"

She hesitated, her throat tightening as shame and fear swirled within her. "Y-yes, sir," she finally murmured, her voice barely audible.

"Good," he said with satisfaction, stepping closer behind her.

His dick pressed against her tunnel, and to her surprise, he didn't struggle at all sliding right past her already wet lips, completely filling her insides.

Why is this happening? Veronica's mind raced as she struggled to process the overwhelming sensations coursing through her. *I don't want this ... I hate this ...* Yet, to her horror, her body seemed to betray her. Her breathing quickened, her skin tingled, and her limbs trembled—not just from fear, but from something she couldn't understand.

Why am I reacting like this? she thought, panic rising with her shame. *This isn't right. This isn't me.* She tried to will herself to fight, to push back against the unwelcome reactions her body was having, but the dissonance between her mind and body only deepened.

Am I broken? she wondered, tears pricking her eyes. *How can I feel this way when every part of me is screaming to stop?*

Her thoughts spiraled further into confusion, each unwanted response fueling a growing sense of helplessness. *I don't want this. I don't want any of this... so why does it feel like my body isn't listening to me? Why am I so turned on?*

This isn't right ... this isn't supposed to happen. Veronica's mind fought to make sense of the storm inside her. At first, it had been pure terror—sharp, raw, and all-consuming. But now, the fear had dulled, morphing into something else entirely.

He slammed into her tight, dripping opening, over and over again.

Why does this feel different? she thought, her breath hitching as a foreign, unwelcome heat began to rise within her. A wave of shame crashed over her as she realized her body was responding in ways she couldn't control.

No, no, no ... I don't want this, she told herself, the disgust bubbling in her chest. But as much as she tried to focus on the revulsion, there was no denying the pull of something deeper, darker—a flicker of pleasure that made her stomach churn.

What's wrong with me? she asked herself, tears prickling her eyes. *How can I be feeling this? How can I be... enjoying this?*

She clenched her fists, trying to suppress the sensations that were threatening to take over.

No... no, this can't be happening, Veronica thought, panic surging as the sensation deepened, overtaking her mind's protests. Her breath hitched, and her body tensed, but not in defiance. Instead, an unbearable pressure was building inside her, one she couldn't ignore, couldn't suppress.

Stop it, stop it now! she screamed internally, her tears spilling down her cheeks. *How can I feel this? I hate this. I hate him. I hate myself!*

Her mind scrambled for control, but her body had long since ignored her commands. The tension grew, relentless and consuming, until it felt like she might break.

His pace quickened, it started to build with a rhythm like he was answering her body's call. Like his veiny cock had a direct line with what her pussy needed.

And then it happened—a soft, unbidden sigh escaped her lips. The sound was quiet, but it rang in her ears like a thunderclap.

Veronica froze, her heart pounding in her chest as shame engulfed her like a wave. *Did that just come from me?* she thought, horrified. Her breathing quickened, the tears flowing freely now as the disgust welled up inside her.

He laughed. "See that's it, you get it now. Your body wanted me all along. Enjoy it, take it all in, my little whore."

What is wrong with me? her mind screamed, her entire body trembling. *Why did I do that? Why… why does this feel so good?*

The realization hit her like a freight train, leaving her reeling. She had never felt more betrayed— by the situation, but most of all, by herself.

No … please, no, Veronica thought, her mind screaming as her body betrayed her completely. The tension that had been building inside her hit a crescendo, an overwhelming wave of sensation she couldn't hold back.

Her breath caught, and despite her protests, her body seized with an uncontrollable euphoria that rolled over her like a tidal wave. Her muscles trembled, her back arched slightly, and a rush of warmth overtook her.

A guttural sound escaped her lips—a mix of shock, shame, and undeniable pleasure—as the release tore through her.

Tears streamed down her face as the euphoric surge ebbed, leaving her trembling and breathless. *This isn't real. This isn't me …* she told herself, her mind frantically trying to reconcile what had just happened.

Her body slumped in exhaustion, and a deep shame settled in her chest. I can't believe I let this happen. How could I lose control like that?

As Veronica lay there, motionless and breathless, her chest rising and falling with the effort of catching her breath, she barely registered the man standing up. Towering over her petite frame, his shadow loomed as his words cut through the haze in her mind.

"This is your life now," he said coldly, his tone commanding and devoid of any compassion. "You belong to me, and you'll do as I say. Do you understand me?"

Veronica didn't respond. Her body remained still, her mind racing, caught between shock, exhaustion, and disbelief. She didn't have the strength to fight, nor the will to acknowledge his words.

Suddenly, a strange warmth startled her, and her eyes fluttered open, confusion clouding her expression as she processed the sensation. The moment was both surreal and humiliating, pulling her further into the depths of disbelief and degradation. Her mind was still foggy, her senses dulled from the overwhelming ordeal, but as the reality of what was happening hit her, a wave of revulsion surged through her.

Oh my God… she thought, her breath hitching as the truth sunk in. *He's … he's pissing on me.*

A flood of emotions overtook her—shock, humiliation, anger, and an unbearable shame that clawed at her insides. *How could this be happening?* she screamed internally. *How have I fallen this far?*

Tears welled in her eyes again, but this time, they weren't from fear or pain—they were from the sheer humiliation of being reduced to this. Her body tensed as the degrading act continued, her mind spinning.

I don't deserve this... I don't... she thought, but the weight of her powerlessness bore down on her, crushing any shred of defiance she might have had left.

The sensation finally stopped, leaving her laying there, frozen and drenched in her humiliation. *What am I supposed to do now?* she thought, her mind fracturing.

Suddenly, a voice rang out, cutting through the haze—a voice she instantly recognized.

"I did not give you permission to fucking piss on her," the voice said, sharp and full of fury.

Her head jerked up slightly, her heart skipping a beat as she tried to place it. It was Grip. His voice was unmistakable, and it carried an edge that sent a chill through her.

The man froze, his smug expression faltering as he turned toward the sound. "Y-yeah, I went a little freestyle on that part," he stammered, attempting to defend himself.

The crack of a gunshot echoed through the trees. The man's eyes widened, his body jolting before collapsing lifelessly to the ground in front of her.

Veronica blinked, her mind reeling as she tried to comprehend what had just happened. Her gaze slowly lifted, following the sound of measured footsteps crunching over the forest floor.

Standing there, calm but with unmistakable rage simmering just beneath the surface, was Grip. His presence was commanding, and in that moment, he looked like both savior and executioner.

The scene around her faded into silence, leaving only his gaze and the promise of safety—or judgment—in his stance.

Grip knelt down, his hands steady as he untied the ropes binding Veronica's wrists and ankles. Her body trembled, tears streaming down her face as he gently wiped away the remnants of her humiliation with a cloth from his bag. His movements were firm yet careful, a quiet reassurance of his presence.

As soon as she was free, Veronica collapsed into his arms, her sobs wracking her small frame. She clung to him tightly, burying her face in his chest. "I didn't know if I was going to live," she choked out between sobs. "I was so scared… I didn't know what to do."

Grip's arms encircled her protectively. "There's something I have to tell you," he said, his tone serious.

Veronica sniffled, pulling back slightly to look up at him, her tear-streaked face filled with confusion. "What do you mean?"

Grip exhaled deeply, meeting her gaze. "I set this up," he said plainly, watching her reaction carefully.

Her breath caught in her throat, her mind struggling to process his words. "The drone?" she asked, her voice shaky as the pieces started to click into place.

Grip nodded. "Yes, the drone. I've been following you the entire time."

"But… but why?" Veronica stammered, her voice a mixture of disbelief and lingering fear.

He cupped her face gently, his expression unwavering. "During our last talk, you told me you wanted to try something new. That CNC felt too fake and safe. I needed it to feel real for you. So I called Mistress Blue and asked for a favor. She's used this man before for other clients. I met with him this morning, laid out the rules—what he was allowed to do and how far he could go. If everything had gone as planned, I wouldn't have killed him."

Veronica stared at him, her emotions a whirlwind of shock, relief, and something else she couldn't quite place. The realization that she was safe, that Grip had been watching over her the entire time, slowly settled in.

A small grin tugged at the corners of her mouth, a mix of disbelief and amusement breaking through her tears. "You cheeky fuck," she muttered, shaking her head as she wiped her eyes.

Grip raised an eyebrow, a faint smirk playing on his lips. "Are you mad?"

Veronica took a deep breath, her hands still gripping his shirt. "I was terrified," she admitted, her voice soft. "But it was thrilling. I've never felt anything like it."

He held her close, his voice steady as he said, "That's what I wanted for you, doll. To give you something you couldn't find anywhere else. And to keep you safe the whole time."

She leaned into him, her heart still racing but now with a mixture of excitement and relief. "You're insane," she whispered, her grin widening. "But maybe I am too."

Grip chuckled, pressing a kiss to the top of her head. "That's why we're perfect for each other."

Veronica shifted in Grip's lap, her breathing finally steadying as the adrenaline began to wear off. She glanced down, her cheeks flushing slightly as she noticed the unmistakable bulge pressing against his pants. Her eyes flicked back up to his face, a mischievous smirk forming on her lips.

"And what exactly did you think of all this?" she teased, nodding toward his obvious arousal.

Grip's lips curled into a sly grin. "I think," he said, his voice low and rough, "I can't wait to get you home and take you back for myself."

Veronica chuckled, her fingers idly tracing the edge of his shirt. "Why wait?" she said playfully. "Why not take me now?"

She paused, her gaze flicking back toward the lifeless body sprawled a few feet away, blood pooling around him. For a moment, she hesitated, the absurdity of the situation making her laugh softly. "Well," she said, looking back at Grip with a wicked grin, "I guess he can watch."

Grip raised an eyebrow, amused, as Veronica leaned in, her hands moving to undo the buttons of his shirt. Her playful confidence returned, the fear and humiliation of the past hour melting away as she focused entirely on him.

She took off his pants, revealing his throbbing, impressive and familiar cock. She straddled him, gasping as she slid him into her extremely sensitive pussy and rocked rhythmically back and forth on his dick.

The comfort she felt in his arms was unmatched, as she felt another orgasm quickly building. She rocked on his dick vigorously as she felt the familiar throb of the head of his dick, she knew he was about to cum.

Was he that turned on watching me be taken? she thought, feeling her own release come as soon as his hit her.

They both jolted with uncontrollable pleasure. As the climax subsided she grinned at him, tightening her pussy muscles around his shaft to evoke another moan of pleasure from him.

Veronica slid off of him, still catching her breath and glanced over at the lifeless body lying nearby. Her brow furrowed slightly, though the playful glint in her eyes remained. "Now what do we do with him?" she asked, her voice soft but tinged with curiosity.

Grip leaned back, adjusting his pants as he gave her a reassuring smile. "Don't worry about it, doll," he said, his tone calm and matter-of-fact. "I'll have a crew come take care of it. Mistress Blue will get an explanation. It might cost a little extra, but your dignity is worth every cent."

Veronica couldn't help but smile, her cheeks flushing as she bit her bottom lip. "You'd really do anything for me, wouldn't you?" she teased, though the warmth in her voice was genuine.

Grip brushed a strand of hair from her face. "You don't have to ask. This scene here," he said, gesturing to the aftermath around them, "should tell you that already."

She leaned in, placing a soft kiss on his lips, her heart swelling with both love and pride. "You're one Hell of a man, Grip," she said, her grin widening.

"And you're one hell of a woman, Veronica," he replied, pulling her close once more.

They lingered for a moment, wrapped in the intimacy of their connection, before Grip stood, straightening his shirt and pulling out his phone.

"Let's get this cleaned up," he said with a smirk. "Can't leave a mess lying around."

Veronica nodded, her playful grin returning as she stretched, completely at ease despite the days' chaos .

CHAPTER 9

THE JOKE

The low hum of conversation and the soft clinking of silverware filled the air in the exclusive downtown Houston restaurant. Its modern decor and dim lighting created an intimate atmosphere, perfect for couples seeking a private escape from the world. Veronica and Grip sat at a corner table, dressed impeccably for the occasion—him in a tailored black suit, her in an elegant, yet form-fitting dress that turned more than a few heads as they walked in.

As the waiter approached, Grip leaned back in his chair, exuding his usual composed confidence. "I'll have the Wagyu beef," he said smoothly, handing the menu to the server, "medium-rare, with the chef's recommended pairing of red."

The waiter nodded, jotting down the order before turning to Veronica.

She smiled politely, setting her menu down. "I'll go with the surf and turf," she said, her voice warm but with an air of sophistication. "The lobster tail and filet, please. And I'll take a glass of the Sauvignon Blanc."

"Excellent choices," the waiter said with a nod, collecting their menus before disappearing toward the kitchen.

As the server left, Grip turned his attention to Veronica, his sharp eyes softening. "You look stunning tonight," he said, his tone low and sincere.

A faint blush crept up her cheeks, though her grin was playful. "You don't look so bad yourself, Mr. Williams," she teased, her fingers brushing lightly against the stem of her wine glass. "Feels like it's been a while since we've done this."

Grip shrugged slightly, his smile subtle. "Been busy lately. But it's important to slow down once in a while."

Veronica nodded, swirling the water in her glass before taking a small sip. "It's nice to feel normal for a night," she admitted, her eyes darting around the bustling restaurant around them.

Grip smirked, leaning in slightly. "Normal isn't really our style, though, is it?"

Veronica laughed softly, shaking her head. "No, it really isn't."

As the waiter returned briefly to re-fill their wine, Veronica swirled the glass in her hand, taking a sip before setting it back down. A playful glint flickered in her eyes as she leaned forward slightly, her lips curving into a smirk.

"Along that note," she began, her voice carrying a hint of mischief, "I've been wanting to talk about what happened."

Grip raised an eyebrow, mirroring her smirk as he met her gaze. "The thrilling event last week?" he asked, his tone teasing.

Veronica nodded, her eyes holding his. "Exactly."

He chuckled, leaning back in his chair, the light catching the wine glass in his hand. "Go ahead. What about it? Are you already craving something like that again?"

"Well..." Veronica tilted her head, "here's the thing—yes, kind of."

Grip's grin widened as he shook his head slightly. "Of course."

"But," she continued, her tone softening slightly,

"there was a part of that whole experience I liked that wasn't just the thrill itself." Her fingers traced the edge of her wine glass as she stared at him. "It was that feeling I had when I found out you were there. Watching the whole time."

Grip's smirk faded into a thoughtful expression as he listened, his focus fully on her.

"That," Veronica said, her eyes locked on his, "that safety net you gave me, even without me knowing it ... I want to have that thrill again, but also know you're there to protect me. Always."

Grip let out a soft chuckle, his smirk returning. "Mistress Blue was understanding the first time," he said, raising his glass slightly, "but I doubt she'll lend me another hand in that matter. You're going to make me get creative, aren't you?"

Veronica grinned, raising her glass to meet his in a playful toast. "You're the mastermind, aren't you? I'm sure we can figure something out."

As their glasses clinked softly, the atmosphere between them lightened, the weight of the conversation shifting into something electric.

Veronica leaned back, swirling the wine in her glass thoughtfully.

"You know," she began, her voice casual but her words deliberate, "the news has been buzzing nonstop about all these women being attacked near downtown lately. It's awful, really."

Grip raised an eyebrow, his expression sharpening. "I've seen the reports," he said. "The rapist at that downtown park."

Veronica nodded, her eyes flicking up to meet his.

"Exactly. They think it's the same guy. He's been targeting women for weeks now, and no one's been able to catch him." She paused, her lips curving into a mischievous smile. "What if we used that to our advantage?" Grip tilted his head slightly, studying her as she continued.

"Hear me out," she said, leaning forward. "What if I … let myself be taken? You guard me, just like last time, but we let him think he's in control. We wait until the moment becomes… perfect," she said, her voice dropping as her smile widened. "And then, you take him out."

Grip's eyes narrowed slightly, his smirk returning as her plan started to sink in.

"Think about it," Veronica added, excited now. "We hit so many birds with one stone. Our pleasure, and we save countless vulnerable women from this predator."

Grip leaned back in his chair, rubbing his jaw thoughtfully. "That's bold, doll," he said after a moment, his tone laced with intrigue. "Bold, dangerous … and maybe genius."

Veronica grinned, taking another sip of her wine. "I knew you'd like it."

Grip leaned forward, setting his glass down on the table, his expression serious. "There are a lot of variables to this," he began, his voice low and measured. "It's extremely risky, Veronica. For one, this guy isn't under our control. What if he decides to murder you before I have the chance to save you? What if he abducts you, and I lose track of you altogether?"

Veronica held up a hand, cutting him off with a confident smirk. She tapped the sleek ring on her finger, then pointed to the smart watch on her wrist. "Both of these connect to our account. You can monitor my location, my heart rate, my oxygen levels—everything in real-time. You'll know exactly where I am and how I'm doing every second of the way."

Grip raised an eyebrow, his expression still skeptical, but he didn't interrupt as she continued.

"Yes," she admitted, "murder is a risk. But this guy has a pattern. He's targeting women my age, taking what he wants, and leaving. He hasn't killed anyone yet. He's methodical, not chaotic."

Grip leaned back in his chair, his jaw tight as he considered her argument. "That's still not a guarantee he won't escalate," he said, his tone grim. "If something goes wrong—"

Veronica reached across the table, placing her hand over his. "I trust you," she said firmly, her eyes locking with his. "I know you wouldn't let anything happen to me. And think about it—we could stop him, Grip. We could make sure he never hurts anyone else again."

Grip's fingers tightened slightly around hers as he exhaled, his mind clearly working through every possible outcome. After a moment, he smirked faintly, though his eyes remained sharp. "You're not going to let this go, are you?"

Veronica grinned, leaning back with a sip of her wine. "Not a chance."

Grip studied her for a long moment, leaning back in his chair. "You've actually put a lot of thought into this."

"Yep," Veronica replied confidently, swirling her wine before taking a sip. Her eyes sparkled with mischief as she added, "Once you have a shiny sports car, it's hard to go back to a sedan."

Grip let out a low laugh, shaking his head as he

reached across the table to lightly tap her hand. "That sedan still gets the job done," he teased, his tone dripping with mock offense.

Veronica leaned forward, her grin widening. "You, sir," she said firmly, her voice playful but final, "will never be a sedan."

Grip chuckled again, raising his glass in a toast. "Good to know," he said with a smirk.

The tension of the earlier conversation melted away as the playful exchange lingered between them, the connection that defined their unique relationship shining through as they enjoyed the rest of their evening.

CHAPTER 10

THE FIRST HUNT

The morning sun streamed through the glass walls of their sleek condo, bathing the living room in a warm glow. Veronica sat cross-legged on the plush rug, leaning forward with curiosity as Grip laid out his gear across the coffee table.

"Alright," Grip began, picking up a compact rifle with a sleek black suppressor attached to its barrel. "This is the main tool I'll be using to keep things under control from a distance. Suppressed and compact, perfect for staying mobile in a public setting."

Veronica nodded, her fingers lightly brushing over the smooth metal of the rifle. Her eyes flicked to the Beretta pistol next, which also had a suppressor fitted. "And this?" she asked.

Grip smirked, picking up the sidearm and holding it for her to see. "Backup," he said simply. "In case things get a little closer than expected."

He set the pistol down and turned his attention to a piece of wearable tech, a slim black band designed to wrap around his forearm. "This," he said, strapping it on, "is where it gets fun."

He activated the small screen, which curved slightly with his arm. The display lit up, showing a live map with a green dot blinking near the center. Grip held up his arm so Veronica could see. "That dot? That's you. Right now, you're one point five feet away from me."

Veronica leaned closer, intrigued. "You're tracking

me?"

Grip nodded. "Not just tracking your location," he said, swiping the screen to show her another set of readings. "This is your heart rate, oxygen levels, and a few other vitals. It'll keep me updated on how you're holding up during the event."

Veronica raised an eyebrow, impressed. "And what about audio? How will you know what's happening?"

Grip reached over to her hand, lightly tapping the sleek, smart ring on her finger. "I've modified this," he said, "so it's continuously sending audio straight to my earpiece. I'll hear everything."

Her lips curled into a small smile. "You've thought of everything."

"Almost everything," he corrected, his expression serious now. "We need a way to ensure I know when to step in if things go too far. A safe word."

Veronica tilted her head, considering. "Safe word? Okay. What should it be?"

Grip thought for a moment, then smiled. "Clover. Simple, memorable, and doesn't sound like something you'd say by accident."

Veronica repeated the word softly, nodding. "Clover. Got it."

Grip placed a reassuring hand on her knee. "This will work," he said confidently. "I'll be right there, every second, ready to step in if anything goes wrong. You're in complete control, Veronica."

She smiled at him, her confidence bolstered by his meticulous preparation. "I trust you," she said, her voice steady.

Grip smirked as he stood, neatly packing his gear

back into its designated cases. His movements were efficient and methodical, each piece of equipment placed with precision. "So," he began, glancing at Veronica as he secured the last latch, "my research shows that all the attacks are happening between 0000 hours and 0300 hours near the fountain downtown."

Veronica tilted her head, listening intently.

"The last two girls said the man approached them wearing a hoodie," Grip explained, "asked to borrow their phone, and as soon as they handed it over, he tossed it into the fountain. Then he dragged them into the wooded pathway nearby and took what he wanted before running off."

Veronica frowned slightly, her fingers absentmindedly tapping the edge of her smartwatch.

"Of the seven known victims," Grip added, "four were blonde, one was a redhead, and two were brunettes. So it doesn't look like he has a specific type other than one thing: all of them were small enough that he could easily overpower them."

He met her gaze, his expression serious. "I think we're good there."

Veronica nodded, absorbing the information. She crossed her arms, her confidence unwavering. "Then we allow him to take me, but he is in for quite the surprise." She smirked.

Grip gave her an approving nod, closing the gear case with a final snap.

"Can I make one request?"

Grip looked up, curiosity flickering in his eyes as he straightened. "I'm listening," he said, anticipation evident in his expression.

Veronica hesitated for a moment, then stepped closer,

her gaze steady as she spoke. "The way it felt ... when the dignitary died, right at the moment of release," she began, her voice dropping slightly. "I want to feel that again. The life leaving his body as he fills me."

Grip's initial reaction was a raised eyebrow, followed quickly by a deep, amused laugh. "Simple," he said, interrupting her train of thought. "You moan, whisper, or scream the safe word—clover—and one perfectly aimed shot will make that happen for you, my love."

Veronica's lips curled into a wicked smile, a mix of anticipation and satisfaction flashing in her eyes. "I knew you'd understand," she said, her voice tinged with excitement.

Grip smirked, stepping closer to brush a strand of hair from her face. "You should know by now, doll. There's nothing I won't do for you."

The soft glow of the park's lampposts cast long shadows across the deserted pathways, and the gentle trickle of the fountain filled the air with an eerie calm. Veronica stood near the edge of the fountain, her lips locked with Grip's in a passionate, lingering kiss. As they broke apart, his hand lingered on her cheek for a moment before he turned and melted into the shadows, leaving her alone under the dim light.

She exhaled slowly, her heart pounding—not from fear, but from adrenaline coursing through her veins. The park was quiet, almost desolate, with only the occasional jogger or cyclist passing by. Each time someone came into view, a thrill rippled through her.

"Is this him?" she whispered under her breath, her lips curling into a sly smile, knowing Grip could hear every word through her modified smart ring. When the figure passed without incident, she giggled softly. "Oh, nope.

Never mind."

Her excitement grew with each passing moment, the anticipation building as she strolled casually around the fountain. She glanced down at her outfit—a short, fitted mini skirt that barely grazed her thighs and a low, tight tank top, her hard nipples visible under the thin fabric. She was the very picture of bait, her provocative appearance daring anyone to approach.

She trailed her fingers along the edge of the fountain, the cool stone grounding her as her gaze flicked around the park. The occasional passerby barely spared her a glance, but it didn't matter. She whispered again, her voice light and teasing, "How about this one, Grip? No? Oh well."

A biker pedaled past, his wheels humming against the pavement. He glanced her way and couldn't resist shouting, "My god, the confidence in you!"

Veronica laughed out loud, watching him disappear into the darkness. Her fingers tapped the edge of the fountain, her heart racing as she turned her attention back to the quiet pathways surrounding her. The thrill of the hunt was intoxicating, and she knew it was only a matter of time before the real game began.

Time dragged on, and Veronica found herself growing restless. She glanced down at her phone, scrolling through social media to pass the time, a quiet giggle escaping her lips at the occasional funny clip. The once-thrilling anticipation had started to fade, replaced by a dull impatience.

Suddenly, a voice cut through the stillness. "Excuse me, miss?"

Veronica looked up, her heart skipping a beat as a hooded figure approached her. He was a large white man, easily 6′6″, with a heavy, lumbering frame, probably weighing somewhere around 275 or 300 pounds. His face, dimly lit by the park's scattered lights, was distractingly unpleasant—his features uneven, his expression unnervingly blank.

"May I borrow your phone? I need to make a call." he asked, his voice low and slightly strained. "My sister was supposed to pick me up an hour ago, and she hasn't shown up."

Excitement surged through Veronica, almost bubbling over as she forced herself to stay composed. This is it. This is him. Her smile was a touch too eager as she held out her phone. "Sure, hun," she said sweetly, her voice steady despite the pounding of her heart.

The man took the phone, fumbling with it briefly before raising it to his ear. Veronica's pulse quickened as she observed his movements, her mind racing. This has to be him.

Her suspicions were confirmed when, without warning, he flung the phone into the fountain. The splash echoed through the park, and before she could react, she felt his massive hands clamp around her throat.

The pressure was immediate and overwhelming, cutting off her breath as he dragged her backward into the darkness. Her vision blurred, her heartbeat thundered in her ears, and she clawed instinctively at his grip, but his strength was unmatched.

This is it, she thought, her mind spinning even as her body fought for air.

The sound of the fountain faded as he pulled her further into the shadows, leaving the park's open space behind. The thrill, the terror … it was all-consuming.

Oh my God, this is it, Veronica thought as the pressure

on her throat eased, and she gasped for air. Her chest burned, and her body ached from the force of being thrown to the ground. All of his weight pressed on top of her. She could feel his unexpectedly large cock throbbing through his pants, but none of it mattered. *This is the rush I've been craving.*

Her mind raced as sensations overwhelmed her—fear, excitement, and a deep, dark thrill she couldn't deny. *I need this. I want this. Why does this feel so… intoxicating?*

He fumbled between her thighs and let out a breath as he realized she wasn't wearing any underwear. "You're out here with your pussy free and bare? You wanted this, you little slut!" He lowered his lips to her neck, kissing and sucking.

Her heart pounded harder. *Bare? Of course, I'm bare. I'm here for this. For you to lose control.* The thought sent a shiver through her, her body betraying any notion of resistance.

This is real. This is raw. The chaos of the moment engulfed her, and even as the situation spiraled, a wicked satisfaction stirred within her. *Grip is watching. He's there. I'm safe, but it feels so dangerous.*

Her breath hitched as she processed the overwhelming sensations. *This is what I've been chasing!* He positioned his cock at her mound, never stopping his kisses. He pushes the head of his dick past her already anticipating lips and she felt herself stretch to accommodate his very thick rod.

"God, you're so wet" he moaned, rising up on his arms to look at her, his hips swinging with intent. As his pace quickened, and his dick slammed repeatedly against her cervix, she let out a moan. "Oh you do like it, bitch," he snarled. "You want it harder? Faster?" His pace reached an unexpected speed for his body size.

Through the scope of his rifle, Grip's gaze remained locked on the scene unfolding before him. His breathing was slow and steady, his hands firm yet relaxed on the weapon. He didn't flinch, didn't waver, his years of precision training allowing him to focus entirely on Veronica.

She was a vision, even in the chaos, her body arching, her expression a mix of raw intensity and bliss. Grip smirked to himself, the glint of amusement in his eyes betraying his otherwise stoic demeanor. She really does look wonderful, he thought, adjusting the scope ever so slightly for a clearer view.

His gaze shifted briefly to the man, hulking and oblivious, his movements frantic and uncoordinated. This poor bastard has no idea, Grip mused, the corner of his mouth twitching into a subtle grin. He thinks he's in control. He doesn't realize he's fallen into her web.

Grip's finger hovered near the trigger, ready but patient. She's enjoying herself, he observed, his focus returning to Veronica as she writhed beneath the man. Every movement, every sound—it's all part of her thrill, her chase.

The familiarity of the scene didn't dull its impact on him. Instead, it fueled a quiet pride in knowing he could give her this—something no one else could. She's mine, he thought, his grip tightening slightly on the rifle. And when the moment's right, I'll be there to finish it for her.

Veronica's mind swirled in a storm of sensations as the intensity built with every thrust. Her breath hitched, her body trembling under his weight. *This is it. This is what I've been chasing. That edge… that uncontrollable thrill.*

She could feel his rhythm faltering, his breathing becoming ragged as he neared his release. The pressure within her own body grew to a fever pitch, her pleasure threatening to crash over her like a wave. So close, she thought, her heart pounding in sync with the mounting tension.

Her lips curled into a small, wicked smile, unable to hide her satisfaction. The man, noticing, looked down at her with a sneer. "What are you smiling at?" he growled, his voice thick with lust. "You want this cum from me, don't you, you little slut?"

Veronica's grin widened, and she locked eyes with him, her voice barely a whisper. "Clover."

In an instant, the man's body jerked violently, his movements halting as a sudden, sharp sound cut through the night. His final release was unlike anything she'd ever felt—the heat flooding her insides from his cum and her orgasm mingling with the shudder of his convulsing body as life left him.

The combination sent her spiraling. A euphoric wave surged through her, her body trembling uncontrollably as she let out a cry of pure bliss. The intensity of her orgasm hit like a tidal wave, overwhelming every nerve as her pleasure mingled with the raw power of the moment.

Her breath came in ragged gasps, her chest heaving as the lifeless man collapsed onto her, his weight pressing her further into the ground. A drop of warm blood trickled down from his temple, staining her cheek as she turned her head.

A mixture of relief and exhilaration coursed through her. Perfect shot.

She shifted slightly, pushing the lifeless body off her, her grin returning despite the mess. "You always know how to finish with a bang," she whispered under her breath, her voice trembling with adrenaline and satisfaction.

Veronica stood, smoothing her skirt and adjusting her hair, her breaths uneven as she steadied herself. Without so much as a glance at the lifeless body behind her, she walked forward, her composure returning with every step.

From the shadows, Grip emerged, his sharp eyes scanning her as he approached. He smirked, his usual calm confidence firmly in place. "Well, doll," he said, slipping an arm around her waist and pulling her close, "how was that?"

She leaned into him, a satisfied grin spreading across her face. "Fucking absolutely perfect, darling," she replied, her voice tinged with exhilaration. "My knees are weak. I couldn't be more satisfied."

Grip chuckled softly, lifting his hand. He licked his thumb and gently wiped away the streak of blood left behind from the fresh kill, his touch tender.

As they embraced, Veronica nestled her head against his chest, her lips brushing against his ear. "Come on," she whispered, her tone playful, "let's take the slow route home. I want to give that tool between your thighs some nice well-deserved head while you drive."

Grip laughed, his deep, rumbling amusement echoing in the quiet park. "You never fail to surprise me, doll," he said, guiding her toward the car.

They walked together to the parking lot, the cool night air wrapping around them as they left the scene behind. The sound of Veronica's mouth pleasuring Grip's cock accompanied them as they drove through the city, the thrill of the night still lingering between them.

CHAPTER 11

THE MORNING NEWS

The early morning sun crept through the blinds, painting golden streaks across the living room floor of the condo. Veronica sat on the couch, her legs tucked beneath her as she flipped lazily through the channels. The muted sound of static and snippets of shows filled the air, blending with the faint hum of the refrigerator.

Grip leaned against the kitchen counter, a mug of coffee in his hand, though it had long since gone cold. He wasn't drinking it; his mind was elsewhere, replaying the events of the night before with sharp clarity.

"God, there's never anything on," Veronica muttered, her voice cutting through the silence. She pressed the remote button again, her frustration mounting.

Then, the steady tone of a news anchor's voice stopped her.

"Breaking news this morning: a body has been discovered in Franklin Park," the anchor announced, her polished voice grim. "Authorities identified the victim as twenty-two-year-old Caleb Neal, a man previously linked to multiple attacks on women. While no charges were ever filed, Neal was considered a person of interest. Investigators are asking for the public's help as they look into his death."

Veronica sat upright, the remote slipping from her hand. "Well, would you look at that," she said, her voice dripping with satisfaction.

Grip pushed himself off the counter and walked into

the living room, his brow furrowed but calm. He sat on the arm of the couch, his attention fixed on the television as they played a clip of Franklin Park, now sectioned off with yellow police tape and crawling with investigators.

The anchor continued, "Authorities suspect foul play, though no further details have been released. Neal's death comes after years of accusations from multiple women. Police are looking into whether his past may have caught up with him."

Veronica leaned back, her lips curling into a sly grin. "Caught up with him? That's one way to put it."

Grip allowed a faint smirk but didn't comment. Instead, his eyes stayed locked on the screen as the footage transitioned to an image of Caleb Neal. The grainy photo showed him in a suit, likely from a court appearance, his face devoid of remorse.

"You'd think they'd lead with the fact he was a predator," Veronica said, her tone dripping with sarcasm. "But no, poor Caleb Neal. Found dead in the park." She shook her head. "He got what he deserved."

Grip finally spoke, his voice low and steady. "The news will milk this for a week, but they'll run out of leads fast. People like him always have enemies. Nobody's going to care enough to dig too deep."

Veronica nodded, picking up the remote and flipping the TV off. "Exactly. Guys like that? Everyone wants them gone. We're just the ones who actually did it."

Grip leaned back, resting his arms on his thighs. "It's done. That's all that matters."

She turned to him, her grin widening. "You know, we should celebrate. The world's one monster lighter thanks to us."

Grip chuckled, a rare sound that broke through his

usual stoicism. "Yeah? And what do you suggest?"

Veronica tilted her head playfully, her dark eyes sparkling with mischief. "Oh, I'm sure I can think of something."

The tension from the morning news broadcast melted away as Veronica stood, sauntering toward the kitchen with a sway in her hips. Grip watched her for a moment, his smirk lingering, before he followed her lead. The thrill of the hunt was gone, but the high still lingered.

For now, their work was done.

The midday sun cast a warm glow through the floor-to-ceiling windows of the condo. Veronica stretched languidly across the bed, the soft hum of the city below drifting into the room. She turned her head toward Grip, who was leaning against the headboard, his shirtless chest rising and falling steadily.

"What are you feeling for lunch?" she asked, breaking the comfortable silence.

Grip glanced at her, his dark eyes thoughtful. "Something quick. Surprise me."

Veronica smirked, grabbing her phone from the nightstand. She slid off the bed, her oversized T-shirt just barely brushing her thighs as she walked toward the kitchen. "Takeout it is," she called over her shoulder.

Fifteen minutes later, the soft chime of the elevator echoed through the condo. Veronica looked up from the couch, where she'd been scrolling through her phone, and set it down. "That was fast," she muttered, rising to her feet.

When the doors slid open, both of them froze.

Mistress Blue stepped into the condo, her sharp heels clicking against the hardwood floor. She held two takeout bags in her gloved hands, her striking figure wrapped in a tailored black trench coat. Her icy blue eyes sparkled with amusement as she glanced between them, her crimson lips curling into a knowing smile.

Grip and Veronica exchanged a quick, silent look. Mistress Blue's presence wasn't just unexpected—it was unheard of. She never came to them.

Mistress Blue strode confidently into the room, setting the bags down on the kitchen island. "I was coming over to thank you when I saw the delivery guy was headed up. I figured I'd tip him for you and bring it up myself. Consider it a small gesture of my appreciation." She removed her gloves, sliding them into the pocket of her coat with calculated elegance. She turned to face them, leaning casually against the counter as if she belonged there, her eyes glinting with something between mischief and satisfaction.

Mistress Blue's lips parted into a disarming smile as she regarded them both. "I thought it was time I expressed my gratitude in person," she began, her voice smooth and commanding. "The skillful, non-eventful execution of the Russian job was flawless. Exactly the discretion I was hoping for."

Grip leaned against the counter, his arms crossing over his chest as he studied her. Veronica perched herself on the edge of the couch, her curiosity piqued, but her expression unreadable.

Mistress Blue's smile grew a touch sharper as she let her gaze linger on them. "And, well, I couldn't help but notice a certain … electricity in the air. Lustful things, perhaps?" She tilted her head slightly, her tone playful but deliberate. "I can imagine the adrenaline from a job like that stirs up all sorts of appetites."

Veronica raised an eyebrow, a small smirk tugging at

her lips. Grip remained silent, his eyes narrowing slightly.

"Well," she said, her tone taking on a feigned note of sadness, "I know how the abduction ended. A pity, really. That man you had to kill—he had a reputation for going a bit overboard. But alas, he no longer has to worry about that. And neither do we."

She straightened, adjusting the cuffs of her coat with meticulous precision. "Which brings me to my question," she said, her eyes flicking between the two. "Have you considered coming back to another one of my events? Or …" she paused, a knowing smile playing on her lips, "are you two starting to freestyle your own adventures?"

Mistress Blue let the words hang in the air, her sharp gaze awaiting their response.

Grip's eyes followed Mistress Blue as she leaned casually against the counter, her sharp presence commanding the room. Veronica stood, smoothing her shirt before walking over to join them.

"Things aren't quite as easy as they used to be," Veronica said, her tone light but with an edge.

"Takes more and more to reach that … point of release."

Grip nodded subtly, his jaw tightening. "Yeah. Seems like the lustful urges keep pulling deeper the more you experience."

Mistress Blue tilted her head slightly, a faint, knowing smile playing on her lips. "Ah, yes. That's the nature of it, isn't it? The things that once came so easily … well, sometimes you have to get creative." She spoke as if imparting a truth she'd long since mastered, her tone smooth and unhurried.

Veronica smirked. "Guess we're learning that as we

go."

Mistress Blue let out a soft chuckle and stepped away from the counter. "If you ever find yourselves in need of any… special accommodations at the network, don't hesitate to ask. You know I have my ways." She smiled, her words laced with double meaning.

Veronica tilted her head in acknowledgment, her sharp gaze matching Mistress Blue's. Grip stepped closer to the elevator, holding it open as Mistress Blue turned to leave.

"Until next time, darlings," Mistress Blue said as she stepped into the elevator. The doors slid shut behind her with a soft chime, leaving the room in silence once more.

Veronica leaned against the counter, eyeing the takeout bags. "She really knows how to make an entrance, doesn't she?"

Grip smirked faintly, grabbing one of the bags. "And an exit."

The condo was quiet once again, the faint hum of the city outside their windows the only noise. Grip and Veronica settled back onto the couch, the aroma of their takeout filling the air. Veronica picked at her food, her movements slower than usual, her mind clearly elsewhere.

After a moment of silence, she spoke, her voice soft but tinged with unease. "I've been thinking about it," she began, not looking up from her plate. "What if I get to the point where what we're doing, or trying, just isn't cutting it for me anymore?"

Grip's fork paused mid-air, his dark eyes shifting to her. "What do you mean?"

Veronica set her plate down on the coffee table, leaning back against the cushions. "What if I'm broken?" she asked, her voice trembling slightly. "What if I require… something more? Something darker. Something you're not willing to allow or provide?"

The weight of her words hung in the air, the tension between them palpable. Grip set his plate aside, turning to face her. His gaze was steady, his voice calm and deliberate.

"There isn't anything on this earth I wouldn't provide for you, my sweet," he said, his tone unwavering. "Whatever you need, whatever it takes, you'll have it. Always."

Veronica's lips curled into a faint smile, her eyes searching his for any sign of hesitation and finding none. She leaned her head back against the couch, exhaling slowly. "Good," she murmured. "Because I'm not sure where this road ends, but I'm glad you're on it with me."

Grip reached over to take her hand in his. They sat in silence, the shadows of their shared darkness stretching out before them.

Grip leaned back against the couch, a sly grin tugging at the corner of his mouth as he stretched his arms across the backrest. "What would you like to do next?" he asked, his tone casual yet laced with intrigue. "This last excursion went off a little too well. He just fell right into your little trap."

Veronica smirked, twirling a strand of her dark hair between her fingers. "He really did, didn't he?"

Grip chuckled, leaning forward slightly. "But how will we find your next victim? Someone who thinks you're their victim?" His grin widened, the gleam in his eyes unmistakable.

She tilted her head thoughtfully, her voice playful. "I'm not sure, baby. I guess I could pretend to be drunk at bars again, see who bites. Or maybe …" She paused, a mischievous smile crossing her lips. "Maybe we start looking at other areas with high volumes of sexual assault. It's not like we're short on targets."

Grip rubbed his chin, his expression contemplative. "So it seems our thing is to find men who are sexual predators... and turn them into your prey?" His lips curled into a sharp grin.

Veronica giggled, leaning closer to him. "Yeah, seems so," she said, her voice soft and dripping with satisfaction. "That feeling from last night, Grip ... it's such a high."

"Well, I know you love that feeling," he began, his voice steady, "but what if we could get to that high without the risk? No public setups, no chance of you getting hurt for real. We control all the variables."

Veronica's brow arched, her curiosity piqued. "I'm listening," she said, leaning in slightly.

Grip continued, his tone growing more deliberate. "What if we create a room? A secure place where we call all the shots. We lure the victims there, on our terms. No outside interference, no chance for surprises."

Veronica's lips curling into a small smile. "And how exactly do we lure them?"

Grip's expression darkened slightly, his tone shifting into something almost disgusted. "There's no shortage of predators on the internet. Men looking for young women, desperate for an easy target. And then there are the real sickos—" he paused, his voice dripping with disdain, "even those who go after kids."

Veronica's eyes widened briefly before a look of fierce agreement settled over her face. "Now that," she said, her voice firm, "that does sound good. Not having to risk getting caught, and fuck yes, let's remove some of those child predators. Sick fucks." She sat back with a satisfied smirk, her dark eyes gleaming. "We'd be doing the world a favor."

Grip nodded, his grin returning as he leaned toward her. "Then let's start planning. It's time to make our playground."

Grip's fingers drummed lightly on the armrest as he continued. "You know," he began, "my company has a pretty damn skilled hacker. Code name Monroe. She's been with us since almost day one—been on more successful operations than I can count."

Veronica's curiosity deepened, and she tilted her head. "Monroe, huh? And you trust her with this kind of thing?"

Grip nodded. "Completely. Monroe's sharp—always five steps ahead. She can scour the internet for targets, find the ones hiding in plain sight, and bring them right to us. And I mean any type of predator, even the ones most people don't know how to track."

A smirk crept across Veronica's face. "Sounds like she's exactly what we'll need."

"As for the playground—or playpen, if you will—I think Mistress Blue could assist with the setup. She's got the resources and connections to make something like this happen quietly. I'll shoot her a message and subtly break down what we're planning. She'll catch on fast."

Veronica's eyes lit up, her excitement growing with each word. She clapped her hands together, her smile widening. "Oh, this is going to be so much fun! No risk, total control, and—" she leaned closer to Grip, her voice dropping, "we get to wipe those sick fucks off the face of the earth."

Grip chuckled, leaning back as he watched her enthusiasm build. "Glad you're on board. Let's make this happen."

Veronica nodded, practically vibrating with energy. "Let's do it."

CHAPTER 12

THE PLAY PEN

The sun was setting as Grip parked the car in front of an unassuming house on the outskirts of Houston. The area was quiet, with no immediate neighbors, just a few scattered homes down the long road. Grip stepped out and glanced around, ensuring no prying eyes were watching, before making his way to the front door. Veronica followed, her brow furrowed as she took in the quaint appearance of the property.

"This is it?" she asked, crossing her arms. "It's not exactly how I envisioned it."

Grip smirked as he unlocked the door and stepped inside. The house smelled faintly of fresh paint and cleaning supplies, as though it had recently been staged. The inside looked like any other suburban home—a cozy living room with a worn couch, family photos on the walls, and a dining table set with placemats as if a family might sit down for dinner any moment.

Grip glanced over his shoulder at Veronica, who was still staring at the faux normalcy. "Just wait," he said, a knowing grin spreading across his face.

He led her through the house, past the kitchen with its sparkling countertops and spotless fridge, to a door at the back of the hallway. He opened it to reveal a set of stairs leading down into a basement.

Veronica hesitated. "What's down there?"

"You'll see," Grip said, his voice steady as he descended the stairs.

She followed him, her heels clicking softly against the wooden steps. The air grew cooler, the faint scent of metal and disinfectant wafting up to meet her. When they reached the bottom, Grip stepped aside, letting her take in the room.

Veronica's eyes widened as she slowly turned in a circle. The basement was vast, much larger than the house above would suggest. The walls were reinforced with soundproof padding, the faint hum of electrical equipment filling the air.

On one side of the room, a collection of BDSM devices stood neatly arranged—restraints, chairs, and frames, each gleaming under the soft overhead lights. Across the room was a medical area, complete with a cold, metal autopsy-style bed and a counter lined with tools. The wall above the counter was covered with an array of instruments, some sleek and medical, others crude and intimidating.

In the far corner, a control room sat behind a pane of glass. Monitors displayed live feeds from cameras placed throughout the house and around the perimeter. Each angle showed the quiet facade of the property above, blending seamlessly with its suburban surroundings.

Veronica walked further into the room, her fingers brushing lightly over one of the frames as she took it all in. Her gaze traveled from the medical area to the control room and back to Grip, her expression unreadable.

"So?" Grip asked, his voice cutting through the quiet.

A slow smile spread across her face. "It's perfect."

Grip's phone buzzed, the screen lighting up with a message. He glanced down, a smirk spreading across his face. Sliding the phone back into his pocket, he looked at

Veronica. "I'm glad you like it," he said. "Because Monroe just informed me that your first 'victim' is nearly here."

Veronica's head snapped up, her eyes wide with surprise. "Already? Someone to play with?"

Grip nodded, leaning casually against the counter in the medical area. "Yeah. Monroe actually knew about this guy. When I told her what I was wanting her to do, she nearly jumped out of her chair. Apparently, this man got away with sexually assaulting someone in her family."

Veronica's expression darkened. "So this one's personal."

"Exactly," Grip said. "But just so you know how this is going to go down… you're going to answer the door under the assumption that your 'husband' sent a friend over to check out some leaking pipes."

Veronica tilted her head, waiting for more.

Grip continued, his tone shifting slightly. "But he's under the impression that your ex-best friend hired him to rape you."

Veronica blinked, the intensity in her gaze growing. "Oh, so he's going to attack me."

"That's the plan. And as you can tell," he gestured around the room, "I'll be watching. Nowhere in this house can my cameras not see or hear."

She glanced toward the control room, taking in the monitors again, then back to Grip.

"So," he continued, his voice calm but deliberate, "you've got options. You can lure him to the bedroom, let him think he's about to have his way with you, and then—when you say 'clover'—I take control. Subdue him and bring him down here. I don't want any blood upstairs if possible."

Veronica folded her arms, her smile sharp and calculating. "And if I don't want to go that route?"

Grip shrugged. "Then you can lure him straight down here. I'll take care of the rest and strap him to whichever device you want for playtime."

Veronica's eyes gleamed as she glanced around the room again, the possibilities swirling in her mind. "I like having choices," she said, her voice dripping with satisfaction.

Grip pulled his phone back out and glanced at the time. "Good. Because he'll be here any minute."

As they climbed the stairs, Veronica glanced over her shoulder at Grip. He gave her a quick, reassuring smile and leaned in to kiss her. "Ah, our guest," he said as the doorbell rang through the house. Without another word, he turned and descended the stairs, leaving her alone to greet their new visitor.

Veronica paused, taking a deep breath to steady herself before approaching the door. She opened it slowly, her expression neutral as her eyes fell on the man standing on the porch.

He was a revolting sight—a fat white man in his forties with greasy hair clinging to his forehead and a sweat-stained shirt stretched across his bloated stomach. His unkempt beard was flecked with crumbs, and the stench rolling off him hit her like a wall. The combination of body odor and stale fast food made her stomach churn.

"Hey there, Mrs. Martin," he said, his voice low and gravelly. "Jim sent me to take a look at some leaks?"

Veronica forced a polite smile, shuffling to the side to let him enter. "Yep, right down the stairs to your right," she said, her tone even.

As he stepped past her, the smell grew worse, and she

wrinkled her nose, holding her breath. *Fuck that,* she thought, *there's no way this guy's going to touch me.*

The man shuffled toward the basement door, oblivious to her disdain. He didn't even glance back as he began descending the stairs, his heavy boots creaking against the wooden steps.

Veronica lingered at the top, as his clumsy footsteps faded into the basement. Moments later, there was a sudden scuffle—a loud thud followed by a short, muffled struggle. She hurried down the stairs, her pulse quickening.

When she reached the bottom, she found Grip standing in the center of the room, dragging the disgusting man by his arms. The man's face was pale with terror, his shirt torn, and his heavy breathing filled the space.

Grip looked up at Veronica, his expression calm and collected. "Where do you want him, dear?" he asked, his tone almost casual.

Veronica's eyes scanned the room, taking in the array of devices. Her gaze landed on a padded contraption in the corner—a peg-like apparatus designed for someone to kneel over, their legs spread, and their ass raised in the air.

She pointed at it with a satisfied smirk. "There," she said simply.

Grip nodded, dragging the man toward the device as Veronica stepped further into the room, the door above closing softly behind her.

Grip secured the man to the apparatus, his movements calm and deliberate, ignoring the man's pleas filling the room. "Please! You've got the wrong guy! I don't know anything!" the man stammered, his voice thick with desperation.

Grip didn't respond, tightening the straps around the man's wrists and ankles, forcing him into position.

The man struggled weakly, his face turning red as the restraints bit into his skin. Grip walked to the corner of the room, returning with a large metal box on wheels, its surface polished and sterile like something out of a medical lab. He rolled it next to the apparatus and unlocked it with a soft click.

As the man continued to plead, Grip pulled out a bright red ball gag, holding it up briefly before securing it tightly around the man's mouth. The man's cries were immediately muffled, reduced to pitiful whimpers as tears streamed down his cheeks.

Grip turned to Veronica, who was silently watching, her expression unreadable. He gestured to the metal box. "Everything you might possibly need is right here," he said, his voice smooth. He stepped back, his dark eyes glinting as he nodded toward the restrained man. "Your toy awaits."

Veronica walked forward, her eyes never leaving the trembling, pathetic figure before her. She circled him like a predator assessing its prey, her lips curling into a faint smile.

As she reached the toolbox, her hand hovered over its contents before selecting a sleek, sharp knife. The fluorescent light above reflected off the blade as she turned back to the man.

"You won't be needing these," she muttered, her tone low and mocking as she began cutting away the remainder of his clothing. Fabric tore easily under the blade, falling away piece by piece until his bare, sweat-slicked body was exposed.

The man's muffled cries grew louder, his struggles feeble against the restraints.

As Veronica stepped back to take in the sight of the trembling man strapped to the apparatus, she wrinkled her nose in disgust. The stench was unmistakable. She noticed the man's soiled pants, the unmistakable evidence of filth smeared across his skin.

Her gaze dropped to the floor, where a large industrial drain was embedded in the concrete. An idea sparked, and she couldn't help but smirk.

"Grip," she called, gesturing him over. "Do we have a water hose or something to clean up? Because this is … revolting."

Grip's lips curled into a wide grin, his amusement unmistakable. "I've got just what you need," he said, walking across the room to a large steel closet built into the wall. With a metallic clink, it opened, revealing a coiled-up fire hose mounted neatly inside.

Veronica blinked, brimming with curiosity. *Damn. What do they expect to be cleaning down here?*

Grip pulled the hose free and handed her the nozzle. She ran her fingers over the sleek, heavy metal, testing its heft as she laughed. "Now this," she said, turning toward the restrained man, "is going to be fun."

The man's muffled cries turned frantic, his body writhing against the restraints as Veronica pointed the nozzle directly at his bare ass. Her laughter echoed through the room, sharp and delighted, as she rested her finger lightly on the lever.

Grip stepped back, his arms crossed and a smirk playing on his lips as he watched her, his eyes glinting with anticipation.

Veronica braced herself, gripping the heavy nozzle as

she unleashed a powerful jet of water directly into the man's exposed rear. The stream hit with such force that he tensed and squirmed, his muffled cries growing more frantic as the relentless spray penetrated him. The sheer pressure of the hose made her arms strain, the nozzle threatening to slip from her grasp as she adjusted her stance.

"Hold still, you filthy pig," she muttered, grinning wickedly as she aimed the jet across his body. She sprayed him thoroughly, directing the water over his legs and up his torso, washing away the filth. With a flick of her wrist, she swung the stream to his face, laughing as he jerked back, his cries muffled by the ball gag. Water splashed off his face, soaking his hair and dripping down his trembling body.

Veronica finally dropped the hose, droplets still trickling from the nozzle as it clanged softly against the floor. She planted her hands on her hips, tilting her head as she surveyed him. "See? How hard is that? Clean yourself from time to time. It's not rocket science."

Her gaze drifted to the assortment of tools and devices on the wall. One in particular caught her eye: a massive, studded paddle. She grabbed it by the handle, its weight satisfying in her grip. "Wow," she said, her voice dripping with playful malice as she swung it lightly through the air. "This looks fun."

She positioned herself behind him, the paddle raised high. With a quick motion, she brought it down hard against his exposed cheeks, the loud crack echoing through the room. The man's body jerked violently against the restraints, his muffled screams intensifying as she swung again and again, the paddle connecting with rhythmic precision.

Welts began to rise on his skin, angry and red.

"Look at that," she said, swinging harder with each strike. "Now we're getting somewhere."

After several more blows, she walked around to his side, studying him for a moment before positioning herself behind his bare back. She aimed carefully between his shoulders and swung with intense speed, the paddle connecting with a sickening thud. The man writhed, his cries desperate and incoherent as she lashed him five, six times in rapid succession.

Veronica stepped back, the paddle resting in her hand as she admired her handiwork. His skin was marked with welts, his body trembling from the onslaught. She grinned, the adrenaline coursing through her veins as she considered her next move.

Veronica's eyes scanned the wall of tools and toys until they landed on something particularly grotesque—a large, black dildo shaped like a horse cock. Her lips curled into a wicked grin as she walked over to it, her fingers wrapping around its thick base.

She giggled as she pulled it from its stand, its absurd size and wobbliness making her laugh harder. She swung it through the air like a long, wobbly sword, the exaggerated motion adding to her amusement.

Turning toward the restrained man, she took a few steps closer, the massive object still in hand. "So," she began, her voice mockingly sweet, "you like to prey on women, huh?" She twirled the dildo in her hand, her grin growing wider.

"You like to take our bodies, do you?" she asked, her tone sharpening as she planted the dildo in front of her, wielding it like a weapon as she stood before him.

The man's muffled cries were incoherent, his head

shaking wildly as his wet hair clung to his face.

Veronica's grin widened as an idea struck her. Without hesitation, she began slipping off her clothes, each movement deliberate and confident. She discarded her shirt and bra, letting them fall to the floor, then slid her pants and underwear down her legs in one fluid motion. Standing completely bare, she flaunted her flawless figure under the harsh basement light.

She stepped closer to the restrained man, her movements slow and calculated, ensuring he saw every curve. With a devilish smirk, she turned her back to him, bending over just enough to give him a perfect view of the valley between her thighs. She straightened with a flourish, swirling around to face him once again.

Her piercing gaze locked onto his as she stepped right up to him, her tone dripping with venom. "See this body?" she said, her voice low and mocking. "It will never be yours. You'll never have the pleasure of touching another woman again."

The man's muffled sobs grew louder, his eyes wide and filled with terror. Veronica leaned in slightly, her smirk unrelenting, before swiftly grabbing the oversized horse dildo from the floor. Without breaking stride, she walked behind him, her steps light and playful.

With a sharp swing, she smacked him on the ass with the massive toy, laughing as the impact made his body jolt. "Playful, aren't we?" she teased, gripping the base of the dildo firmly as she positioned it at his exposed opening.

She leaned in closer, her voice a low, taunting whisper. "Let's see how much you enjoy being on the receiving end."

Without any lube, she forced the massive object into

the man, eliciting a guttural, muffled scream as she pushed it as deep as it could go. His body strained and tore to accommodate the foreign object. With a mischievous grin, she flicked the end of the dildo, laughing wildly as it wobbled back and forth like a door stop.

Veronica left the massive object inside the man as she turned to the toolbox, her eyes scanning its contents for her next choice. Her fingers landed on a large vice clamp. With a mischievous grin, she walked back to the restrained man, noting how his balls and limp dick swung below the padded pedestal.

Without hesitation, she grabbed his sack and carefully placed it in the vice, positioning it just right. She began tightening it, click after click, as the man squirmed in discomfort. His muffled cries grew louder, rising to desperate squeals as she continued to turn the handle. His testicles turned a deep, alarming shade of blue, appearing on the verge of bursting.

As she applied one final turn, she suddenly felt the vice loosen. Confused, she leaned in to observe what had just happened. Her eyes widened in realization—she had clicked one time too many. One of his testicles had ruptured.

The man's muffled screams turned to guttural cries of agony as he thrashed against the restraints. Veronica blinked and glanced back at Grip, a mix of amusement and disbelief on her face. "Well," she said with a wicked grin, "I guess that happened."

Grip gave a squeamish look paired with a slight grin as Veronica picked up the clamp again and turned her attention to the man's remaining testicle. "Well," she said, "can't leave you with just one, now can we?" She began tightening the vice once more, counting aloud with each click. "One, two, three, four …" Her voice grew more animated as she continued. "Five, six, seven …"

On the eighth click, the clamp suddenly loosened again, and the man let out a guttural cry before slumping forward, limp from the overwhelming pain. Veronica leaned in with a wicked smile, her tone mocking as she said, "Oh, don't pass out on me now—we're not nearly done."

Grabbing the hose, she sprayed the man with a powerful jet of water, the icy blast shocking him back to consciousness. He jerked against the restraints, groaning and squealing as Veronica laughed. "There's my little pig," she teased, circling him like a predator savoring its prey.

Her eyes landed on the oversized toy still lodged in the man's bleeding asshole. With no hesitation, she gripped it tightly and began thrusting it in and out with vigor, slamming it deeper into him as he writhed in agony. Blood streaked down his thighs as she finally yanked the toy free, her grin widening.

Turning back to the man, she swung the massive toy like a baseball bat, striking him across the face with a sickening crack. His head snapped to the side, his muffled screams echoing in the room as Veronica let out another laugh.

She tossed the toy to the side and walked back over to the table, looking at the various tools. She pointed to the cold medical table. "Let's move him over there." Grip walked over and unstrapped the man. He didn't fight; he was defeated and limp from the pain. Grip dragged him to the table and strapped him to the cold metal frame.

Veronica walked over, examining the medical tools. "Hmmm, what to do, what to do," she murmured as she picked up a small scalpel. "Wow, this is sharp," she said, placing it against his cheek and sliding it across, opening the skin. Blood instantly dripped down. "Very, very sharp," she added with a grin.

She walked to his side, reached down, and grabbed the man's sack. "Let's see what's left of those balls," she said, cutting into his sack. Blood and fluid begin to drain out. She pulls out what looked like a clot of meat and sliced the veins holding it in place. As she freed the destroyed testicle, she said, "Well, that's nasty," plopping it on the table beside the man's face before returning for the other.

"This is like high school science all over again," she quipped as she removed the second one. She unfastens the ball gag and forced both testicles into the man's mouth. "Now look at you, taking your own load like a good little pig," she said, her voice dripping with mockery as she replaced the ball gag over his mouth.

As Veronica continued to make tiny little cuts into him, she felt the urge building; she wanted release. "Grip, my love," she said lustfully as she climbed onto the table, positioning herself above the man's face so he was staring directly at her pussy. "Come over here and take me."

Grip wasted no time as he undressed, walking toward her. "Anything for you," he said as he climbed onto the table, straddling the man's head. Grip's balls nearly dragging across the man's forehead as he entered Veronica's awaiting pussy. She let out a pleasurable moan as Grip began to fuck her on top of the man.

"My god, yes," she sighed as Grip's massive, throbbing cock slid deep into her passage. He began to thrust vigorously. "Faster," she commanded. As his body slammed into hers, he couldn't help but notice the man below them squirming as Grip's balls slid up and down his fat face.

Veronica's pussy tightened around him as the tension built. "FUCK," she screamed, leaning forward and arching her back perfectly for Grip to see her face lying near the man's limp dick. To his amazement, she opened her mouth and started to suck on it.

Veronica let out a growl of pleasure as the orgasm pulsed inside her. Grip felt her pussy convulsing, and right on time, he let loose with his own orgasm, shooting a massive amount of warm cum deep into Veronica's pussy. As he slid out of her, he slowly and deliberately dragged his dick across the squirming man's face, watching as a glob of his newly deposited cum dripped from Veronica's pussy right onto the man's cheek.

Grip looked up to see Veronica had blood in her mouth. Confused, he glanced back down and saw she had nearly bitten the man's dick clean off.

"Well, damn, he won't be using that again," Grip laughed.

She spit out the rest of the blood. "I don't know what got into me; it just happened."

"Sometimes we lose control. That's why we're here, right?" Grip stated.

"That's why we're here," Veronica agreed.

Veronica, looking around and taking in everything in front of her, noticed the man was bleeding heavily.

"Should we stop the bleeding or just let him die?" she questioned Grip.

"Well, doll, I guess that depends. Do you think you've gotten enough fun out of him?" he replied.

"Yes, I think I'm ready for a shower and a nap," she said before continuing, "What do we do now? How do we get rid of the evidence?"

"Ah, don't worry about that," Grip said, and pressed a

button on the wall.

A roll-up door Veronica hadn't noticed in the far corner by the closet swung open, and a two-man team walked in, wheeling a bed over.

As they prepared to move the dying man, Veronica shouted, "Wait!"

She grabbed the scalpel off the table again and reached over to grab the man's dick that was barely hanging on. She cut it off and looked back at Grip. "My trophy," she said with a grin.

As Veronica slipped back into her clothes, she glanced one last time at the now lifeless man strapped to the table. Grip pulled on his shirt, buttoning it up quickly, and motioned for her to follow him. They walked through the house in silence, the faint hum of activity from the basement fading behind them as they stepped outside into the cool night air.

Veronica's eyes scanned the area. She noticed something was missing. "Where did his car go?" she asked.

"The crew," Grip replied casually, his hands in his pockets. "I'm sure they've already taken care of it."

Veronica furrowed her brow, her curiosity growing. "How many people are involved in this?"

"We've got a four-man crew here," he explained. "They handle the property, disposal of the body, evidence cleanup—everything. Then there's Monroe, of course, and us. That's it."

Veronica crossed her arms, processing the information. "And the bodies? What are they going to do with them?" she asked.

Grip shrugged, his voice matter-of-fact, "Probably incinerate them. It's the easiest way to get rid of everything."

Veronica shook her head, a sharp edge to her voice. "Don't do that. Have them make sure there's no DNA left on the body, and then dump the naked body somewhere public."

Grip raised an eyebrow, intrigued. "Public, huh?"

"Yeah," Veronica said with a smirk. "Humiliate these sick fucks. Let the world see what they are. It's what they deserve."

Grip pulled his keys from his pocket as they approached their car. "Noted," he said, unlocking the doors. "I'll pass that along."

Veronica slid into the passenger seat and glanced back at the house as Grip started the engine. A small smile lingered on her lips as she looked over at him. "You really do think of everything, don't you?"

Grip smirked, pulling the car out of the driveway. "That's why you keep me around."

Back at the condo, the warm glow of the evening light cast a soft ambiance over the living room.

Grip and Veronica were curled up together on the couch, freshly showered and wrapped in soft robes, the faint scent of lavender lingering in the air. The TV flickered as Veronica lazily flipped through the channels, her head resting against Grip's chest.

"This is nice," she murmured, her voice relaxed and content.

Grip'sarm draped around her shoulders. "Told you a shower and some downtime would do the trick."

Just as she landed on a local news channel, the anchor's grave tone caught their attention.

"Breaking tonight: Terrance Miller, who was acquitted of sexual battery charges last year, has been found mutilated and murdered near the city pool. Authorities are asking for the public's help in identifying any leads regarding his death."

Veronica's hand paused on the remote, her lips curling into a sly smile as she glanced up at Grip.

"Well," Veronica said softly, her voice dripping with satisfaction, "it looks like someone finally got what they deserved."

Grip gave a low chuckle, pulling her closer. "Guess the city's a little safer tonight."

CHAPTER 13

JUDGE AND JURY

The aroma of freshly brewed coffee filled the condo as Grip and Veronica sat at the small kitchen table, enjoying a quiet morning together. The sunlight streamed through the blinds, casting soft patterns across the hardwood floor. Grip sipped his coffee, his sharp eyes scanning the skyline through the window, while Veronica absent-mindedly stirred hers, lost in thought.

The buzz of Grip's phone broke the silence. He picked it up from the table, his expression sharpening as he read the message. A moment later, he glanced up at Veronica.

"I know it's only been four days since we used the playpen," he said, setting his cup down, "but Monroe just sent me a lead."

Veronica raised an eyebrow, intrigued. "What is it?"

Grip leaned back in his chair, his tone steady but cold. "It's a corrupt judge. Monroe says he bought and trafficked a young teenage girl. He's been posting about it on the dark web—putting her up for sale."

Veronica's grip on her coffee mug tightened, her jaw clenching slightly as she listened.

Grip continued, his voice growing darker. "Monroe attached clips of the judge abusing her. It's sickening. He's already put the girl up for auction, but Monroe hacked the auction to make us the winner. She's arranging for the delivery to happen at the playpen."

Veronica exhaled, setting her mug down. "So, the judge delivers the girl … and then?"

"Then we take the judge. While you handle him, I'll have the network take the girl to safety. They'll make sure she's convinced she didn't see or hear anything and she somehow escaped. She'll be free."

Veronica's eyes softened for a moment before they hardened with resolve. "That bastard deserves everything we give him."

Grip nodded, his gaze meeting hers. "We'll make it happen."

#

The soft hum of the surveillance monitors filled the room as Grip and Veronica stood side by side, watching the live feed. On the screen, a black sedan pulled into the driveway, its headlights cutting through the darkness before shutting off. Grip glanced at Veronica, giving her a small nod before the two made their way upstairs to the front door.

The doorbell rang, and Grip opened the door to find Judge Hawthorn standing there, his broad, smug grin sending a wave of revulsion through both of them. Behind him, a young girl stood with her head down, trembling slightly.

"Well," Judge Hawthorn said, his voice dripping with satisfaction, "I want to thank you for your purchase. Here, as expected, is nineteen-year-old Summer." He gestured dismissively to the girl as though she were nothing more than a commodity.

Grip stepped aside, his face calm but unreadable. "Come in," he said, his voice steady.

Judge Hawthorn grinned and stepped past him, guiding the girl roughly by her arm. She stumbled slightly as he dragged her into the living room before tossing her to the ground like a discarded toy. She fell with a soft cry, her hands trembling as she curled into herself on the floor.

Hawthorn let out a laugh, glancing around the room. "Oh, I didn't realize you'd both be enjoying the merchandise," he said, his eyes lingering on Veronica.

Veronica stood near the doorway, her arms crossed and her gaze sharp as it locked on the judge. A sly smile spread across her lips, her hips swaying as she approached him . "Oh, she's not for me," she said softly, her voice dripping with seduction as she gestured toward Grip. "She's for him."

Her finger traced along the judge's neck, her touch light but commanding as her smile deepened.

"You, however," she murmured, her voice growing darker, "are for me."

Veronica grabbed his collar, her fingers curling into the fabric as she yanked him forward. The judge blinked in surprise but didn't resist, his grin faltering slightly as she led him toward the back bedroom.

"Come along," Veronica said, her voice smooth and commanding. "We're going to have a little fun."

Hawthorn chuckled nervously, his bravado slipping. Grip watched silently, his sharp gaze following them before shifting to the trembling girl on the floor. His jaw tightened as he knelt down, his voice calm but firm. "It's okay, Summer. You're safe now."

As soon as Veronica disappeared with Judge Hawthorn, Grip spoke to the trembling girl on the floor. "Come on," he said gently, offering her his hand. She hesitated for a moment before taking it, her wide, tear-filled eyes searching his face for any sign of malice. He helped her to her feet, keeping his tone calm and reassuring. "Let's get you out of here."

Grip led her to the front door and opened it, revealing two men dressed in scrubs, their professional demeanor radiating calm and trustworthiness. The men stood beside a sleek black suburban parked in the driveway, its back door open and ready.

Summer looked up at Grip, confusion and fear still clouding her face. "What's happening?" she whispered, her voice trembling.

"You're safe now," Grip explained, his voice steady and comforting. "Your family has already been contacted. They'll be meeting you at the hospital soon. These men are going to take care of you, but you need to understand something." He crouched slightly to meet her gaze directly. "You cannot tell anyone what happened here. Do you understand? For your safety, you're going to tell the hospital staff that you escaped from the judge by jumping out of a moving car."

Summer's lips quivered, fresh tears spilling down her cheeks. "I … I don't know what to say. Thank you. Thank you for saving me," she sobbed, throwing her arms around Grip in a desperate hug.

Grip's expression softened as he gave her a brief but firm pat on the back. "You're safe now. Just remember what I said."

The two men in scrubs approached, gently taking Summer by the arms and leading her to the suburban. One of them spoke in a calm tone. "We'll take good care of her."

Grip watched silently as they helped Summer into the vehicle and shut the door. The engine started, and the suburban disappeared down the road, its taillights fading into the night.

With a heavy sigh, Grip stepped back into the house,

closing the door behind him. The quiet was broken by a series of pleasurable sighs coming from the back room. Grip made his way down the hallway and saw the door at the end on the left slightly ajar.

Grip pushed the door open and stepped into the room. The dim light cast long shadows against the walls, and his eyes immediately fell on the scene before him. Veronica was perched on top of Judge Hawthorn, riding him in reverse cowgirl, her movements slow and rhythmic. The judge's hands were strapped to the bedposts, his face a mixture of discomfort and pleasure.

Veronica's head tilted slightly as she felt Grip's presence. She turned to look over her shoulder, her dark eyes meeting his. A wicked grin spread across her face, her movements never faltering.

"Enjoying the show?" she teased, her voice low and sultry, a playful glint in her eyes.

Grip leaned casually against the doorframe, his lips curling up. "Always," he replied, his tone cool but approving.

Veronica chuckled, her gaze lingering on him for a moment before turning her attention back to the man beneath her.

Veronica, never missing a stroke, asked, "Is she safe?"

Grip nodded, his smirk deepening. "Yep. She's on her way back to her family."

Before Veronica could respond, Judge Hawthorn's confused voice broke through the tension. "What's going on?" he stammered, his voice shaky and weak.

With a single motion, Veronica slid off him, her body bare as she stood at the foot of the bed. The judge lay helplessly tied to the bedposts, his body exposed and vulnerable. He squirmed, his eyes darting between her and

Grip, fear beginning to show in his expression.

Veronica leaned forward slightly, her tone sharp and commanding. "You've been a disgusting man," she began, her words slicing through the air. "Someone the people elected to trust. Someone meant to set judgment on others. Yet you've corrupted yourself—and the very system you swore to uphold—by becoming the kind of predator you pass judgment on."

The judge's face twisted with discomfort, his breathing growing erratic. He attempted to speak, but no words came out.

Veronica's gaze bore into him, unwavering. She stood tall, unashamed of her bare form, her presence dominating the room. "You, sir," she continued, her voice cold and resolute, "will now meet your own jury… and it's me, myself, and I."

Veronica smirked as she looked down at the restrained judge. "Let's get him down to the playpen," she said, her voice carrying an edge of excitement.

The judge's face twisted in confusion and panic. "What the fuck is the playpen? Let me go! I'll have you both arrested for this!" he barked, pulling against the restraints in vain.

Grip, calm but deliberate, pulled a pistol from his waistband and leveled it at the judge's forehead.

The cold steel glinted in the low light, making the judge freeze instantly. "She's going to untie you," Grip stated evenly, his voice carrying a lethal edge. "You're going to follow her without stopping. If you so much as hesitate, I'll put a shot of lead straight through your fucking skull. Do you understand?"

The judge's mouth opened and closed like a fish gasping for air. "What the fuck are you two—?"

"Shut the fuck up and do as you're told," Grip snapped, his tone sharp and unwavering.

Veronica leaned over the judge, her perfect erect nipples dangling teasingly in front of his face as she reached for the restraints. Her fingers worked deliberately, unfastening each one, her eyes flicking between his and Grip's pistol with a taunting grin.

The judge sat up, rubbing his wrists as he cast a frantic look toward the door. Grip didn't flinch, keeping the weapon trained on him. "Don't even think about it," he warned.

Veronica turned, her hips swaying as she strolled toward the door leading to the basement. She cast a quick glance back, her voice laced with amusement. "Come along, Judge. Don't keep us waiting."

Defeated and naked, the judge stood and followed her, his shoulders slumping as he shuffled hopelessly behind. The tension in the room followed them down the stairs, the only sounds the judge's hesitant footsteps and Grip's steady, calculated pace behind him.

The judge stumbled into the playpen, his eyes darting around the room in shock. The dim lighting illuminated the array of devices and tools scattered across the space. His breath hitched as he took in the intimidating sight—the medical table, the restraints, the control station in the corner, and finally, the towering wooden X with shackles at each end.

"What the hell is this place?" he muttered, his voice trembling.

Veronica stepped in front of him, her bare form exuding confidence as she pointed to the wooden X.

"There," she said, her voice firm but playful. "Face me and back into the frame."

The judge hesitated, his lips parting as though to protest, but one glance at Grip—still holding the pistol steadily—silenced him. Slowly, he obeyed, backing up until his arms and legs aligned with the shackles. Veronica moved closer, fastening the restraints one by one with an almost sensual precision.

With the judge now bound and helpless, Veronica leaned in, her finger trailing lightly across his chest. She traced a slow, deliberate path down his abdomen, her touch teasing yet unnerving. Her finger stopped at its mark—the judge's still-erect dick.

Veronica tilted her head, her eyes gleaming with amusement as a sly smile played on her lips. "Well," she murmured, her voice dripping with mockery, "isn't that interesting? Still hard, you must be enjoy this?"

Veronica's finger continued to tease its way along the judge's length, her voice soft but laced with disdain. "You have an impressive tool, Judge," she said, her eyes locking onto his with an almost pitying expression. "Why must you go down such a dark path? Aren't women easy enough to obtain with your power and wealth? Real women, not these innocent girls."

She stroked his dick slowly, her touch light and deliberate. "You felt really good inside me moments ago," she said with a sly smile. "I'm sure plenty of women have complimented you on this… tool."

Her words hung in the air, her tone a mix of mockery and seduction. Without breaking eye contact, Veronica knelt down in front of him, her bare knees pressing against the cold floor. The judge's manhood pointed directly at her supple lips as she tilted her head, her expression unreadable.

She took him deeply, swallowing his whole dick without so much as a sound. Grip watched as she worked vigorously, cupping and stimulating him rhythmically. Slurping as she worked on him for a while, building up momentum.

When the judge let out a solid grunt, she accepted the release without faltering, not missing a single drop of the judges cum, holding it in her mouth. Standing up, she used her fingers to pry open the judge's mouth and spat himself between his lips, then quickly covered them, forcing him to swallow.

"I hate to tell you this, Judge," Veronica said, her tone sweet, "but that's going to be your last nut. So I wanted you to keep it with you for what comes next."

The judge coughed and gagged, his body convulsing slightly as he struggled against the restraints. His eyes darted between Veronica and Grip, panic written all over his face.

Veronica reached into the nearby toy box, her fingers rummaging through its contents before pulling out a curling iron. She held it up, her lips curling into a mischievous grin. "What the heck could this be used for?" she giggled, her tone playful. "Let's see."

She plugged it into a nearby outlet and set it on the counter, letting it heat up while she continued to sift through the assortment of toys. Her eyes lit up as she pulled out another item. "Nipple clamps?" she mused, holding them up for inspection. "I think so."

Her hand brushed against something else—a pair of spurs like those worn by cowboys. She held them up, laughing. "Oh, why the heck not?"

Finally, she dug deeper and pulled out a familiar item. Her grin widened as she held up a metal-tipped flogger, a tool she remembered well from an event at Mistress Blue's. "Now this," she said, her voice filled with excitement, "I remember."

Turning her attention back to the judge, she strolled toward him, the flogger swinging lightly in her hand. Without hesitation, she lashed it across his stomach, leaving a trail of small, stinging scratches. The judge flinched, his body tensing against the restraints as Veronica laughed softly, savoring the moment.

Veronica reared back and struck the judge across the face and neck with the flogger, the metal tips leaving a small blood trail dripping from his cheek. She tilted her head slightly, a smirk forming as her eyes wandered down to his still-erect manhood.

Without hesitation, she swung the flogger again, this time with precision, letting the metal tips catch the sensitive tip of his manhood. The judge let out a guttural cry, his body convulsing against the restraints as he begged her to stop.

She reached over and grabbed the nipple clamps, positioning them onto the judge's nipples with deliberate care. A small bell dangled from each clamp, and she flicked them lightly with her finger, causing them to jingle softly.

Stepping back, she raised the flogger again and lashed it across his stomach and thighs, the sharp metal tips leaving thin, red trails in their wake. She delivered seven or eight swings in quick succession, moving in a back-and-forth motion that formed an X across his trembling body.

"Oh, you like this, don't you?" Veronica asked, her tone dripping with mockery.

The judge screamed in response, his voice filled with anger and desperation, "No, bitch, I don't! Let me fucking go right now!"

Before he could say another word, Veronica interrupted him, dragging the sharp spurs quickly across his thighs. He flinched, his body trembling as the pain shot through him.

"Oh, don't be like that," she said with a grin, tracing the spurs lightly across his torso. Each drag of the metal left thin, angry lines on his skin.

Without warning, she pressed the spur directly into his side, driving it into his abdomen with a sudden, forceful punch. The judge's body convulsed, a shockwave of pain ripping through him as he let out a guttural cry.

"Please!" he begged, his voice cracking as he writhed against the restraints. "Let me go! Please!"

"I bet Summer begged you to let her go, didn't she?" Veronica said coldly, her voice slicing through the room like a blade.

The judge's tone shifted as panic took over. "Please, I'm sorry," he begged, his voice trembling. "I'm truly sorry. I wish I could take it all back." He stammered, his words rushing together as he tried to justify his actions. "My wife ... she hasn't touched me in ages. Ever since she started chemo, it's been—"

Veronica's eyes narrowed, and she interrupted him sharply. "Cheating on your sick wife?" she asked, her voice dripping with disgust. "That's your excuse?"

Veronica lowered the spur and turned to Grip. "Grip, dear, message Monroe. Find out anything you can about this man's wife."

Grip nodded. "Sure thing," he said, pulling out his phone and stepping to the side as he made the call.

Veronica turned her attention back to the judge, her expression cold and unrelenting. "You sick fuck," she said, her voice steady but filled with disgust. "This woman has given you everything, and you treat her like this? And then you turn around and treat Summer the way you did?"

The judge opened his mouth as if to respond, but Veronica's piercing glare silenced him. She leaned in closer, her voice low and deadly. "I'm going to tell you right now—you're not going to live to see the morning. Your body will be found in your courtroom, along with all the evidence to prove what you've done. The world will know. Your wife will know."

She straightened, her eyes never leaving his as his face contorted in terror.

Grip returned, his phone still in hand. "I've got a contact number for her," he said, his voice calm and measured. "It looks like she doesn't have any appointments today, so we could call her if we want. There's a VPN here, so there's no way the call could be traced."

Veronica turned her attention to him, a slow grin forming. "You know what? Yes," she said, holding out her hand. "Hand me the judge's cellphone."

Grip retrieved the phone and passed it to her. Veronica held it up to the judge's trembling face. "Unlock it," she commanded.

The phone recognized his face and unlocked. Veronica began scrolling through his contacts, her brow furrowing as she came across a particularly jarring entry. She looked up at him, her eyes blazing with fury. "Dead wife?" she spat, incredulous. "What the actual fuck … How could you?"

The judge stammered, his face pale, but Veronica didn't give him the chance to respond. She tapped the contact and hit the call button. The phone rang twice before a soft, weak voice answered. "Hello? Clint?"

Veronica smirked. "Hi," she began, her voice laced with mock politeness. "I'm sorry to bother you, but I think you should know the truth about your husband."

There was a pause on the other end of the line. "The truth about what?" the woman asked, her voice trembling slightly.

"Well," Veronica said, her tone turning sharp and vehement, "he's been caught with an abducted young woman. He sold her to the highest bidder. Oh, and quite frankly, he hasn't been very nice to you, either."

The line went silent for a moment before the woman on the other end whispered, "What … what do you mean?"

Veronica let out a cold laugh. "Did you know you're saved in his contacts as 'dead wife'?"

Another heavy silence filled the air as Veronica waited for the woman's response, a wicked grin playing on her lips

The silence on the other end of the call broke with a shaky voice. "I know he's been messing around with the nurses who come here to take care of me," the woman said, her tone filled with anguish. "I saw one of them … pleasuring him in his study. I know he's counting on me to die. He basically calls me a waste of money and a burden."

Her voice cracked as she continued, now clearly crying. "But there's nothing I can do. I have no family, no friends, no money, and I have this fucking cancer …" Her sobs grew louder, the sound of her pain filling the air. "He's done everything to hurt me without actually laying a hand on me. But I'm sure he's thought about that, too."

There was a sniffle on the line before she asked, her voice trembling, "But… how do you know all of this?"

"Well, darling," Veronica said, her voice laced with mock sweetness, "let's just say your problems are about to be solved."

The woman paused. "How so?" she asked, her voice still thick with tears.

Veronica smirked and tapped the screen to turn on the video call. She pointed the camera directly at the bound and bleeding judge, who was visibly shaking and crying as he begged to be released.

"For what he's done to you and so many others," Veronica said calmly, her tone taking on a darker edge, "I'm going to give it back to him tenfold."

The judge's cries filled the room as Veronica held the camera steady, her wicked grin growing as she waited for the wife's response.

"I don't know why, but I'm not upset about this," she said, her tone soft yet firm. "If I weren't so weak, I'd come down there and help."

Veronica chuckled darkly. "Oh, don't worry, my dear. I can leave the camera on and take my time with him if you'd like."

The wife hesitated, then asked, "What are you going to do with him? What if he comes after me?"

Veronica's eyes gleamed as she tilted her head slightly. "Well, my sweet, beautiful Mrs. Hawthorne, I hope you have a good life insurance policy. Because by morning, his body—and all the evidence of his crimes—will be discovered in his own courtroom."

The wife let out a shaky, relieved sigh. "Well then, yes. If I'm safe, fuck it. I want to watch the prick burn in hell."

Veronica's grin widened, her face lighting up with

twisted delight. "Well, fancy you mention burn," she said, her tone dripping with anticipation. She handed the phone to Grip, positioning the camera so the wife could see everything.

Walking over to the counter, Veronica picked up the curling iron she had plugged in earlier. "You know," she mused, holding it up, "I didn't quite know what to do with this until now."

She unplugged the iron, the faint smell of its heated coils filling the room. Turning back toward the judge, she smiled coldly. "This prick deserves to rot in hell, and I'm going to send him there."

She moved toward him slowly, the curling iron gripped tightly in her hand, as the judge's weak cries filled the room.

Veronica leaned closer to the judge, her eyes cold and commanding. "Look at the camera," she ordered, her voice sharp. "Apologize for being a sick fuck."

The judge hesitated, his lips trembling as his gaze flickered to the phone. He let out a shaky breath before stammering, "I'm … I'm sorry for being a sick fuck."

Veronica's smirk deepened, her satisfaction evident. "Good. Now, stick your tongue out."

The judge froze, panic flashing across his face. "Do it before I shove it up your ass," Veronica snapped, her voice like a whip. Slowly, he complied, his tongue trembling as he extended it from his mouth.

Without hesitation, Veronica pressed the hot curling iron against his tongue, pinning it to his bottom lip. His muffled screams filled the room as the sound of sizzling flesh crackled in the air. The acrid smell of burning taste buds made Grip wrinkle his nose as he watched from the side.

Veronica removed the iron and tilted her head, her smile wicked. "There," she said mockingly. "That tongue won't be spreading any more lies."

The judge whimpered, his head slumping forward as his body shook with pain and humiliation.

"His nipples!" the wife suddenly called out through the speakerphone, her voice cutting through the air. "He hates his nipples being touched!"

A malicious grin spread across Veronica's face as she turned her attention back to the judge. "Well, isn't that just delightful," she said, yanking the nipple clamps off with two quick motions. The judge flinched, a yelp escaping his lips.

Without hesitation, Veronica pressed the hot curling iron directly against one of his exposed nipples.

The searing heat made him scream out in agony, his body writhing against the restraints. "Please! Please stop! I'll do anything!" he begged, his voice cracking with desperation.

Veronica tilted her head, her expression thoughtful. "Anything?" she asked, her tone dripping with sarcasm. "Hmm… how about this: go to Hell."

With that, she pressed the iron against his other nipple, his screams filling the room as the acrid smell of burning flesh lingered in the air.

"I have an idea," Veronica said, her tone calm yet chilling. She plugged in the curling iron and pointed to a padded stand in the corner of the room, its design leaving no doubt about its purpose. "Get down from there," she ordered, unstrapping the judge from the wooden X.

The judge stumbled forward and fell to his knees, his body trembling as he looked between Veronica and Grip. Grip stood steady, holding the pistol in one hand and the phone streaming the video in the other. His cold, unwavering stare made it clear that compliance was his only option.

Veronica gestured toward the stand. "Go over and strap yourself in," she commanded.

The judge hesitated for a moment, his eyes darting between them. "Why should I? You're just going to kill me anyway. At least the gun is quicker."

Grip lowered the pistol slightly, aiming at his dick, which seemed to spur him into action. Slowly, he shuffled toward the padded apparatus, his shoulders slumping in defeat. He positioned himself over it, bending forward and spreading his legs as instructed. His movements were sluggish and heavy, his breaths shaky as he strapped one leg in, then the other.

He placed one hand in the restraint, fastening it himself, before pausing, his body trembling as he waited for someone to secure his other hand. His head hung low, his face etched with fear and humiliation.

Veronica approached him, her heels clicking softly against the floor as a wicked grin spread across her face. "Good boy," she muttered. She reached for his remaining hand, snapping the strap tightly into place with a deliberate, sharp tug

As Veronica circled the judge, her steps slow and deliberate, she glanced at the curling iron heating up on the counter. "Mrs. Hawthorne," she said with a sly grin, "do you see anything you'd like me to use on him?"

Grip, ever the composed assistant, shifted the phone to point at the array of tools on display. The camera panned over clamps, blades, floggers, and other assorted devices.

She scanned the scene silently for a moment before

suddenly exclaiming, "That!" Her voice was loud and clear, filled with malicious satisfaction as she pointed toward a section of the toolbox visible on the screen.

Veronica's eyes lit up as she followed the direction of the camera. She reached into the toolbox and pulled out a reciprocating saw, a long dildo affixed to the blade. Holding it up, she smirked and turned it over in her hands.

"This?" she asked, her voice dripping with mock curiosity. "What an interesting choice," she added, giving the saw a quick test, its motor whirring ominously as the dildo wobbled back and forth. She chuckled, looking into the camera. "Well, this should be fun."

Veronica circled the judge, a predatory grin spreading across her face as she held the saw in her hand. She placed the tip of the dildo against his trembling lips. "Open your mouth," she commanded, her voice cold and unyielding.

She pressed the trigger lightly, letting the motor whirl to life. The dildo slapped against his face, the sound echoing in the room as the judge flinched. Humiliated, he hesitantly opened his mouth, his eyes filled with terror. Without missing a beat, Veronica pushed the toy into his mouth and squeezed the trigger fully, the saw buzzing loudly as the toy jerked back and forth between his lips.

Suddenly, she shoved the toy deeper, forcing it down his throat as the motor continued to whirl at full blast. The judge gagged violently, his body jerking against the restraints as he desperately tried to pull away, his muffled cries filling the air.

She continued to throat fuck the judge with the crude tool. Gagging and motor noises were all that could be heard until, out of nowhere, a giggle came through the speaker phone. Veronica looked pleased as she could see the judge's wife enjoying the show.

Veronica pulled the toy out of the judge's mouth, her smirk widening as she leaned in closer. "Does the good boy want this in his ass?" she asked, her tone dripping with mockery. She stood silently, waiting for his response, her gaze unrelenting.

The judge, his will broken, whispered, "Yes."

Veronica raised an eyebrow, her grin turning wicked. "Say please," she demanded.

The judge's voice cracked as he obeyed. "Please ... use that thing on my ass."

"Good boy," Veronica cooed, repositioning herself behind him. The toy, still slick with his own slobber, pressed firmly against his exposed entrance. As she adjusted her grip, her finger accidentally squeezed the trigger, causing the dildo to shoot forward with force.

The judge cried out in pain and shock, his body jerking against the restraints. Veronica giggled, amused by the mishap. "Oh well," she said with a playful shrug. "It's in now."

She pressed the trigger fully, sending the toy into full speed. The buzzing filled the room as the judge writhed helplessly, his muffled cries blending with the sound of his wife's hysterical laughter on the phone.

Noticing the judge's balls juddering violently from the relentless force of the machine plowing his entrance, Mrs. Hawthorne's voice crackled through the phone, laced with wicked amusement. "I should have those turned into a necklace and wear them around my neck."

Grip interrupted her train of thought, his tone steady and calculated. "Well," he said with a smirk, "I just so happen to have an idea." He set the phone down at an angle, ensuring Mrs. Hawthorne could still see everything as Veronica continued her relentless assault on the judge.

Grip disappeared into the closet, reemerging moments later with a propane tank and a round metal pot. He placed the pot on a portable cooking stand and ignited the propane, the blue flames licking at the base. Reaching into a small case, he pulled out a chunk of silver-looking metal and dropped it into the pot, the clink echoing in the room as it settled.

Picking up the phone again, Grip held it steady, pointing the camera toward the makeshift setup. "You see," he explained with a calm, almost educational tone, "silver has a low melting point. And as a collector of fine metals, I just so happen to have some of my personal stash on hand. We'll have liquid silver in just a few minutes."

Mrs. Hawthorne's face lit up on the screen, her grin growing malicious. "You say the word, Mrs. Hawthorne," Grip added, his voice steady and dark, "and you'll have them around your neck by tomorrow."

The wife laughed wickedly through the speaker, her voice trembling with excitement. "Do it," she said, her grin practically glowing on the screen.

Grip nodded, his smirk deepening as he set the phone back down. The propane hissed steadily, the silver beginning to melt as Veronica continued her merciless work on the judge, who was now sobbing uncontrollably.

Veronica noticed the machine start to slow, its buzzing growing faint. "Well, shit," she muttered, tossing the device back into the box. "That was fun while it lasted."

As she turned around, her attention shifted to Grip, who was carefully pouring a molten liquid into a heat-resistant container, his gloved hands steady. "What do you all have going on over there?" she asked, curiosity sparking in her voice.

Grip smirked as he walked toward her, holding the container of liquid silver. "Darling, be a dear and grab the judge's crown jewels," he said smoothly. "Dip them into this."

Veronica's eyes gleamed with intrigue as she moved behind the restrained judge, her hands deftly grasping his sensitive and swollen parts. With a malicious grin, she lowered them into the molten silver. The smell of burning flesh filled the room, and the judge's screams of agony echoed off the walls. Mrs. Hawthorne, watching intently through the propped-up phone, remained silent, her face cold and emotionless.

After about ten seconds, Grip pulled the judge's seared parts from the container, letting them cool briefly before dipping them again. This process repeated four or five more times, each dip bringing fresh screams from the judge as Veronica laughed softly at his torment.

Finally, Grip set the container back near the propane tank. Veronica knelt down, tapping the judge's hardened, silver-coated skin with her fingernails. "Clink, clink, clink," she murmured, her tone filled with fascination. "Holy shit, that's pretty nice."

Through the phone, Mrs. Hawthorne's voice broke the silence. "Now cut them off," she demanded. "Get them to me—dick and all."

Veronica raised an eyebrow, her lips curling into a mischievous grin. "Well, sorry, Mrs. Hawthorne," she said as she turned toward the medical table. "But the dick is mine."

She reached for a scalpel but hesitated, her hand moving toward an older, rusted medical saw that looked like it had seen use in World War I. With a wicked laugh, she picked it up and walked back toward the judge, the dull teeth of the blade gleaming under the light.

Veronica walked back to the judge, the dull, rusty saw clutched in her hand. She held it up to the phone, showing the jagged blade to Mrs. Hawthorne, who watched with wicked anticipation. "This ought to work just fine," Veronica said with a sly grin.

The judge writhed in pain and begged for death, his body jerking as the burning agony of the molten silver adorning his testicles continued to overwhelm him. Veronica leaned in close, her lips brushing against the hardened silvered surface of his mutilated jewels. She placed a slow, mocking kiss on them before straightening.

Grabbing the silvered remains with one hand, she pressed the dull blade against the tender, unsilvered flesh where his genitals met his body. Her voice was cold and cutting. "You, sir, are a disgrace to men. Since you want to own women, how about you become one and see how hard it is?"

With deliberate force, Veronica began to saw, the rusty blade tearing into the skin. The judge let out guttural screams, his body straining against the restraints, but there was no escape. Veronica pushed and pulled, the dull blade slowly working its way through the flesh. Blood dripped onto the floor, pooling beneath him as she worked methodically.

Finally, with one last determined pull, the severed jewels came free. Veronica held them up triumphantly, crimson-streaked silver glinting in the light. Turning to the phone, she smiled sweetly at Mrs. Hawthorne.

"Mrs. Hawthorne," she said with a mockingly cheerful tone, "your order is ready. You'll have this custom piece as soon as we can get it to you."

Veronica laughed softly, twirling the grotesque trophy in her hand as she admired her work.

She placed the severed pieces on the table next to her and smirked. "I'm not done," she said, her tone cold and commanding. "You're still a man with that tool dangling there, so it's time I take my reward as well."

She walked back over, gripping him firmly in her hands. With a mocking laugh, she mused aloud, "I wonder if he can still cum after losing his nuts?" Her actions were deliberate, and the judge screamed as she started stroking his cock, using his own blood as lubricant.

Veronica tilted her head, studying him intently. "Interesting," she said with a twisted curiosity. "It seems like he's still trying …"

She looked toward Grip with surprise and amusement. "My god," she said, shaking her head, "is this even possible? Look at him—he's actually trying."

The judge instinctually thrust into her hand as his reflexive movements took over. "Oh wow, it feels like he's actually cumming!" Veronica leaned back, laughing coldly. "Aww, look at that," she mocked. "He tried so hard … but nothing came out. Sad. But what a good boy you are."

She stepped back, the tension in the room still palpable, as the scene settled into silence, save for the muffled cries of the broken man.

Without a warning or so much as a hint, Veronica took the dull blade and, with one forceful push, sawed clean through the judge's manhood. It fell to the ground with a wet thud. She threw her head back, laughing hysterically as the judge's screams ceased and he slumped forward, passing out from the unbearable pain.

"Here, darling, hand me the curling iron," she said, looking over her shoulder at Grip. Grip walked over, unplugged the device, and handed it to her. Veronica took it, inspecting the bloodied stump where the judge's manhood once was. Without hesitation, she pressed the hot iron firmly against the gushing wound.

The room filled with the sickening sound of sizzling flesh and the faint hiss of blood meeting extreme heat. The metallic scent of burning blood and skin hung heavy in the air. "Huh," Veronica mused, tilting her head as she noticed the bleeding had stopped. "Well, I'll be damned—the TV shows aren't lying. You really can stop bleeding like this. Who knew?"

She pulled the curling iron away, examining it with a twisted grin as blood and charred remnants clung to the surface. Glancing over at the judge's unconscious form, she turned to Grip. "He's passed out, isn't he?"

Grip looked up from his phone, casually confirming, "Yeah, he's out cold."

Veronica's grin widened as a wicked thought crossed her mind. "Well, this should wake him up."

With that, she shoved the still-hot curling iron directly into the judge's recently destroyed asshole. The iron slid in with ease, the seared tissue offering no resistance. The judge's body twitched slightly, though he remained unconscious.

Veronica tried to pull the iron back out, but it didn't budge. Frowning slightly, she tugged harder, only to realize the burned tissue inside had fused to the iron's surface. "Oh, for fuck's sake," she muttered.

Veronica bent down and picked up the still-erect severed manhood from the floor, holding it up with a twisted grin. Walking over to the pot of molten silver, she stirred it carefully. "Well, we shouldn't let this go to waste," she mused, dipping the severed piece in headfirst.

She pulled it out, examined it briefly, and then dipped it back in again, repeating the process over and over. Finally, she withdrew it, now fully encased in shimmering silver. Despite the mutilation, about six inches remained intact. Satisfied, she placed it on the counter to cool.

Turning to Grip, she asked with a playful tone, "Hey, do we have anything to wake him up? I've got an idea."

Grip tapped his chin thoughtfully before pointing to the nearby medical tools. "Hmm... take that fingernail file over there. Shove it under one of his fingernails—that should do the trick."

Veronica grabbed the file as she walked toward the judge. Following Grip's instructions, she slid the file under a nail on his hand, pressing it in firmly. The reaction was immediate. The judge shot awake, his eyes wide with horror as a guttural scream escaped his lips. His body jerked violently as the burning rod sticking out of his ruined body registered in his mind.

"Kill me!" he screamed hoarsely, his voice mangled by his burnt tongue. "I can't take anymore!"

Veronica let out a mocking laugh, shaking her head. "No, ma'am," she said coldly, a deliberate emphasis on stripping him of his manhood. "You, little lady, now have a task."

She began untying the judge, moving with a casual ease as though the horrors she inflicted were second nature. In her haste, the fingernail file fell loose from his hand and clattered to the floor. "Oops," she muttered with a chuckle before continuing to release him.

Once the restraints were undone, she walked over to

the counter, picked up the now-cooled silvered manhood, and tossed it lightly between her hands. "Ah, yes," she said with delight. "It's nearly cool enough."

Veronica walked to a padded massage table, hopped up onto it, and reclined leisurely. Spreading her legs, she held the silvered manhood in the air, her grin wide and sinister. "Come," she said, her voice dripping with mockery. "Take this and pleasure Mommy."

The judge, now overwhelmed by pain and barely able to stand, shuffled toward her, clutching the severed silver tool in his trembling hand. His face was pale, and his movements sluggish, as if his mind was too fogged by shock to resist. As he raised it hesitantly, Veronica's voice sliced through the air.

"No, no, no," she snapped. "You don't just get to skip to the fun part. You have to earn it. Be a good girl and suck it first."

The judge froze, his defeated eyes darting between her and the grotesque object in his hand. His breathing was shallow, a mix of humiliation and desperation etched across his face. Slowly, he bent his head and obeyed, taking the severed organ into his mouth.

"That's right," Veronica purred, her voice low and taunting. "In and out, just like that. You're such a good little girl, aren't you?"

As he continued, she suddenly slapped his hand, forcing the tool deeper than he expected. The judge gagged.

"Choke on it," she sneered. "Bet you like that, don't you?"

Suddenly, a phone rang, interrupting the moment. Mrs. Hawthorn's voice came through, calm and steady. "I'm sorry, I must go now. My children are coming to take me to dinner. But rest assured, I'll keep everything that's happened to myself and happily replay these memories until this disease takes me from this world. Thank you both, from the bottom of my heart." With that, the call disconnected.

The judge spit the object out, coughing and trembling as tears streamed down his face. He looked up at her, utterly broken. "Please … Mommy… just end it. I can't—I just can't anymore."

Veronica smirked, tilting her head in mock pity. "Poor baby," she cooed. "Let's see how good you can make me feel, and maybe I'll think about it."

As the judge placed the tool between her thighs, easing it into her anticipating mound, she let out a soft moan. "Yes … yes, just like that," she murmured.

Veronica, now thrusting back against the judge's hand, began to move with increasing force, her breaths growing heavier. She moaned deeply, her voice raw and unrestrained. "Oh God," she gasped, her body shuddering as her climax overtook her. Her juices sprayed from her quivering mound, coating the judge's forearm in warm, slick wetness as she let out a final cry of release.

As Veronica caught her breath, she sat up slowly, her body still trembling slightly from the aftershocks of pleasure. She reached out and took the severed toy from the judge's trembling hand, inspecting it with a smirk.

"This is mine now," she said, her voice firm yet playful. She leaned in close, brushing her fingers under his chin. "But you did such a good job, baby girl. I'll let you choose how this ends."

Her eyes glinted with dark amusement as she stood and strode across the room to the medical table. "I'll give you a couple of options," she added, her tone almost singsong.

With deliberate movements, she picked up a scalpel, twirling it briefly between her fingers. Then, she grabbed a long, sharp rod, its pointed end gleaming under the light, and a heavy hammer. Turning back to face the judge, her lips curled into a wicked smile.

"Now," she said, holding up the tools, "let's see which one you prefer."

"You've got three choices," Veronica said with a smirk, holding the scalpel and the rod up for emphasis. "Option one: take this scalpel, slice an artery, and bleed out like the pathetic worm you are." She paused, letting the words sink in before grinning. "Option two: the creative route. Hold this sharp rod to your temple, and I'll drive it straight into your sick little mind with this hammer." Her tone was gleefully menacing.

"And finally," she continued, raising a hand dramatically, "option three: Grip shoots you in the head. Quick, clean… boring."

The judge, trembling and broken, immediately blurted out, "Shoot me!"

Veronica scowled, rolling her eyes. "Now, that's no fucking fun." She marched over to him and shoved the rod into his hand. "Veto! Hold this to your temple," she demanded.

The judge hesitated but obeyed, his hands shaking as he positioned the rod against his head.

Veronica took a practice swing with the hammer, her petite frame vibrating with anticipation. "Alright, baby girl, let's do this."

Rearing back, she swung with all the force her small body could muster.

THWACK.

The hammer missed the rod entirely, connecting with

the side of the judge's skull instead. Bone cracked loudly, and a jagged fragment of his skull flew across the room, hitting the wall with a sickening thud. The judge's body crumpled to the floor, limp, his chest rising and falling weakly. Gurgling and wheezing escaped his lips as he took his final breaths.

Veronica stared at the scene in mock surprise, her lips curling into a devilish grin. "Oh shit… my bad!"

Grip, watching from the sidelines, crossed his arms and chuckled. "Well, doll, you never fail to amaze me with your creativity."

Veronica exhaled, brushing her hair back as she composed herself. With a satisfied smile, she strode over to a small panel on the wall and pressed a button to call in the staff. Moments later, the door opened, and a team entered, led by a tall man with a no-nonsense demeanor.

Veronica pointed to the judge's limp body with a flick of her wrist. "Clean him up. Get all the DNA and evidence off him," she instructed, her voice sharp and commanding. "Then take him to his courtroom and set him in his chair. Leave a folder beside him—everything we have, all the proof of his sick exploits."

She turned to face the team fully, her expression chillingly casual. "Oh, and one more thing," she added with a smirk, gesturing toward a pile on the table. "Find a nice silver chain for those balls over there, get them wrapped up, and sent to his wife. Make it thoughtful."

With a flick of her wrist, Veronica tossed the silvered severed tool into the air, catching it effortlessly. "I'm keeping this one for the collection," she said with a grin.

Turning toward the door, she glanced at Grip, who had been watching quietly from the corner. "We're done here."

Together, they left the playpen, the door swinging shut behind them as the staff moved into action, the eerie silence of the room broken only by the sound of their preparations.

CHAPTER 14

SERIAL KILLERS NOW?

Veronica stepped out of the shower, steam billowing into the bedroom as she wrapped herself in a plush towel. Her damp hair clung to her shoulders as she padded barefoot into the kitchen. The rich aroma of coffee filled the air, and she poured herself a cup, savoring the warmth against her palms.

Grip sat at the kitchen table, casually flipping through a newspaper. With a mischievous grin, he slapped it down on the table in front of her. "Look at this," he chuckled, leaning back in his chair.

Veronica glanced at the bold headline on the front page:

Judge Hawthorn of the 7th District Court Found Mutilated and Murdered in His Courtroom

Her eyes scanned the article as she sipped her coffee.

Sources say police discovered a mountain of evidence allegedly proving Judge Hawthorn was involved in a vast sex trafficking ring. His wife released a statement on her late husband's actions, calling them 'disgusting,' and vowed to donate 50% of his wealth to organizations combatting human trafficking.

Veronica smiled, setting her coffee mug down. "See? We're making a real difference," she said with a satisfied smirk.

Grip raised an eyebrow, smirking as he folded his

arms. "Yeah, well, now I think we're officially serial killers," he said, his tone light but questioning.

Veronica tilted her head, amused. "Oh, really? Do we get a fancy name?"

Grip shrugged, leaning forward as if in thought. "I guess when the news finally puts the pieces together, maybe. Wonder what it'll be?"

Veronica chuckled, taking another sip of her coffee. "Whatever it is, I hope it has a nice ring to it."

Grip grinned, his dark humor evident. "Something classy, right? Gotta keep up appearances." The two exchanged a knowing look, their twisted sense of accomplishment hanging in the air.

Veronica picks up the paper again, the faint sound of sirens echoing in the distance.

#

A month passed since Judge Hawthorn's grotesque end, and Veronica and Grip hadn't let the trail go cold. They'd begun following leads unearthed from Hawthorn's deep web of connections, each thread leading to the next. One trafficker after another, broken in the playpen, had ratted out their cohorts, forming a grim chain that brought them closer to their ultimate target. Five victims later, they stood at the precipice of uncovering the head of the operation.

Veronica lounged on the couch, idly swirling her coffee mug as she watched the darkened video screen. On it, Monroe's figure was faintly illuminated by the glow of her multi-monitor setup, her voice calm and analytical as it filtered through the condo speakers. Grip leaned against the kitchen counter, arms crossed, his eyes flicking between Veronica and the screen, his expression one of cautious anticipation.

The quiet hum of the elevator broke the tension, and Mistress Blue stepped into the condo. Her dark, tailored attire hugged her figure, her heels striking sharp notes against the floor as she made her way into the room. She dropped a sleek leather bag onto the table, her piercing gaze sweeping over the trio.

Her brow arched slightly as she glanced at Veronica, then Grip, and finally the faint image of Monroe on the screen. "Problem with the safe house?" she asked, her tone casual but inquisitive.

Veronica smirked but said nothing, taking another sip of her coffee. Grip's lips curled into a faint, knowing grin, but he remained silent as well, letting the moment hang in the air.

Mistress Blue's eyes narrowed, scanning their faces. "Something wrong?" she pressed.

Monroe's voice crackled through the speakers, steady and calm as ever. "All in good time," she said, her words only deepening the mystery.

Mistress Blue's gaze lingered on Veronica, who leaned casually against the couch, her smirk widening ever so slightly. The silence thickened.

Grip pushed off the counter, flashing a casual grin. "Thanks for coming, Mistress Blue. And no, nothing's wrong with the safe house. Best purchase I've made this year, actually," he said, his tone light but genuine. "Your men's quick customization and skills are top-notch. It's the perfect place for us."

Mistress Blue arched a brow. "So, why the summons?"

Grip's grin lingered as he folded his arms, his tone taking on a more serious note. "We've been following some leads … things that have come to light recently."

He paused, studying her expression. "You heard

about Judge Hawthorn?"

Mistress Blue leaned back slightly, a small smirk forming on her lips. "Yes, wild story, wasn't it? Someone really had it out for him."

Her gaze shifted to Grip's sly grin, then to Veronica, who sipped her coffee with an unmistakable glint of amusement in her eyes. Mistress Blue's smirk widened as realization dawned. "Oh, you kinky, cheeky fucks," she said with a low laugh, shaking her head. "Well, what do you need from me?" she asked, folding her arms and leaning against the table.

Veronica set her mug down on the table, rising from the couch with an air of practiced confidence. "Monroe, you're up," she said, gesturing to the screen.

Monroe's voice came through, smooth and steady. "Gladly. What we've uncovered so far paints a pretty grim picture. Hawthorn wasn't just a player in this trafficking ring; he was one of the cornerstones. Every lead we've squeezed out of his associates points to a sprawling, international network."

Grip crossed his arms, his gaze fixed on the screen. "We've taken down five of his little pawns already, but there's always someone bigger in the shadows, pulling the strings."

Monroe nodded, the glow of her monitors reflecting in her sharp eyes. "I've been tracking their movements online—encrypted messages, payments, the works. The network's head isn't just sitting back quietly. They've noticed their chain unraveling, and they're taking steps to tighten security. If we want to get to the top, we'll need to move fast."

Mistress Blue listened intently, her expression hardening. "And how exactly do you plan to do that?" Veronica exchanged a glance with Grip.

"We're thinking it's time for a more direct approach." Monroe's voice sounded off through the speakers, calm yet purposeful. "This is where you come in, Mistress Blue. The next name we've uncovered is Anthony Freeman."

Mistress Blue arched an eyebrow, crossing her arms as she waited for Monroe to continue.

"But here's the intriguing part," Monroe added. "I caught his name on one of your party invite lists."

Mistress Blue's expression hardened. "How do you have access to my lists?" she asked, her voice sharp.

Monroe smirked, her silhouette tilting slightly on the screen. "Ma'am, you may make men bend to your will," she said with a touch of dry humor, "but coding is my bitch. There's nothing I can't access."

Veronica hid a smirk behind her coffee mug as Mistress Blue's eyes narrowed.

Before she could respond, Monroe continued, her tone shifting to reassurance. "Relax. I'm not here to dig through your business—or ruin it. My intent isn't malicious, and I can even patch some of your security issues if you want. Consider it a professional courtesy."

Mistress Blue studied the screen for a long moment, her lips pressed into a thin line. Finally, she let out a sharp breath and waved a hand dismissively. "Fine. Let's say I believe you. How can I help with sir Freeman?"

Monroe's voice came through the speakers, steady but laced with a hint of frustration. "Since the last few men have turned up in the news—mutilated, with all their dirty laundry laid bare—the trafficking network has gone dark. Completely. All chatter has stopped. I can't find this Sir Freeman linked to anything viable. Just small hints here and there."

She paused, her tone sharpening as she laid out the plan. "What we want to do is simple: host another party. Use it to draw him out. Cater it to his personal desires. I'm sure you know what it is he likes."

"I might have a few ideas," she said coolly, her eyes flicking toward Veronica.

Monroe continued, "With the right bait, we can make sure Freeman walks right into your hands."

The room fell quiet for a, tension hanging in the air as Mistress Blue considered her response.

Mistress Blue let out a small sigh, her expression shifting as she leaned against the table. "Okay, so just so you're aware," she began, her tone measured but carrying an undercurrent of discomfort, "Sir Freeman has a very particular taste ..."

The room grew still, all eyes fixed on her as the pause stretched uncomfortably.

"Well," she finally continued, "he is a very neat, clean freak kind of guy, he doesn't touch doorknobs or anything that hasn't been frequently cleaned, and there's no easy way to say this ... he likes the cold ... the non-moving ... Well the dead, to be frank."

Her words lingered in the air, heavy and grotesque, as the room fell completely silent. Even Monroe's usually confident voice remained quiet on the other end of the feed.

Mistress Blue let out a breath, her expression hardening. "He likes freshly expired women in their twenties," she said bluntly, her tone void of emotion. "But there's more to it. He always travels with a rather large group of men—his personal entourage. If I were to lie and claim we had something for him and didn't deliver, it wouldn't end well. His reach within the network is vast, financially and otherwise. Crossing that line would be problematic."

Her gaze swept across the room, meeting Veronica's eyes before shifting to Grip's. "However," she continued, her tone calculated, "I can give you a live feed to the room when he visits. After he leaves, you can set up some sort of ambush or whatever else you have planned. But it cannot happen on our grounds. That wouldn't be good for the network." Mistress Blue adjusted her posture, smoothing the hem of her tailored jacket. "That's my offer. Take it or leave it."

Grip nodded. "That will work just fine," he said. "I can have my men extract him once he leaves your facility. Having him there gives us what we need. We can record his actions for the media. Afterward, the fallout will be perfect. Everything will work out just right."

Mistress Blue tilted her head, her sharp gaze meeting his. "Perhaps," she replied, her tone skeptical. "But there's one issue. It's not exactly easy or cheap to find a freshly expired, beautiful woman." She folded her arms, her voice tinged with dark pragmatism. "So … any ideas there?"

Her question hung in the air, heavy with implications, as the room once again fell into silence.

Veronica leaned forward, setting her coffee mug down with a quiet clink. "Let's just say, Mistress Blue, money isn't an issue," she began, her eyes narrowing thoughtfully. "Do you have a …" She paused, searching for the right words. "… a vendor for that type of thing?"

"Oh, my darling," Mistress Blue purred, "I have a 'vendor' for anything you could possibly desire. My job is to provide people with everything they can dream of—no matter how twisted."

"With a blank check," she said with a wink, "I'll make a call."

She stepped to the side of the room, her heels clicking softly against the floor, and began speaking softly into the phone, her tone low and discreet. Veronica and Grip exchanged a glance, the faintest hint of a smirk tugging at Veronica's lips.

Mistress Blue returned to the center of the room, slipping her phone into her pocket with a satisfied smirk. "Well, we're in luck," she announced. "A young woman just overdosed. She was pronounced dead nine minutes ago. Seems fate is on your side tonight." She glanced at Veronica and Grip as if discussing a mundane delivery. "I'll have her cleaned, prepared, and delivered to the facility. And I'll send Freeman's invite shortly." Her gaze shifted to the video screen, where Monroe's silhouette glowed faintly. "I'd offer you camera access, but I assume you're already there?"

Monroe's voice came through, calm and confident. "Yep. I'm guessing it's the room with the weird autopsy table?"

Mistress Blue let out a small laugh. "That's the one."

"Well, happy hunting," she said, turning on her heel, stepping toward the elevator. The soft chime announced its arrival as the doors slid open. Without another word, Mistress Blue disappeared into the elevator, leaving the room in silence.

Grip crossed his arms, his expression dark but focused. "I'll have the guys prepare the extraction and handle the delivery to the playpen after. So, I guess, Monroe, if you want to document whatever sick shit he does with this poor girl, that's your cue."

Monroe's voice crackled through the speakers. "Already on it. I'll make sure every moment is captured. This guy won't have a shred of plausible deniability left when we're done."

Grip turned toward Veronica with a faint smirk. "I'll drop you off at the playpen to get everything ready. You know how to make it … welcoming."

Veronica returned his smirk, her eyes glinting with anticipation.

The room grew quiet again, tension thick as the pieces began falling into place.

#

Time had passed, and now the moment had arrived. Monroe sat in her dimly lit workspace, the glow of her monitors illuminating her sharp features. Her fingers danced over the keyboard as she cycled through the live feeds, her eyes narrowing as the camera at the network's entrance flickered to life.

On-screen, Freeman's entourage strode into view. The group of men surrounded him in a tight formation, their movements sharp and no-nonsense, as if choreographed for maximum efficiency. Freeman, a tall man with slicked-back hair and an air of unsettling calm, walked in the center of the group, his presence commanding despite the silence.

"They move like clockwork," Monroe muttered to herself as they made their way directly to the secure room.

The camera feed shifted, following their progress into the room. Inside, the space was pristine and cold, dominated by the autopsy table where a delicately displayed red-haired woman lay motionless, her pale skin and soft features frozen in unnatural stillness.

Freeman's men wasted no time. Splitting up, they methodically swept the entire room, checking every corner, every piece of furniture, ensuring the space was secure. Satisfied, they exited without a word, taking up positions outside the door to stand guard, leaving Freeman alone with his carefully prepared prize.

Monroe's gaze flicked to another feed on the screen. In the parking garage, a man in dark clothing appeared near Freeman's sleek black vehicle. He moved with precision, crouching beneath the car and placing something underneath it. Within seconds, he stood, adjusted his hood, and vanished into the shadows.

Monroe raised an eyebrow. "Huh," she muttered, cracking her knuckles. "That's interesting. Let's see what sick shit you're into, Sir Freeman."

She switched her focus back to the secure room feed. Freeman stood motionless for a moment, his head tilted as if admiring the lifeless form in front of him. Slowly, he unbuttoned his suit jacket. Piece by piece, he shed his clothing, hanging each item neatly on the back of a nearby chair.

Monroe's expression hardened, her eyes glued to the screen. The eerie silence of the room seemed to creep into her workspace as she watched the man prepare to reveal the depths of his depravity.

Freeman reached for a small device on the table and turned on a classical music playlist, the soft, elegant strains filling the sterile room. He moved slowly around the lifeless body, his fingers tracing up her thighs, over her supple breasts, and up to her cold, parted lips. His touch lingered briefly before pulling away, his expression unreadable.

On the table beside the body was an assortment of

neatly arranged items: brushes, clothing, and other accessories. Freeman reached for a hairbrush and carefully dragged the woman's body to the edge of the table. With deliberate precision, he began to brush her hair, each stroke slow and meticulous.

Monroe, watching through the live feed, leaned back in her chair, eyebrows furrowing. "What the fuck?" she muttered, her voice dripping with disbelief as she continued to monitor the bizarre scene.

Freeman's low voice broke the unsettling silence, his tone eerily gentle. "It's been a while, Sarah Lew. I hope you haven't missed me too much … because I've missed you."

Monroe blinked. "What the absolute fuck is going on here?" Her tone was laced with incredulous humor, though her discomfort was evident.

On the screen, Freeman placed the hairbrush down carefully, as if it were a sacred relic, and reached for another item on the table—a toothbrush. He leaned closer to the body, cradling her chin as he opened her mouth with unsettling tenderness. "Let's get those teeth clean for Daddy," he murmured.

He began to brush her teeth, his movements unnervingly thorough, as if preparing her for some grotesque reunion.

Monroe's mouth hung open as she stared at the screen, her fingers hovering over the keyboard. "Nope. Nope. This is … next-level insanity," she muttered, her voice thick with disbelief.

Freeman tilted her head back slightly, pouring a small stream of water into her mouth from a glass on the table, letting it spill messily onto the sides of her face before wiping it away with a cloth. "There," he said softly, almost lovingly. "Now we're all fresh, Sarah."

He turned back to the assortment of items laid out neatly on the table, selecting a small razor. He examined the blade, ensuring its sharpness, before turning back to the lifeless body. "Now," he said softly, "let's get this body hair under control."

Freeman shaved her underarms, his strokes slow and meticulous. Monroe's face twisted in disbelief as she leaned closer to the screen, unable to tear her eyes away.

Freeman moved on to her legs, dragging the razor carefully up each thigh with an almost obsessive focus. The silence in the room, broken only by the faint classical music and the subtle scrape of the razor, made the scene all the more unnerving.

Finally, he worked his way to her pubic area, his hands steady as he continued his task. Every motion was deliberate, as if performing some twisted ritual.

Freeman placed the razor back on the table, his motions calm and deliberate. Reaching for a wet rag from a nearby bowl, he began to gently bathe the lifeless body, running the cloth over her pale skin with unsettling tenderness.

As he worked, he spoke softly, his voice steady and conversational, as if addressing an old friend. "You missed it, Sarah," he said with a faint edge of disappointment. "You weren't there for the gala. You know how important it was to me. All those people watching, waiting. You let me down."

He paused, his hand lingering on her collarbone as if considering his next words. "But it's okay," he continued, his voice softening. "I forgive you. You always had a habit of letting your priorities slip, didn't you? But …" He tilted his head, a faint smile crossing his lips. "You know there has to be consequences, don't you? You'll have to be punished. Just a little."

Freeman resumed bathing her, his movements disturbingly intimate as he carefully wiped down her arms, legs, and torso. The rag moved slowly, as though he were savoring every second of the ritual.

Watching through the feed, Monroe's jaw clenched. She leaned closer to the screen, her hands tightening into fists. "This guy…" she muttered under her breath. "What the hell kind of mental gymnastics is he doing? Punished? She's dead, you lunatic."

Her fingers hovered over the keyboard, tempted to turn the audio off, but she resisted, morbid curiosity keeping her locked on the scene.

Freeman placed the rag aside, his demeanor calm as he reached for a large saw on the table, its blade gleaming under the fluorescent light. The sharp teeth of the saw reflected his unsettling focus as he turned back to the lifeless body.

Monroe's eyes widened as she noticed something that made her stomach turn—Freeman was becoming visibly erect.

"What the absolute shit?" she exclaimed, her voice rising in disbelief. "He's turned on? What the hell is he about to do with that saw?"

Her reaction escalated, taking on the tone of someone in a horror movie theater, practically yelling at the screen. "Oh, hell no! Don't you dare! What is this sick-ass lunatic doing?"

Freeman stood over the body, gripping the saw tightly, his focus never wavering as the classical music played in the background.

In one well-positioned push, Freeman drove the saw into the poor girl's throat. The blade tore through, and on the return stroke, it sliced completely through her neck. The lifeless head tumbled to the floor with a dull thud, rolling slightly before coming to rest at his feet.

Freeman bent down, picking it up with both hands as if cradling something precious. He pressed his lips gently to hers, the grotesque tenderness of the gesture sending a chill down Monroe's spine.

"My Sarah," he whispered softly, his voice dripping with a disturbing mix of affection and delusion.

"Don't worry. Everything's going to be okay. You get to watch."

With that, he carefully placed the severed head on the lifeless body's stomach, positioning it so it faced the empty space where the neck once was. He brushed stray strands of hair away from the head's unseeing eyes.

"There," he murmured, straightening the hair with his fingers. "Now you can see."

Freeman returned to the neck of the body, his motions disturbingly calm and deliberate as he repositioned himself. The faint strains of classical music played on, an eerie contrast to the scene unfolding.

Monroe's knuckles tightened around the edge of her desk. "What the hell am I even watching?" she muttered under her breath, her voice low, filled with disbelief.

Freeman grabbed the lifeless body by the shoulders, positioning himself with a disturbing tenderness. His erect manhood hovered over the bloody stump of the neck before he slid himself into the gaping wound. A grotesque grin spread across his face as he looked at the severed head resting on the body's stomach.

"See, my darling?" he murmured, his voice low and

almost affectionate. "You liked this the last time."

He began to thrust, his movements slow at first, his hands gripping the body's shoulders tightly. As he built up momentum, he reached over and lifted the head into the air, holding it aloft like a prized possession.

"Oh, my sweet Sarah," he groaned, staring into the lifeless eyes. "I've missed your touch."

His pace quickened, the act growing more frantic as his breathing grew heavier. He pressed his lips to the head's mouth, kissing it passionately while letting out moans and sighs, his body shuddering with grotesque pleasure.

Back in her dimly lit workspace, Monroe sat frozen, her face blank. Her eyes were wide, her mouth slightly open, and for the first time, she had nothing to say.

A loud grunt broke the eerie quiet as Freeman's body jerked violently. He trembled for a moment, his grip tightening on the head as he let out a guttural moan.

Monroe blinked, her voice monotone but tinged with disbelief. "He just … no. No, no, no, no. He didn't just—" She paused, her voice rising in pitch. "Did he just fucking cum in her dead throat!"

Freeman pulled himself free from the neck, holding the head up. He pointed it toward the room's entrance, tilting it slightly.

"See what you did, Sarah?" he said with a sickeningly tender smile. "Always such a good girl."

He gently placed the head back onto the body, adjusting it so the eyes seemed to watch him. Calmly, he grabbed a cloth and cleaned himself off before moving back to the table to retrieve his clothes. With practiced ease, he began dressing, as if nothing out of the ordinary had occurred.

Freeman straightened his tie and smoothed his suit as he left the room. His entourage, waiting just outside, immediately fell into formation around him. Without a word, they escorted him through the compound, their footsteps echoing in the quiet halls.

Monroe's eyes stayed glued to the monitors, tracking his every move. She watched as they exited the building, Freeman striding confidently to his sleek black car. His men opened the door for him, ensuring everything was secure before taking their positions in nearby vehicles.

As Freeman settled into the back seat, Monroe grabbed her phone, typing quickly to Grip.

Well, he's all yours. They're leaving now.

She set her phone down and leaned back in her chair, staring blankly at the monitors. For a moment, she said nothing, her mind replaying everything she had just witnessed.

Finally, she muttered to herself, her voice tinged with both disbelief and exasperation: "What the absolute fuckity fucking fuck fuck shit was that?"

The camera feed showed Freeman's car pulling out of the compound, his convoy following close behind. Monroe exhaled sharply, running a hand over her face as she turned off the computer and walked away.

CHAPTER 15

BREAKING FREEMAN

The night was quiet, save for the low hum of tires on asphalt as Freeman's convoy moved steadily along the highway. His sleek black car, sandwiched between two SUVs filled with his loyal men, cut through the darkness like a predator returning to its lair. Inside, Freeman sipped from a crystal tumbler, his demeanor relaxed after his twisted exploits at the compound.

He had no idea what was coming.

A few miles ahead, hidden in the shadows of a bridge, Grip's men lay in wait. The plan was flawless, executed with military precision. Their vehicles, fitted with disabling devices and reinforced bumpers, were parked strategically for a textbook ambush. They had practiced this scenario countless times, and tonight, the target was finally within their grasp.

As the convoy approached the trap, the first vehicle in Freeman's convoy hit a spike strip laid across the road. Tires screeched, and the SUV swerved violently before grinding to a halt. The black car came to an abrupt stop behind it, its driver scanning the area with rising panic.

Before Freeman's men could react, Grip's team moved in. Two vehicles blocked the road from behind, cutting off their escape. Masked figures emerged swiftly, armed and efficient. Smoke grenades filled the air, creating chaos and confusion as Freeman's guards shouted orders, disoriented by the sudden attack.

Freeman's car door was yanked open, and a masked

figure grabbed him, dragging him out into the chaos. He struggled briefly, shouting obscenities, but his resistance was met with a sharp jab from a stun baton. His body convulsed, and he slumped forward, unconscious.

Grip stood nearby, his arms crossed as he watched the abduction unfold with ruthless efficiency. His men worked quickly, disarming Freeman's guards and neutralizing any resistance. Within minutes, the scene was cleared. Freeman's men were left unconscious or restrained on the side of the road, their vehicles rendered useless.

"Load him up," Grip ordered, his voice calm but commanding.

Freeman's limp body was thrown into the back of an unmarked van, its interior fitted with restraints designed for maximum security. Grip climbed into the passenger seat, pulling out his phone to text Veronica.

The package is on its way. Have fun.

Veronica stood silently, her expression cold and calculating, as Grip's men brought in the unconscious form of Mr. Freeman. They strapped him securely to a heavy chair in the center of the room, its metal frame bolted to the floor. Around him, the walls were adorned with an array of tools—implements of torture, sharp and gleaming, alongside the familiar trappings of BDSM. The atmosphere was a sinister blend of seduction and menace.

One of Grip's men approached her, handing her a small vial of smelling salts. "Miss," he said respectfully, "break this and let him smell it when you're ready for him to wake up."

Veronica took the vial without a word, nodding as the team exited the room, leaving her to her devices. As the heavy door clicked shut, Monroe's voice crackled over the intercom, her tone dripping with controlled rage.

"Take your time with this one, Veronica. What he did to that poor girl deserves … special attention."

Before Veronica could respond, the door opened, and Grip stepped in. Without a word, he crossed the room, cupped her face gently, and pressed a kiss to her lips. "Have fun," he said with a smirk, his voice low. He turned and exited through another door, disappearing into the adjoining security room to watch.

Veronica turned back to Freeman, her heels clicking softly on the floor as she approached. With a measured calm, she cracked the vial of smelling salts, holding it slightly under his nose.

Freeman jolted awake, his eyes wide with confusion and fear. His breathing quickened as he struggled against the restraints, taking in the ominous surroundings. "What the hell is going on here?" he demanded, his voice sharp but edged with panic.

Veronica crouched slightly, bringing her face level with his. Her lips curled into a slow, predatory smile. "Hi, love," she said smoothly, her voice sweet and chilling. "I'm your newest admirer. I've been following your work for a little while now, and I have some questions."

She straightened, the soft click of her heels echoing in the room as she slowly circled him.

Veronica leaned in closer, her lips curling into a sly smile as she spoke. "Do you remember Judge Hawthorn? Or should I say Ms. Hawthorn, after I was through with him?"

Freeman's eyes widened in recognition, and his face twisted with rage and fear. "Oh, fuck no—it's you! You're the one responsible for our guys' deaths!" he shouted, his voice rising. "You crazy bitch, what the Hell do you want?"

Veronica raised an eyebrow, unfazed by his outburst. She opened her mouth to speak, but before she could get a word out, soft strains of classical music began playing over the intercom. She turned her head, her expression shifting to mild confusion.

Before she could ask, Monroe's voice crackled through the speakers. "Mr. Freeman here loves classical music and torture," she explained. "I thought it'd be a nice touch to make him feel welcome."

Veronica let out a light chuckle, shaking her head. "Oh, well, if you say so, Monroe, I don't mind." She turned back to Freeman, her expression darkening as she stepped closer to him, her heels clicking ominously against the floor.

She leaned in, her eyes narrowing. "Ms. Hawthorn and those other scumbags were all part of your little group of 'men,'" she said, her voice dripping with disdain. "A group that abducts young women from other countries and sells them all over the world."

She straightened, her voice growing colder as she added, "And they led me right to you. So… here we are."

Her gaze locked on Freeman's panicked eyes. "Anything to say for yourself, Mr. Freeman?"

Freeman's face twisted in rage as he shouted, "Fuck you, bitch! There's no proof. You don't know shit! You can't prove anything!"

Veronica smirked, tilting her head slightly. "I'm not trying to prove anything," she said smoothly. "I won't have to prove anything to anyone because you'll be dead."

Freeman snarled, leaning forward as far as the restraints would allow. "The fuck I will! You can't touch me!" His voice rose in desperation as he added, "He's probably already aware of what's happening here, and he's sent a team to kill you and burn this place to the ground."

Veronica let out a soft, mocking laugh, stepping closer to him. "Well, I doubt anyone can help you, my friend," she said, her tone light and teasing. "See, my real man is really good at his job." Her voice darkened as she leaned in slightly. "But now that you mention it, we do want to know who's running this little network of yours. Who's this mysterious man who's going to save you?" She straightened, taunting him with a wicked grin. "Come on, tell me. Who's your big, bad savior?"

Freeman's confidence wavered, his defiance visibly cracking as beads of sweat formed on his forehead. "You'll find out soon enough," he muttered, his voice shaking slightly. Then, with a sudden burst of bravado, he added, "His power is unmatched. He knows judges, congressmen, prime ministers—Hell, if they're in control of the world, he knows them personally. There's nowhere, no one, he can't get to!"

Veronica raised an eyebrow, her lips curling into a faint smirk. "Well, who is he, then?" she asked calmly, her tone deceptively sweet.

Freeman's eyes burned with hatred as he spat, "Fuck you. You'll see. And when you're dead, I'll get to play with your little body."

Veronica's expression darkened, but she didn't respond. The room grew tense, the air heavy with unspoken threats.

Veronica smirked, stepping back slightly as her eyes locked onto Freeman's. "Oh, this little body you say?" she teased, her voice dripping with mockery. With deliberate precision, she began to undress, sliding her top off her shoulders and letting it fall to the floor. Her movements were slow and methodical, almost like a dance as she circled around him.

"This body you want to play with, huh?" she continued, cupping her breasts in her hands and lifting them slightly before letting them fall back into place, still perfectly perky. Her eyes drifted to the growing bulge in Freeman's pants.

"Oh, but Mr. Freeman," she purred, her voice both taunting and amused, "I'm still warm. I'm very much alive. I guess you can't control your own body, huh?"

She knelt down in front of him, her hands moving deliberately as she unbuttoned his pants. Pulling them down, she revealed his erect manhood, her grin widening.

"See? You don't mind the breathing as much as you thought," she said, her tone laced with malice.

"Fuck you, cunt," Freeman spat, his voice trembling with both rage and humiliation.

Veronica leaned forward, taking him into her mouth. Her motions were slow and methodical, every move calculated to disarm him further. The wet sounds filled the room as she slurped, her mouth working him with deliberate precision.

Freeman, caught off guard, groaned despite himself. "Yeah … you suck my dick, bitch," he muttered, his defiance faltering under the sensation.

With a loud pop, Veronica pulled away, letting his manhood slip out of her mouth as she grinned wickedly. "Well, that's where you're wrong," she said, her voice calm and cold. She gestured to a clear jar on the table beside them. "If you'll look over there, you'll see my rather growing collection," she said.

Freeman's eyes darted to the jar, his face twisting in horror as he noticed the severed dicks floating in the murky liquid.

"This dick," Veronica continued with a chilling laugh, "isn't yours. It's mine."

Standing up, she walked over to the table, picking up a sharp pair of scissors. Returning to her place kneeling in front of him, she twirled the scissors playfully in her hand.

"So," she said, her tone mockingly sweet, "how about you tell me who this big savior of yours is?"

Freeman's face contorted with rage and fear. "You sick cunt," he spat, his voice shaking.

Veronica smirked, her grip tightening on the scissors.

She knelt in front of Freeman, her expression cold and unrelenting as she slowly began to close the scissors around his erect manhood. The sharp blades pressed tighter, nearly closing, and blood began to trickle down the handles. Freeman thrashed in his restraints, screaming in panic.

"Please! Stop! Don't do this!" he begged, his voice cracking. "I don't know his name—I don't know anything!"

Veronica's gaze didn't waver as she tightened her grip, the blades biting deeper into his flesh.

Freeman let out a high-pitched squeal, tears streaming down his face. "Please! Stop! Please, please, please! I'll do anything!"

Veronica tilted her head, her voice calm but deadly as she said, "Then tell me who the fuck is running this cesspool of degenerates."

Freeman whimpered, shaking his head desperately

before shouting, "Okay! Okay, okay! I'll tell you! Just loosen up, please!"

Veronica paused for a moment, her grip relaxing ever so slightly, but the scissors remained firmly in place.

"I-I don't know his full name," Freeman stammered, his words tumbling out in a panic. "All I know is it's not just him. He and his wife—they run and fund the network. I just manage the collection of the girls to be sold. They handle everything else. I deliver the sold girls. That's it!"

Veronica's eyes narrowed, her grip on the scissors tightening again as she shook them slightly, making Freeman yelp in pain. "Who. Is. It?" she demanded, her voice sharp and unforgiving.

Freeman squealed, the words spilling from his mouth. "His name is Mr. Jay! He's the head of the largest investing firm in the world! He owns everything and everyone! And his wife, Penelope, handpicks the victims and sends them to me. That's all I know, I swear!"

Without hesitation, Veronica snipped the scissors closed, severing Freeman's manhood in one clean motion. Freeman let out a blood-curdling scream as his body convulsed in the chair. Veronica picked up the severed organ from the floor, holding it up and studying it for a moment before bringing it to her lips. She sucked lightly on the head, her eyes locking with Freeman's tear-filled ones as she smirked maliciously.

Walking over to the jar, she unscrewed the lid and dropped it in with the rest of her collection. "See? I told you it was mine," she said with a cruel laugh, sealing the jar back up.

Behind her, Freeman was wailing in agony, his voice breaking as he screamed, "I told you what you wanted!

Please! I told you everything!"

Veronica turned back to him, her expression icy and emotionless. "You did," she said, her voice calm, "and thank you for being a good boy. But you still need to be punished."

She leaned in closer, her voice dropping to a menacing whisper. "Based on my experience, you've got about eight minutes before you pass out from blood loss. So let's make this as memorable as possible."

Veronica strolled over to Freeman, her expression cold but teasing as she leaned in close, her voice dripping with mockery. "So, from what I've been told, you're a very clean man," she said, her tone almost conversational. "Not a big fan of messes, allegedly."

Freeman groaned in agony, his head slumping forward, but his gaze snapped back up as Veronica turned around, flaunting her perfectly shaped, bare ass cheeks. Slowly, she began to move her hips, taunting him with a seductive twerk, each movement deliberate and provocative.

Freeman's groans of pain mingled with audible disgust as she backed up closer to his bloody pelvis, her movements slow and deliberate. With a wicked grin, she reached back, spreading her cheeks as she locked eyes with Grip, who was watching silently from the security room viewing window.

Veronica's expression shifted to one of concentration, her eyes never leaving Grip's. With a low grunt, she released herself onto Freeman's lap, the thick, batter-like consistency of her excrement spreading across his thighs and pelvis.

As the sight and the instant smell of fresh shit hit his nose. Freeman screamed in both pain and revulsion, his cries echoing in the room. "What the fuck! You sick, disgusting bitch!" he wailed, thrashing against his restraints, the overwhelming sensation pushing him further into madness.

Veronica stood tall, smirking proudly as she strutted over to the sink. Calmly, she cleaned herself off, taking her time as Freeman continued to scream and struggle in the chair.

Once finished, she reached for a large paintbrush hanging on the wall. Grasping it tightly, she turned back to Freeman, the wicked grin returning to her face.

"Oh, Mr. Freeman," she cooed, her voice dripping with malice as she walked back toward him, the paintbrush in hand.

Veronica stood in front of Freeman, her wicked grin widening as she held up the brush. "Oh, don't worry," she said, her voice sickeningly sweet. "We're just getting started."

With a deliberate motion, she dipped the brush into the pile of grotesque fluids on his lap, swirling it until the red-brown concoction coated the bristles. Lifting the brush, she crouched by his feet and began to paint his toes, dragging the bristles up along his legs in slow, deliberate strokes.

Freeman thrashed weakly in his chair, letting out guttural screams before gagging and vomiting down his front.

Veronica paused briefly, glancing at the new addition to her palette. "Oh, a new color," she said with mock excitement, swirling the brush into the mixture of vomit, blood, and feces.

She continued her work, painting his legs, hips, and

groin with meticulous precision. The disgusting concoction smeared across his skin, staining every inch of exposed flesh. Freeman's suit and tie were no exception—Veronica moved upward, using the paintbrush to cover his white shirt like an artist preparing a canvas with mod podge.

Freeman's screams turned to moans as his energy waned, his head slumping forward slightly.

Veronica tilted her head, watching him closely. "Oh no," she teased, setting the paintbrush down in his lap. "Getting weak, are we? Losing too much blood? Well, not before the main course."

She turned and walked over to the table, her heels clicking ominously against the floor. Her hand hovered over an assortment of tools before she picked up a large serving spoon, her fingers curling around it tightly.

Freeman's head lolled slightly as she returned to him, the grotesque mixture now pooled in his lap. "You know," she said, her tone casual as if discussing dinner plans, "it's impolite to waste food."

Without hesitation, she scooped up a large spoonful of the revolting concoction and held it in front of his face. Dazed and weakened, Freeman was powerless to resist as Veronica shoved the first scoop into his mouth.

His gag reflex kicked in immediately, but Veronica's strength overpowered him. "No, no," she cooed mockingly, forcing his jaw shut. "Chew. Swallow. Be a good boy."

She scooped another portion, then another, shoving each one past his lips as Freeman's muffled cries and gags filled the room. His body twitched and convulsed, tears streaming down his face as Veronica smiled coldly, savoring every second of his humiliation.

As she continued her twisted performance, an unexpected wave of nausea crept up on her. She paused for a moment, internally chastising herself. Okay, this may be a little much, she admitted silently. I know he's a sick fuck, but is there not a line I won't cross?

Taking a deep breath, she composed herself, her expression remaining calm and taunting. "Well," she said aloud, tossing the spoon into Freeman's lap with a faint clatter. "I've had about enough of this. Honestly, I'm feeling a little nauseous myself."

Turning on her heel, she strode over to the closet, pulling out a long hose connected to the wall.

She walked back to Freeman, uncoiling it as she went, and began spraying him off. Freeman shrieked as the cold water hit him, jolting his senses and washing away the revolting mixture from his body. Veronica cut off his shirt and tie as the mess swirled down the drain.

Once he was clean—though still bleeding profusely from his mutilated groin—she reached for a can of air freshener. With exaggerated enthusiasm, she sprayed the area liberally, stopping to spray directly onto Freeman's exposed, raw wound.

Freeman's screams echoed through the room, his voice hoarse and ragged. Veronica looked down at him with a smirk. "Looks like you've got about three minutes left," she said, her tone mockingly sweet. "And since you don't like dirty—or apparently alive and loud—I'll put on a theatrical show just for you."

She motioned for Grip, who had been watching from the sidelines, to come over. Dragging a padded table into position directly in front of Freeman, Veronica climbed onto it with practiced ease. She knelt on the table, her face mere inches from Freeman's, her piercing gaze locking with his terrified eyes. Propping herself up with her hands on his thighs, she smiled wickedly.

"Hun," she said, her voice dripping with playful malice as she looked over her shoulder at Grip, "fuck me like I drank the last cup of coffee."

Grip didn't need to be told twice. With eager vigor, he stripped off his clothes and climbed onto the table. Without hesitation, he grabbed Veronica's hips and slammed into her, his force causing her to lurch forward. Her forehead knocked against Freeman's, eliciting a muffled groan of pain from him as she cried out in pleasure.

"Oh yes!" Veronica screamed, her voice echoing in the room with exaggerated ecstasy. Her moans grew louder and more theatrical with every thrust, her head tilting back as her body rocked in rhythm with Grip's movements. "Oh, my god, YES! Right there! Harder! HARDER! Oh, Grip, you're so big! You're gonna ruin me!"

Her cries were relentless, her tone deliberately over-the-top, every sound designed to disgust Freeman, whose preferences thrived in silence and stillness. She locked eyes with him again, her lips curling into a wicked grin between her moans. "Do you hear that, Mr. Freeman?" she panted. "That's what it sounds like when someone's alive."

Freeman squirmed against his restraints, his face twisted in agony and repulsion as Veronica continued her vulgar display.

Veronica could feel Grip's throbbing cock, her familiarity with him telling her that he was close to finishing. She glanced back at him with a wicked grin, her voice sultry yet commanding. "Oh, hunny, I'm sorry, but I have a request. I want you to stand up and cover Freeman's face with your sweet cum."

Grip let out a deep grunt, his breathing ragged as he awkwardly stood on the surprisingly stable table. With urgency, he gripped his shaft, stroking himself to completion. With the first forceful shot, his warm fluid splattered directly into Freeman's right eye. The second hit squarely on his lips and nose, and the third, with less momentum, dripped onto Veronica's back.

Freeman groaned weakly, his face contorted in disgust and despair, his life slipping away with each passing moment. Veronica leaned in close, her lips brushing against his cheek in a mockingly tender kiss. With deliberate malice, she licked the dripping fluid from his face, savoring the moment as her gaze bore into his lifeless eyes.

"Poor thing," she cooed with a twisted smile, pulling back and standing tall. Freeman's body slumped further into the chair, his head lolling to one side. Veronica studied him for a moment before noticing his chest had stilled completely—his life finally expired.

She smirked, wiping her hands on a nearby cloth as she glanced over at Grip. "Well," she said with dark amusement, "I guess that's one way to send him off."

Veronica, still slightly nauseated, stood up and took a deep breath, brushing her hair back from her face. "I'm sorry, hun," she said softly, glancing at Grip with a faint smile. "That went a little off the rails. But I don't always want to resort to pain—sometimes mental torture is just as important."

She turned toward the room, raising her voice, knowing Monroe was still listening through the intercom. "I apologize to you too, Monroe. You shouldn't have had to see that."

Monroe's voice crackled through the speakers, her

tone blunt but satisfied. "Sick fuck got what he deserved," she replied simply.

Veronica smirked, her expression softening slightly as she looked back at Grip. "Hit the button," she instructed, motioning toward the security system. "And tell the men to display him as usual. The folder with all his damning evidence is over there." She gestured toward a nearby table.

With that, she stretched her arms overhead, her body language easing into calm confidence. "I'm going to take a shower," she said casually. "And then I think we need to find a hot tub."

Grip nodded as he moved to carry out her instructions. The room began to clear, the twisted remnants of their work left behind.

CHAPTER 16

THE EUNUCH COLLECTOR

The morning sun streamed through the windows of the condo as Veronica and Grip sat at the kitchen table, enjoying breakfast. The clink of forks against plates and the soft hum of conversation filled the air until a familiar voice crackled over the security system's speakers.

"Good morning, you two," Monroe said cheerfully, her tone holding a hint of amusement. "Y'all told me to keep an eye out in case the news started talking about you directly. Well ... watch this."

Without waiting for a response, the large TV in the living room flickered to life. Both Veronica and Grip turned their heads as the news anchor began his announcement.

"Local authorities have made a press release regarding the recent string of staged victims," the anchor said, his tone serious. "All of the victims were men involved in heinous crimes; each one found with their genitalia mutilated. Authorities now believe we may have a serial killer on the prowl. The victim count this morning has reached seven—possibly eight—with the latest being a Mr. Anthony Freeman, a prominent Wall Street executive."

The anchor continued, "Freeman's body was discovered early this morning on Wall Street, along with evidence accusing him of necrophilia and other heinous crimes. While police have not disclosed everything, we took to the streets to ask local residents their thoughts."

The scene shifted to an anchor on the street, microphone in hand, standing in front of a bustling cityscape.

She approached a woman who looked directly into the camera with a confident expression.

"It looks like someone is cleaning up the streets," the woman said firmly. "Like Batman or Superman or something. I don't see anything wrong with it."

The camera shifted to another interviewee, a man in a business suit. He adjusted his tie and said, "It's about time someone took out the trash. Whoever's doing this is giving those creeps what they deserve."

Finally, the scene cut to a rougher-looking man leaning against a lamppost. "Looks to me like someone's cleaning the streets and collecting eunuchs," he said bluntly, giving the camera a knowing smirk.

The broadcast returned to the news anchor in the studio, his expression cautious but intrigued. "For those unfamiliar, a eunuch is a man who has been castrated. And while authorities are still piecing together the details of this case, it seems the public has already coined a name for the killer. They're calling them… The Eunuch Collector."

The anchor leaned forward, his tone grave. "Whether or not this 'collector' sees themselves as some sort of vigilante, we can only hope the authorities can put an end to these gruesome murders soon."

Veronica let out a sharp laugh, leaning back in her chair. "Oh, I kinda like that!" she exclaimed, grinning as she turned to Grip. "The Eunuch Collector. It has a nice ring to it, don't you think?"

Grip smirked, shaking his head as he took another bite of his toast. "You sure know how to leave an impression," he said dryly.

Monroe's voice chimed back in over the speakers. "You're trending now, sweetheart. Congratulations.

Can't wait to see how you top this."

Veronica raised her coffee mug in a mock toast. "To the Eunuch Collector," she said with a smirk, clearly enjoying her newfound infamy.

Veronica leaned back in her chair, swirling the last of her coffee in her mug as she addressed the room with a sly grin. "Oh, Monroe, you beautiful keyboard warrior," she said, her voice dripping playfully. "Have you found any information about this Mr. Jay and his lovely wife, Penelope?"

Monroe's voice crackled over the speakers, her tone smug yet professional. "Well," she began, pausing for dramatic effect, "as it just so happens, I do have a little something ..."

Veronica set her mug down, exchanging a knowing glance with Grip. "Oh, do tell, darling," she said, her tone filled with anticipation.

"All right, you two," she began, her tone shifting to business. "Let me give you the rundown on our new targets: Mr. Jay and Penelope. They're a real piece of work, let me tell you." Veronica leaned back in her chair, sipping her coffee as Monroe continued.

"Mr. Jay is a high-ranking executive at one of the world's largest investing firms. Publicly, he's a 'pillar of the community'—philanthropist, devout Christian, staunch advocate for anti-abortion legislation. You know, the usual cover story. But privately, he's one of the key leaders of one of the world's largest racist organizations."

Grip raised an eyebrow, crossing his arms. "Racist? Figures."

"Extremely racist," Monroe confirmed. "To them, anything non-white is a sin. They don't let the public know, of course, but it's no secret in their private circles. They use their influence and money to fund extremist causes worldwide, all while keeping up their squeaky-clean public image. And that's just him."

She paused for a moment before continuing. "Penelope, his wife, isn't any better. The two of them have been inseparable since high school. The perfect couple, according to their autobiography. High school sweethearts, first and only sexual partners, devoted to their faith ... and apparently, their trafficking network." Monroe's voice hardened. "Penelope's role is equally twisted. She's the one who handpicks the victims, personally selecting the girls to be trafficked. She even oversees some of the operations herself. Oh, and for added hypocrisy, they're extreme advocates against abortion. Can't have an innocent life snuffed out, right? Except, you know, when they're abducting and selling girls for profit."

Veronica's lips curled into a smirk. "Classic holier-than-thou scum."

"And here's the kicker," Monroe added. "They don't have kids. Apparently, Mr. Jay was diagnosed as infertile years ago, which he's publicly described as 'God's will.' They've embraced it as part of their religious narrative, though I'm sure it eats at his pride every day."

Grip shook his head. "So, let me guess—they're the type who think they're untouchable?"

"Exactly," Monroe replied. "Their money and influence shield them from everything. They're used to being worshipped by their circle and feared by everyone else. They've worked hard to keep their private activities out of the public eye. But," she said, her voice taking on a sly edge, "I've been digging, and I've got some leads that might pop their perfect little bubble."

Monroe let the weight of her words hang in the air

for a moment. "That's the rundown. These two are as vile as they come." Monroe's voice crackled back over the speakers, breaking the brief silence. "Now, here's the good stuff. I've dug into their schedules, their habits, and their little social circle. These two may think they're untouchable, but they're creatures of habit, and that's where we'll get them."

Veronica leaned forward, resting her chin on her palm. "Go on," she said, a glint of anticipation in her eyes.

"They're scheduled to attend a very exclusive charity gala in two weeks," Monroe explained. "The event is one of their big public appearances every year. It's all about pushing their anti-abortion advocacy while conveniently rubbing elbows with other high-profile figures who share their warped views. It's their way of staying relevant and laundering their reputation."

Grip frowned. "Sounds like tight security, though. How do we get in?"

Monroe chuckled softly. "Oh, it'll be tight, no doubt. Guest lists, private security, and surveillance all over the place. But here's the thing—this gala isn't just a public show. It's also where Mr. Jay likes to network with certain… associates. He uses these events to conduct business, trafficking deals included."

Veronica raised an eyebrow. "And let me guess—Penelope's role is to charm the crowd and distract everyone while he gets down to business?"

"Exactly," Monroe confirmed. "They work as a team. While she schmoozes the donors and plays the saintly philanthropist, he handles the dirty work. And here's where it gets even more interesting—Penelope is obsessed with divine signs and miracles. Apparently, she's convinced that her success in life is due to direct blessings from above. We might be able to use that against her."

Grip smirked. "Religious zealots. They're the easiest to manipulate."

"Bingo," Monroe said. "We can't just crash this gala—it's too well-guarded, and their paranoia is off the charts. But if we play this right, we can convince them to let their guard down. I've already started forging some credentials for you two as potential allies. Wealthy, devout, and just racist enough to blend in with their inner circle."

Veronica wrinkled her nose. "Oh, joy. Pretending to be a bigot. My favorite."

Monroe's voice turned serious. "It's a means to an end. Once we're in, we'll isolate them. Penelope's faith can be exploited with a little theatrics, and Mr. Jay's ego will make him easy to manipulate. We just need the right bait to lure them into a secluded spot."

Grip crossed his arms, leaning back in his chair. "Sounds doable. What's the bait?"

Monroe paused for a moment. "Still working on that part," she admitted. "But I've got a few ideas. These two are so full of themselves, they'll probably walk right into the trap if we push the right buttons. Give me a little more time, and I'll have the details locked down."

Veronica smirked, standing up and stretching. "Well, Monroe, you've outdone yourself. I'm liking this plan already. Let us know when you're ready for the next step."

Monroe's voice came back with a hint of amusement. "Oh, don't worry. I'll let you know. In the meantime, you two might want to brush up on your Bible verses." Monroe's voice crackled one last time before signing off. "All right, I'll keep digging and let you know when I have everything ready. Sit tight, you two. This one's gonna take some finesse."

The speakers went silent, leaving Veronica and Grip alone in the condo. Grip leaned back in his chair, his fingers drumming lightly on the table. "So," he said, glancing over at Veronica, "do we have any clue what we're gonna do in the playpen when we get them there?"

Veronica tilted her head, a slow, chilling grin spreading across her face. "Oh, I already have a plan," she said, her tone dripping with dark amusement.

Grip raised an eyebrow. "This'll be the first lady visitor we've had in the playpen. You think we'll need more staff to handle them both? Two targets might be a lot to manage."

Veronica's grin widened, her eyes gleaming with malice. "Oh, yes," she said slowly. "I think we should hire some… let's say non-white help for the evening. Homeless, desperate, and ready to earn some quick cash. Nothing screams poetic justice like hiring the very people they despise to assist in their downfall."

Grip chuckled, shaking his head. "That's bold. You really think we can pull that off without it blowing back on us?"

Veronica waved a hand dismissively, her confidence radiating. "The public loves me. I'm untouchable. Even if whispers about the playpen ever got out, people would be lining up to shake my hand, not question me. This is just another way to remind myself—and them—that I can do whatever I want."

She leaned back, crossing her legs as she picked up her coffee mug again, sipping it leisurely. "Besides, what better way to drive the point home to those two hypocrites than to make them face the very people they think are beneath them? It's poetic, don't you think?"

Grip nodded slowly, a grin creeping onto his face.

"You're a scary kind of genius, you know that?"

Veronica shrugged nonchalantly. "I prefer 'visionary.'"

The two sat in silence for a moment, the weight of the plan settling between them. It was ambitious, audacious, and perfectly tailored to their twisted sense of justice.

The condo fell silent after their conversation, save for the faint ticking of the kitchen clock. Veronica leaned back in her chair, sipping the last of her coffee, her mind still dancing with the thrill of their plans. Her eyes drifted to Grip, who sat across from her, casually scrolling through his phone.

She watched him for a moment, her gaze softening as a sudden wave of desire coursed through her. The intensity of their life—the power, the danger, and the control they wielded—always seemed to manifest in moments like this, where passion burned brighter than any plan or scheme.

Setting her mug down, Veronica stood and walked around the table, her bare feet soundless on the cool floor. Grip barely noticed her movement until she slid onto his lap, her arms wrapping around his neck. He raised an eyebrow, surprised but intrigued.

"What's this about?" he asked, his voice low, a smirk tugging at his lips.

Veronica didn't answer. Instead, she leaned in, her lips capturing his in a fierce kiss. It was sudden and demanding, her nails digging lightly into the back of his neck as she pressed herself against him.

Grip responded immediately, his hands finding her waist, pulling her closer as their kiss deepened. The chair creaked under their combined weight, but neither cared. Veronica's hands slid up into his hair, tugging slightly, earning a low growl from him that sent a thrill down her spine.

"You're insatiable," he murmured against her lips, his voice thick with desire.

"And you love it," she shot back, her voice breathless and teasing.

In one swift motion, Grip stood, lifting her effortlessly as she wrapped her legs around his waist. He carried her to the living room, their lips never parting, knocking over a chair as he passed. They didn't care about the noise, the mess, or anything but each other in that moment.

He lowered her onto the couch, his hands trailing up her thighs, gripping her hips as he hovered over her. Veronica tugged at his shirt, pulling it over his head and tossing it aside before running her hands over his chest, her nails leaving faint marks on his skin.

"You're mine," she whispered, her voice dripping with both possession and passion.

Grip smirked, leaning down to kiss her neck, his lips trailing down to her collarbone. "Always," he murmured against her skin.

Their movements grew more frantic as they shed the rest of their clothing, their bodies pressing together with an intensity that bordered on desperation. The heat between them was palpable, their breaths mingling as they explored each other with practiced intimacy.

The couch shifted beneath them, its cushions falling askew as their passion escalated. Veronica pushed Grip onto his back, straddling him. Her hands roamed his chest as she leaned down, her hair brushing against his skin, her lips finding his once again.

Time seemed to blur as their movements grew more intense, their surroundings fading into the background.

A lamp toppled over, shattering on the floor, but the sound only seemed to spur them on, adding to the chaotic symphony of their love-making.

Veronica's voice filled the room, her cries of pleasure growing louder as Grip's hands guided her hips. His low, guttural moans matched her intensity, their bodies moving in perfect rhythm.

They shifted positions again, this time knocking over a stack of books on the coffee table. Papers scattered across the floor, a testament to their unrestrained passion. Grip pinned her beneath him, his hands gripping the edge of the couch for leverage as their pace quickened.

The clock on the wall ticked away the minutes, but time felt meaningless. Every touch, every kiss, every movement was a testament to their connection—a raw, unfiltered expression of their shared hunger for control, power, and each other.

As their passion reached its peak, the living room was a mess of overturned furniture, shattered glass, and scattered papers. Veronica clung to Grip, her nails digging into his back as their bodies moved in perfect harmony, the climax of their passion leaving them both breathless and spent.

They collapsed onto the disheveled couch, their chests rising and falling in unison as they caught their breath. Veronica let out a soft laugh, running a hand through her hair as she looked around at the chaos they'd created.

"Guess we'll need to clean up before Monroe starts judging us," she said with a smirk.

Grip chuckled, pulling her close. "Let her judge. She's probably already hacking into the Roomba to help out."

Veronica laughed, her head resting against his chest as they basked in the afterglow, the plans for their next move temporarily forgotten in the warmth of each other's embrace.

CHAPTER 17

THE PLAN

The days passed quietly in the condo, Veronica and Grip moving through the routines of their lives. Between bouts of planning, work, and casual exchanges of texts and banter, the condo had been unusually calm—at least by their standards.

Veronica lounged on the couch, her feet propped up on the coffee table as she scrolled through her phone. Grip sat nearby, sipping coffee and reviewing notes on his tablet. The hum of their shared space was interrupted as the large TV on the wall flickered on, Monroe's face filling the screen.

"Hi, guys," Monroe chirped, her expression smug. "I think I've got it all sorted. Grip, your extraction team is already briefed, but I wanted to go over the details with you both before next week's big event."

Grip leaned back in his chair, setting the tablet aside. "All right, Monroe. Let's hear it."

Monroe nodded, adjusting something off-screen before turning back to them. "Okay, so here's how this is going to play out. The charity gala is being held at an exclusive venue in the city. Think luxury, high security, and a guest list full of elites. Mr. Jay and Penelope will be attending, of course, and this event is one of the only times they'll be in the same place and relatively vulnerable."

Veronica smirked, leaning forward slightly. "Relatively?"

Monroe rolled her eyes. "Fine, they'll still be heavily

guarded, but I've been working on some ways to get you two in undetected. The venue's security is tight—top-tier private contractors and police—but their system isn't flawless. I've hacked into the guest list and added your aliases as honored donors. Congratulations, you're now incredibly wealthy and devout benefactors of the anti-abortion cause."

Veronica laughed, shaking her head. "Wealthy and devout? Oh, this should be fun."

Monroe continued, her tone sharp. "Your cover identities are completely watertight. Grip, you're a successful tech investor with traditional family values, and Veronica, you're a philanthropist and advocate for religious education. I've also planted fake donation records to make you look credible. You'll have to act the part, but I trust you two can handle that."

Grip nodded, a slight smirk on his face. "What about their security detail?"

"That's where things get interesting," Monroe said, her grin widening. "During the event, there's a private prayer session planned for a select group of guests. Penelope will definitely attend—it's her pet project for the evening. Mr. Jay, meanwhile, will likely use the opportunity to conduct some private business deals in a separate room. That's our window to isolate them both."

Veronica raised an eyebrow. "And how exactly do we isolate them without tipping anyone off?"

Monroe's tone turned sly. "Ah, that's where the theatrics come in. Penelope is obsessed with divine signs and miracles, so we're going to give her one. I've got control of the venue's lighting and audio systems. With a little creative timing, we can make her think she's experiencing something … supernatural. That'll make her easy to lure into a private room. As for Mr. Jay, he'll already be distracted by his business dealings, so Grip's team can handle his extraction with minimal fuss."

Grip's eyes narrowed. "And once we've got them both?"

Monroe's expression turned serious. "Once they're both secured, they'll be transported to the playpen. Veronica, that's where you take over. I trust you already have some plans for them?"

Veronica's grin widened, her eyes gleaming with anticipation. "Oh, don't you worry, Monroe. I've got plenty of ideas."

Monroe sighed, leaning back in her chair on the screen. "Great. Just remember, subtlety is key until they're in your hands. I've patched the timeline and all logistical details into your devices. Study up, because this isn't going to be easy."

Grip stood, stretching and cracking his neck. "We don't do easy, Monroe."

"Good," Monroe said, smirking. "Because if this works, it'll be our most rewarding job yet." The screen went dark, leaving Veronica and Grip to process the plan.

#

The day arrived. The culmination of weeks of preparation, forged identities, and meticulous planning was about to be put to the test. Veronica and Grip stood side by side in the condo's entryway, both dressed to perfection.

Veronica's long, emerald-green gown hugged her figure, its shimmering fabric catching the light as she adjusted a delicate diamond necklace around her neck. Her hair was styled in soft waves, cascading over her shoulders, giving her an air of elegance. Grip, in a sharp black tuxedo, adjusted his cufflinks with practiced ease, his expression calm and unreadable.

"Ready to play nice with the elite?" Grip asked, smirking slightly as he looked at Veronica.

Veronica returned his grin. "Oh, I was born for this," she said, her voice dripping with confidence. "Let's show these hypocrites what real power looks like."

As they stepped into the sleek, black car waiting for them outside, the tension between them was palpable. Monroe's voice crackled through the small earpieces they wore, hidden carefully to avoid detection.

"Good evening, Mr. and Mrs. Whitmore," Monroe said smoothly, using their aliases. "Your car is en-route to the gala. Everything's set. You've got about twenty minutes until you arrive. You know the drill—blend in, charm their socks off, and stick to the plan."

Veronica smirked, glancing out the window as the city lights blurred past. "Oh, don't worry, Monroe. I'll be the belle of the ball."

Grip chuckled, shaking his head. "Just remember, subtlety is key until we've got them where we want them."

The car pulled up to the grand venue, a sprawling mansion bathed in warm light, with guests in formal attire streaming up the steps. Security guards flanked the entrance, their expressions stoic as they checked each guest's invitation.

Veronica and Grip stepped out of the car, their movements synchronized as they ascended the marble stairs. A staff member greeted them at the door, scanning their forged invitations with a polite smile.

"Welcome, Mr. and Mrs. Whitmore," the staff member

said, gesturing for them to enter.

The grand foyer was a spectacle of wealth. Crystal chandeliers hung from the high ceilings, casting a warm glow over the marble floors. Guests mingled in small groups, their conversations a symphony of polite laughter and whispered deals.

Veronica's eyes scanned the room, her smile poised and practiced as she caught snippets of conversation. Grip stood at her side, his hand resting lightly on her back as they navigated the crowd.

"Eyes on the prize," Monroe whispered through their earpieces. "Mr. Jay and Penelope are at the far end of the ballroom, by the bar. You've got maybe fifteen minutes before the prayer session starts. Make your introductions."

Veronica's smile sharpened as her gaze locked onto the couple. Penelope was draped in an elegant white gown, her hair pulled into a perfect chignon, radiating the image of a virtuous socialite. Mr. Jay stood beside her, exuding an air of authority in his tailored suit, his expression cool and calculating.

"Let's make a lasting impression," Veronica said under her breath, slipping her arm through Grip's as they made their way toward their targets.

As they approached, Penelope's eyes lit up with the false warmth of practiced charm. "Oh, you must be the Whitmores!" she exclaimed, extending her hand. "I've heard so much about your generous donation. It's wonderful to meet you."

Veronica took her hand, shaking it firmly as she returned the smile. "The pleasure is all ours. We couldn't miss an event like this. It's such an important cause, after all."

Mr. Jay's gaze lingered on Grip, his eyes assessing. "And you, sir, are in the tech industry, I believe? I hear it's a lucrative field."

Grip nodded, his demeanor polite but reserved. "It's been good to us. We believe in using our success to support causes that matter."

As the four of them exchanged pleasantries, Veronica's eyes never left Penelope's, her smile unwavering. The game had begun, and the pieces were in motion.

The quartet stood at the edge of the room, their polite conversation blending seamlessly with the hum of the gala. Veronica's every move was calculated, her charm radiating as she subtly guided Penelope into deeper conversation. Grip, meanwhile, handled Mr. Jay, his responses measured and perfectly tailored to maintain their cover.

"So," Penelope said, her voice soft yet laced with curiosity. "What inspired you both to support tonight's cause so generously?"

Veronica tilted her head, her expression the perfect mix of sincerity and warmth. "We've always felt strongly about protecting the sanctity of life," she said smoothly, her hand resting lightly on Penelope's arm. "It's such a privilege to meet others who are equally passionate."

Penelope's face lit up, and she leaned in slightly, her defenses lowering. "Oh, isn't it refreshing? So few people understand the importance of this mission these days." Veronica smiled inwardly. Hooked.

On the other side, Mr. Jay scrutinized Grip, his tone professional but probing. "And what brought you into the tech world, Mr. Whitmore?"

Grip took a sip of his drink, his movements relaxed. "The same thing that brings anyone to success: hard work and faith. My wife and I believe in applying those principles to everything we do, including supporting events like this."

Jay nodded, a flicker of approval crossing his face. "That's good to hear. We need more people like you in our circle."

Monroe's voice buzzed softly in their earpieces. "Nice work. Penelope is completely distracted. Mr. Jay's interest is piqued. Keep them engaged; the prayer session is about to begin."

As if on cue, a staff member approached, tapping a crystal glass to draw the room's attention. "Ladies and gentlemen," he announced, "if you'll please follow me, we'll be transitioning into the chapel for our private prayer session. This is a special moment for a select few of our esteemed guests."

Penelope turned to Veronica, her hand brushing hers lightly. "Oh, you simply must join us. It's such a spiritually enriching experience."

Veronica exchanged a glance with Grip, her smile widening. "We'd be honored."

The group moved through the venue, escorted to a smaller, ornately decorated chapel tucked away from the main ballroom. The room was dimly lit, with golden candelabras casting flickering shadows on the walls. Rows of velvet seats were arranged in a semicircle around a small altar, where a clergyman stood waiting.

Monroe's voice whispered again. "Penelope's in. Jay's lingering outside, as expected. Grip, you've got your team ready, right?"

Grip adjusted his cufflinks as they took their seats, giving a barely perceptible nod. "Always."

The prayer session began, with Penelope clasping her

hands in front of her, her eyes closed in fervent devotion. Veronica mirrored her posture, playing the part flawlessly, though her mind was racing with anticipation.

Outside the chapel, Mr. Jay lingered near the bar, speaking in hushed tones with two men who looked more like bodyguards than guests. Grip, watching from a distance, casually stepped closer, feigning interest in the decor. He touched his earpiece lightly.

"Monroe, any updates?" Grip muttered under his breath.

"Yep," Monroe replied. "The team's in position. Jay's about to step into his private meeting room. Once he's inside, they'll move."

Grip smirked, grabbing a glass of champagne from a passing server to keep up appearances. He watched as Mr. Jay excused himself, nodding to his bodyguards before heading toward the hallway leading to the private rooms.

"Showtime," Grip whispered.

Back in the chapel, the prayer session was winding down. The clergyman raised his hands, offering a final blessing as the guests murmured their thanks. Penelope stood, smiling beatifically as she turned to Veronica.

"Wasn't that just wonderful?" Penelope asked, her voice practically glowing with self-satisfaction.

"Oh, absolutely," Veronica replied, her tone warm. "I can feel the power of faith radiating through this place. It's truly special."

Penelope placed a hand on Veronica's arm. "Would you like to see something even more special? There's a private prayer room just behind the altar. I go there sometimes to feel closer to God. It's transformative."

Veronica's heart quickened, though her face betrayed

nothing but calm enthusiasm. "I would love that. Lead the way."

As the two women walked toward the private room, Monroe's voice buzzed faintly in Veronica's ear.

"Nice work. She's taking the bait. Keep her distracted while Grip's team does their thing."

Meanwhile, Mr. Jay entered the private meeting room, the door shutting behind him. He glanced around, his sharp eyes scanning the luxurious yet discreet space. A figure stepped out of the shadows, one of Grip's men dressed as a staff member.

"Mr. Jay," the man said smoothly, locking the door behind him. "We need to have a chat."

Jay's brows furrowed, his body tense. "Who the hell are you?"

Before he could react further, two more of Grip's men emerged, quickly subduing him with a well-placed injection. Jay's body went limp, and they moved swiftly to extract him through a service corridor, bypassing the main event.

Back in the prayer room, Penelope was too enraptured by the false "miracle" Monroe orchestrated—flickering lights, soft whispers of ethereal chants echoing through hidden speakers—to notice anything amiss. Veronica played along, gasping softly and clutching Penelope's hands.

"Do you feel it?" Veronica whispered, her voice reverent. "It's like Heaven is speaking to us."

Penelope's eyes welled with tears. "Yes ... yes, it is!"

The moment was perfect. As Penelope closed her eyes in rapture, Veronica slipped a small syringe from her clutch, injecting the sedative into Penelope's arm with practiced precision.

The woman gasped, her knees buckling as Veronica caught her, lowering her gently to the floor.

"Monroe," Veronica said quietly, "she's down. Move your piece."

"Copy that," Monroe replied.

Penelope lay unconscious in Veronica's arms, her delicate features slack and pale from the sedative. Veronica worked quickly, adjusting Penelope's dress to ensure she looked like she'd merely fainted.

The door to the chapel creaked open, and a concerned staff member stepped in, their brow furrowed.

"Is everything all right, Mrs. Whitmore?" the staff member asked, their gaze darting to Penelope.

Veronica looked up, her expression radiating polite concern. "Oh, thank goodness you're here! She fainted during the prayer session. I think it was just too overwhelming for her."

The staff member knelt beside Penelope, their worry evident. "Let me call for medical assistance—"

"No!" Veronica interrupted, her voice firm. She softened her tone, smiling gently. "There's no need to embarrass her like that. Poor thing is so proud; she'd be mortified if this turned into a public spectacle."

The staff member hesitated. "Still, I really think—"

Veronica leaned in slightly, lowering her voice. "Here's what we'll do. Let's take her out through the back way, where no one will see her. It'll spare her any embarrassment. I'll have my husband go alert Mr. Jay to bring a vehicle around back for us."

The staff member's resolve wavered, their loyalty to the event's hosts conflicting with their duty. "All right," they relented. "If you think that's best."

Veronica gave a warm, reassuring smile. "Trust me, it's what she'd want."

With the staff member's help, Veronica carefully carried Penelope toward a discreet side hallway. The staff member led the way, unlocking a door that opened into the service areas of the venue.

"I'll make sure the path is clear," the staff member said, moving ahead.

Veronica touched her earpiece lightly, her voice barely audible. "Grip, I need you to 'alert Mr. Jay.' Head to the service corridor and meet us at the back exit."

Grip's response came quickly. "On my way. Monroe, keep an eye on their security detail."

Monroe's voice chimed in. "Already on it. Security's still focused on the ballroom. You're clear for now, but don't waste time."

Grip moved efficiently, slipping through the main hallway toward the service corridor. He intercepted one of Penelope's bodyguards, feigning urgency. "Mr. Jay's wife fainted. She's being taken out the back way to avoid a scene. Mr. Jay said to have a car brought around back."

The bodyguard nodded and turned toward the ballroom, unaware that Mr. Jay was already unconscious and being transported by Grip's team.

Veronica and the staff member arrived at the back exit, the door opening into the underground loading dock. Grip met them there, his movements calm and purposeful.

"Thank you so much for your help," Veronica said to the staff member, her gratitude genuine enough to sell the act. "We'll take it from here."

The staff member hesitated. "Are you sure? I could—"

"No, no, you've been wonderful," Veronica assured them, her tone final. "We wouldn't want to take up more of your time."

Reluctantly, the staff member nodded and retreated, leaving Veronica and Grip alone. They moved quickly, loading Penelope into the waiting van beside Mr. Jay, who was already secured and unconscious.

Grip tapped his earpiece. "Targets are loaded. What's the status?"

"Security's none the wiser," Monroe replied. "You've got a clean window to leave. I've looped the cameras, so no one will see the van."

Grip smirked, shutting the van's door. "We're clear. Let's move."

To further sell the illusion, Veronica and Grip returned to the gala, blending seamlessly back into the crowd. Veronica's charm and poise kept any lingering suspicions at bay, while Grip casually excused himself to "check on his wife."

After mingling briefly, they made their exit through the main doors, thanking the staff for a lovely evening. Their car pulled away from the venue, leaving no trace of the elaborate extraction that had just taken place.

In the back of the van, Mr. Jay and Penelope lay unconscious, the first step of their reckoning complete.

Veronica leaned back in her seat, a satisfied grin spreading across her face. "Flawless," she murmured, her voice dripping with satisfaction.

Grip glanced at her, his smirk matching hers. "Now the real fun begins."

CHAPTER 18

PENELOPE'S AWAKENING

The heavy door to the playpen swung open as Grip and Veronica stepped inside, the cool air carrying a faint metallic scent. The room was dimly lit, with spotlights trained on the two centerpiece attractions. At the center of the room, a large queen-sized bed dominated the space, its crimson sheets framing Penelope's nude, bound body. Her wrists and ankles were strapped securely to each corner of the bed, leaving her completely exposed under the harsh glow.

Opposite the bed stood the imposing padded X-frame, where Mr. Jay was affixed, equally naked and restrained. His arms and legs were spread wide, leaving him immobilized, his face turned toward his wife, forced to take in every detail of her vulnerable position.

Around the edges of the room stood eight staff members—older, unkempt homeless men, their tattered clothing and weathered faces a stark contrast to the luxurious couple. At Veronica's request, they had been hired for the night, their presence an intentional affront to the Jays' deeply ingrained prejudices. None of the men were white.

As Grip and Veronica stepped further into the room, Monroe's voice crackled through the loudspeakers, her tone dripping with humor.

"Ladies and gentlemen," Monroe began, her voice echoing theatrically, "introducing the stars of tonight's performance! Mr. Jay and Penelope, meet your hosts ...

Mr. and Mrs. Eunuch Collectors!"

Grip and Veronica couldn't help but let out a shared laugh at Monroe's dramatic flair, their voices echoing off the walls. The absurdity of the moment only seemed to heighten their satisfaction as they took in the scene before them.

From the X-frame, a groggy groan broke through the laughter. Mr. Jay's head lolled to one side as he blinked against the harsh light. His mind caught up slowly, piecing together the horrifying reality of his situation.

"W-what … where am I?" he muttered, his voice hoarse. His eyes widened as his gaze locked onto his wife's bound, nude body displayed before him on the bed. Panic set in. "Penelope!"

Veronica smirked, leaning closer to Grip as they observed the unfolding chaos.

Behind him, Mr. Jay heard the sound of approaching footsteps. Turning as much as his restraints allowed, he caught sight of Grip and Veronica, their expressions cool and confident as they stood just behind him.

"What the hell is this?!" he shouted, his voice growing louder as he struggled against his bindings. "Do you have any idea who I am? I'll have the full power of the United States government on your heads! They'll find you, and they'll end this charade!"

Veronica tilted her head, her smile never wavering. "Oh, Mr. Jay," she said, her voice dripping with mock sympathy. "You've got this all wrong. We are the ones in control here."

Grip leaned in closer, his tone laced with menace. "Go ahead. Scream and threaten all you want. No one's coming for you. In fact, the people you think are your allies will be the first to bury your name once we're done."

Mr. Jay's eyes darted around the room, landing on the staff members who stood silently, watching the scene unfold. Their disheveled appearances and silent presence only deepened his confusion and rage.

"What is this?" he spat. "Who are these fucking people?"

Veronica stepped forward, her heels clicking sharply against the floor. She gestured grandly to the staff. "These, Mr. Jay, are the men who'll be helping us tonight. Each of them is here because you don't like their skin color. The people you've spent your life despising will now bear witness to your undoing."

Monroe's voice came back over the speakers, her tone gleeful. "Oh, and let's not forget the main attraction. Penelope! Don't you worry, sweetheart. You're not just here as decoration. You'll be playing a very special role in tonight's festivities."

Veronica chuckled, stepping closer to the bed. "But first," she said, her voice silky and teasing, "let's make sure everyone's awake and ready to play."

Grip walked over to the queen-sized bed, his expression cold and calculated. In his hand, he held a small vial of smelling salts. Penelope lay motionless, her wrists and ankles securely strapped to the corners of the bed. He uncapped the vial, waving it gently under her nose.

It took only seconds before she jolted awake, gasping sharply as her eyes fluttered open. Disoriented, her gaze darted around the room, taking in her surroundings. She froze as the reality of her predicament settled in—the straps binding her wrists and ankles, the cold air against her bare skin, and the eerie, silent stares of the men lining the room.

"What … what is this?" she stammered, her voice

trembling as her head whipped toward the padded X-frame. Her eyes widened in horror as she saw her husband, naked and restrained, facing her. "Jay!"

Mr. Jay groaned, his head tilting forward as he met her gaze, his face etched with humiliation and rage.

Penelope's face contorted in disgust as she scanned the room again, her voice rising. "What the hell is going on? Who are these people?"

Veronica stepped forward, her heels clicking on the floor as she approached the foot of the bed. She leaned down slightly, her eyes gleaming with a sinister glint. "Oh, Penelope," she said sweetly, her voice dripping with mockery. "You're about to find out. Welcome to the show."

Veronica paced the room slowly, her heels clicking against the floor as she approached each of the eight men standing along the walls.

"Thank you for your time," she said, her eyes locking with each man as she leaned in, pressing a firm kiss to their lips before moving to the next. By the time she reached the last man, her lips curled into a wicked smile, her confidence unshaken by the chaos unraveling around her.

With the men now visibly more at ease and focused, Veronica returned to the bed where Penelope was restrained. She turned to face the group, her hands on her hips, exuding an aura of absolute control.

"You all enjoy a little … variety, don't you?" she asked, her voice teasing, though her words carried a sharp edge.

The men exchanged glances, their expressions shifting as they began to piece together her implications. Low chuckles and murmurs filled the room as a few of them shifted uncomfortably, though their interest was evident with the bulges now appearing through their pants.

Veronica grinned. "I imagine you were all curious about why you were given a little … boost earlier." She let the word hang in the air for a moment before continuing, her tone light but with a sinister undertone. "Well, I think it's all starting to make sense now, isn't it?" The room erupted in low laughter, the men exchanging knowing looks as they caught on.

Veronica raised her hands mockingly, as if addressing a crowd. "Now, here's the thing about this couple," she said, gesturing toward the bed and the X-frame where Penelope and Mr. Jay were restrained. "These two have a little issue. You see, not only are they stuck in the 1800s with their ridiculous, outdated racist views, but they've also only ever slept with each other. How … quaint."

Her gaze flicked to Mr. Jay, her smile turning into a sneer as she pointed at him. "And as if that wasn't bad enough, it seems Mr. Jay here isn't exactly equipped for the job." She gestured mockingly toward his exposed body, the head of his dick wasn't even fully exposed from the pubic hair surrounding it, earning a few snickers from the group. "Mr. jay has stated that it was God's will that he wasn't able to produce a baby."

Ignoring the growing protests and threats from the restrained couple, Veronica turned back to the group of men. "So, gentlemen, here's the plan. Tonight, we're going to help these two old-souls by helping them conceive a baby!" She squealed excitedly. "A multi racial gift!"

Mr. Jay screamed threats, his voice hoarse and desperate. Penelope joined in, her cries of outrage echoing through the room as Veronica clapped her hands together, mockingly celebrating her declaration.

"Now," Veronica continued, her tone sharp as she addressed the men, "let's get started, shall we? Each of you, drop them clothes stroke your cocks and come to the bedside. This is going to be a night they'll never forget."

The room descended into chaos, with the men following her instructions as Mr. Jay and Penelope's disgusted protests filled the air.

As the fully naked men surrounded Penelope, the pungent, unwashed smell filled the air, causing her to gag. Taken aback by her reaction, Veronica raised an eyebrow.

"Well, that was rude," Veronica said mockingly, her tone dripping with sarcasm. "Does anyone here feel like helping her adjust to the situation? Maybe she'd like to assist with cleaning someone up a bit."

One of the men stepped forward eagerly, his grin wide. "Oh, I haven't had this kind of treatment in ages," he said, quickly climbing onto the bed.

Penelope gasped, struggling for air as he positioned himself over her face. His grin widened as he leaned closer, clearly enjoying the reaction. He began to grind his asscheeks into her face as she gasped for air. He reached down, pinching her nipple as he snarled "oh yea, lick that dirty asshole!"

Meanwhile, from the X-frame, Mr. Jay screamed obscenities, his voice hoarse and furious. "Get off her, you sick bastard! You'll pay for this!"

The man ignored him and continued to grind into Penelope's face, his hands teasing her chest. Her muffled cries and gasps for air were drowned out by Mr. Jay's furious shouts from the X-frame.

Veronica, observing the scene with detachment, turned to one of the other men. "Would you like to give

Ms. Penelope a taste?" she asked, her tone mocking as she gestured toward the bed.

The man's face lit up with excitement, and in broken English, he eagerly responded, "Yes, yes!" Without hesitation, he climbed onto the bed, positioning himself between Penelope's thighs.

Penelope's muffled protests were futile as the man wasted no time, diving in and devouring her with unrestrained enthusiasm. Her body jolted involuntarily under his touch, her cries muffled beneath the weight of the man perched above her.

From the X-frame, Mr. Jay's voice cracked as he shouted, "My God! What are you doing to my innocent wife?"

Veronica turned to him sharply, her eyes gleaming with malice. "Innocent?" she scoffed, her voice laced with venom. "You two are far from innocent. Your network has destroyed countless lives, but it ends tonight."

Jay's eyes widened as her words sank in. His mind raced, piecing together the events leading up to this moment. His voice trembled as he screamed, "The … the Eunuch Collectors! You're them!"

Veronica smirked, crossing her arms as she stepped closer to him. "Now you're catching on," she said smoothly.

Desperation overtook Jay as he thrashed against his restraints. "Please! I'll give you anything! Money, connections—anything! Just stop this!"

The man riding Penelope's face suddenly turned to Veronica, a twisted grin on his face. "May I clean my dick?" he asked, his voice low and eager.

Veronica smirked, folding her arms and tilting her head. "Sure, have at it," she replied casually.

Without hesitation, the man shifted his position, backing up slightly before shoving his cock deep into Penelope's mouth. Her muffled screams and gasps for air were drowned out by the scene unfolding around her.

Meanwhile, the man between her thighs continued his relentless work. Suddenly, Penelope's body tensed, and with a shudder, she released a powerful, uncontrollable orgasm. The man was momentarily startled as he found himself covered in her juices, but he let out a laugh, clearly unbothered. Penelope's body trembled as she came down from the peak of her forced pleasure, her gasps audible between the invasive thrusts at her mouth.

From his restrained position, Mr. Jay froze, his expression a mix of horror and disbelief. He had just witnessed his wife's body betray her, climaxing under another man's touch. His voice cracked as he screamed, "No! My God, no! Penelope, how could you?"

Veronica glanced over her shoulder at Jay, her smirk widening. "How could she?" she mocked. "Oh, I think she just found out what she's been missing all these years."

Veronica's sharp gaze shifted to Mr. Jay, catching sight of his now-erect, four-inch manhood. She smirked, strolling over to him with an air of mockery.

"Well, well," she said, her voice dripping with amusement. "Talk about body betrayal. Look what we have here."

She reached out, grabbing his tiny cock with her hand, giving it a firm yet teasing stroke. Mr. Jay flinched, struggling against his restraints, but he couldn't move away.

"Looks like you're enjoying the show more than you let on," Veronica continued, her tone taunting. "I bet that filthy little mind of yours has a porn history filled with fantasies of your wife being pleased by real men. Isn't that right, Jay?"

His face turned crimson, his eyes wide with a mix of fury and humiliation. "Get your hands off me, you sick bitch!" he spat, his voice trembling as he strained against the straps holding him in place.

Veronica's grin widened as she leaned in closer, her voice softening to a whisper. "Oh, but your body is telling me something very different, darling. Looks like you've been waiting for this moment your entire life."

Mr. Jay's struggles grew more frantic, but the restraints held firm, leaving him powerless as Veronica continued to mock his vulnerability.

Veronica continued her movements, her grip firm as she maintained eye contact with Mr. Jay. Her smile widened as she noticed the subtle twitch of his body, betraying his efforts to resist.

Across the room, the man currently deepthroating Penelope let out a deep, satisfied moan. His posture stiffened as he reached his peak, his actions leaving no doubt about his conclusion. Penelope, unable to protest, was forced to swallow every drop of the man's seed.

Veronica turned back to Jay, her eyes narrowing in a calculated gaze. "Oh, you liked that, didn't you?" she taunted, her voice dripping with malice. "I could feel it. Your body's not exactly hiding the truth."

Jay squirmed, his face contorted with a mix of shame and anger. "You're insane," he spat through gritted teeth.

Veronica ignored him, her attention shifting momentarily as she addressed the man involved. "All right, let's not waste any more seed, it's against the bible," she said with mock cheerfulness. "After all we're here to help them have a baby, how about you be the first to make your deposit?"

The man nodded eagerly, responding in broken English, "Yes, ma'am. Make baby? Okay, yes, yes." He adjusted his position, leaning in with unrestrained focus.

Penelope's reaction was immediate and visceral, her body jolting slightly as she let out an uncontrollable pleasurable moan of shock and confusion. The man's dick easily penetrated her welcoming cunt. Veronica's smirk deepened as she glanced at Jay. "See? Even she's surprised."

Jay's reaction was predictable—he strained harder against his restraints, his words dissolving into garbled protests. Veronica chuckled, maintaining her air of dominance. "Oh, look at you. Every bit of this is written all over your face. You're enjoying this."

Veronica dropped to her knees in front of Mr. Jay, taking him into her mouth. He squirmed, his face a mix of humiliation and reluctant pleasure as his gaze flickered between Veronica and the dark-skinned man taking his wife before him.

Penelope's cries of protest mingled with uncontrolled moans. The room filled with the chaotic symphony of her conflicting emotions—pleas for it to stop and the involuntary sounds of pleasure that escaped her lips. Suddenly, her body tensed, and another overwhelming wave of pleasure overtook her. She let out a sharp, guttural scream, the sound reverberating through the room.

Veronica continued her calculated movements, but her focus was broken as Mr. Jay, without warning, reached his climax, spilling unexpectedly into her mouth. Startled, Veronica pulled away, standing and spitting the contents onto the floor with a look of disgust.

"A little premature, aren't we?" she said.

The air was thick with tension as Penelope's cries gave way to the soft, involuntary sounds of her body coming down. The man between her thighs grunted, his pace quickening with determination. With one final thrust, he buried himself deep, eliciting another uncontrollable gasp from Penelope as her body responded once more, a shuddering moan escaping her lips.

The man withdrew himself, his figure towering over Penelope's restrained body. His breath was heavy as he passed Veronica, muttering in very broken English, "She tight like virgin," a mocking jab clearly aimed at Mr. Jay's noticeably smaller frame.

Veronica burst into laughter, her voice cutting through the room like a sharp blade. "Well, two down," she said, glancing around at the remaining men. "Six more to go. Who's next?"

Another man eagerly stepped forward, his eyes gleaming with anticipation. He replaced the first, positioning himself between Penelope's trembling thighs. Penelope's body shuddered as she whimpered, her protests drowned out by the audible sounds of her body responding involuntarily.

The process repeated itself, one man after another. Each time, Penelope's body betrayed her further, waves of pleasure rippling through her despite her desperate cries. Her gasps and uncontrollable moans filled the air, mingling with the grunts and laughter of the men. With each encounter, her body convulsed, overcome by yet another forced climax, her face twisting in a mixture of disbelief and shame.

As each man finished, he leaned back, panting and satisfied, leaving Penelope's body trembling and visibly overwhelmed. By the time the fifth man stepped away, her body glistened with sweat, her breathing ragged as she lay utterly spent.

Veronica watched it all with a cruel grin, leaning casually against the side of the bed. "Well, gentlemen," she said mockingly, "you've certainly been thorough." Her eyes turned to the last man, who stood by the bed, awaiting her signal. His figure was imposing, his posture one of eager anticipation as he glanced from Veronica to Penelope.

Veronica walked across the room, her heels clicking softly against the floor as she approached a large jar displayed prominently on a table. Inside, a collection of severed male appendages floated in a clear solution. She tapped the glass lightly with a manicured finger, her expression calm but chilling.

"I collect these," she said, her voice casual as if discussing a hobby. Her eyes flicked to Mr. Jay, narrowing slightly. "And Mr. Jay, although small, will still end up in this jar. But as for you, Penelope…" She turned, locking eyes with the trembling woman on the bed.

"To be honest, I don't want to kill you," Veronica continued, her tone deceptively warm. "We're bringing life into the world tonight with this baby, after all. So, I'm going to make you a deal." Penelope's breathing was shallow as she stared at Veronica, her expression a mixture of fear and exhaustion.

Veronica leaned closer, her grin widening. "You've clearly enjoyed yourself tonight. Don't try to deny it. Your body's been very honest, even if your words haven't been." She gestured toward the man standing beside the bed, his figure imposing and still waiting.

"So, here's your choice. If you want to live and walk

out of here, you're going to show us how much you really enjoyed this. I'm going to untie you, and you're going to take this man before you. First, you're going to please him with your mouth—with enthusiasm." Penelope's eyes widened, her lips trembling as she gasped.

"But that's not all," Veronica continued, her voice cool but firm. "While you do, I want you to look at your husband. Let him see every moment. And then, once you've made him ready, you're going to place him on his back, climb on top, and ride him. And while you do, you'll describe exactly how your body feels."

Veronica stepped back, her arms crossed as she regarded Penelope with a sharp, expectant look. "Do you want to live, Penelope? This is your chance. Or do you prefer to join the others?" She tapped the jar again, its contents glinting in the low light.

Penelope closed her eyes, her body shaking as she caught her breath. When she opened them again, her voice was barely a whisper. "Please … I'll do it. I don't want to die."

Veronica's grin returned as she walked slowly back toward the bed.

"Good," she said softly. "Then let's begin."

Veronica leaned over Penelope, unfastening the restraints that bound her wrists and ankles. As each strap came loose, Penelope's limbs trembled, the freedom of movement bringing no relief.

"Up," Veronica commanded sharply, stepping back to give her space.

Penelope sat up slowly, her hands clutching the bed sheets as she glanced nervously at the man standing beside her. He loomed over her, his presence intimidating.

Veronica's tone softened, though it remained laced

with malice. "Go on, Penelope. You said you didn't want to die. Prove it."

Penelope swallowed hard, her face flushed with a mix of shame and fear. Slowly, she crawled toward the edge of the bed, her gaze flicking briefly to her husband. Mr. Jay's face was a mask of anger and humiliation, his fists clenching uselessly against the restraints.

"Don't look at me, Penelope!" he spat, his voice shaking. "You don't have to do this!"

Veronica chuckled, stepping closer to him. "Oh, Jay," she said mockingly, her voice dripping with sarcasm. "Always so protective. But don't forget, this is as much your doing as hers. You built this world you're now trapped in."

Penelope turned her gaze back to the man beside the bed, her body trembling as she hesitantly reached out. The man's grin widened, his confidence growing as she leaned closer. She closed her eyes tightly, as though shutting out the world, and began to do as Veronica instructed. She opened her mouth and slid the man's cock into it. She eagerly licked and sucked on his dick while looking directly at Mr. Jay. Noises of slurping and suction filled the air as her hands followed suit and started to massage the man's balls.

"Good girl," Veronica purred, watching with satisfaction as Penelope carried out her task. She turned her attention back to Mr. Jay, smirking at his visible discomfort. "See, Jay? She's a quick learner. Maybe she'll even discover something about herself tonight."

Jay thrashed against his restraints, his voice cracking as he shouted, "You're sick! All of you! This isn't justice. It's insanity!"

Veronica tilted her head, her smirk deepening. "Justice

and insanity aren't mutually exclusive, Jay. Sometimes, they're one and the same."

As the man groaned audibly, Veronica snapped her fingers sharply. "That's enough. On to the next part, Penelope."

Penelope froze, her body stiffening as Veronica's words sunk in. With trembling hands, she adjusted her position, turning to face the man as he lay back on the bed. Her face was a mask of anguish, but she obeyed, climbing on top of him as instructed, sliding his dick into her awaiting hole.

"Don't forget to describe how it feels," Veronica reminded her.

Penelope's voice was barely audible, her words halting and broken as she forced herself to speak. "It ... it feels strange," she stammered, her tears streaming down her face. "I-I don't know what to say ..."

"Then try harder," Veronica snapped, her tone suddenly sharp. "Because this is the only way you're walking out of here alive."

Penelope choked back a sob, forcing herself to continue as the man beneath her moved with increasing intensity. "It feels good, his dick feels so good. It's so deep inside me I can feel him pushing against my cervix!"

"More!" spouted Veronica.

"I like it, he's fucking me better than I've ever been fucked before, I've never felt this much pleasure. My pussy feels so full like he's taking up every inch inside of me." Every word she uttered was a mix of shame and despair, but Veronica's cold gaze never wavered.

"I love it, fuck me please!" she said, as the man began to quickly thrust into her. "YES! YES! YES! I'M ... CUMMING!"

She fell limp onto the man's chest and he flipped her over. Her face went from pleasure to shock as the man mounted her ass and pushed his cock against her anus.

"NO, FUCK! NOT THERE" she screamed, but the man ignored her and, with a powerful thrust entered her ass.

He vigorously destroyed her ass and she began to moan with surprising pleasure.

"Oh we like that, don't we? Does it feel good?"

"Yes, it really does," Penelope said as the man slammed into her ass. The man's pace quickened, and as Penelope cried, "Pease cum in me," he gave a final thrust and ended his onslaught on her virgin hole.

From the X-frame, Mr. Jay cried with anguish. "Stop this! She's my wife! Just stop!"

Veronica turned to him with a look of icy satisfaction. "Oh, Jay," she said softly, her voice carrying the weight of finality. "We're just getting started."

CHAPTER 19

MR. JAY'S END

As Penelope's freshly used body lay trembling, struggling to catch her breath, Veronica stepped forward with a cold smile. "Very good," she said mockingly, her tone condescending. "You've been such a good girl tonight, Penelope. I expect you're well-seeded by now."

Penelope whimpered softly, her eyes filled with exhaustion and humiliation. Veronica tilted her head, her smile widening. "Now, kiss your husband goodbye and go wait with the staff."

Penelope hesitated but obeyed, leaning toward Mr. Jay, her lips trembling as she pressed a soft kiss to his cheek. His face contorted in disgust and despair, but he remained silent, his tears doing the talking.

"Go on," Veronica said, dismissing her with a wave of her hand. Penelope climbed off the bed, unsteady on her feet, and followed the staff out of the room, leaving Mr. Jay alone with Veronica and Grip. The men, now finished with their task, were also quietly escorted upstairs, awaiting further instruction.

The door clicked shut, and the room fell into an eerie silence. Veronica turned back to Mr. Jay, her heels clicking ominously against the floor. Her eyes gleamed with malice as she leaned in close.

"Well," she said, her voice dripping with venom, "How does it feel to watch your wife become a multi-racial, bred cum slut right in front of you? To see her used in ways you could never dream of? And to learn that she actually enjoys being taken—especially from behind?"

Mr. Jay let out a ragged sob, his face contorted with anguish. "You've ruined everything," he choked out, his voice shaking. "I ... I can't have her as a wife anymore. She's destroyed."

Veronica threw her head back with a cruel laugh, her voice echoing off the walls. "Oh, don't worry, Jay," she said, her tone turning icy. "You're not leaving this room, so her future isn't much of a concern to you."

She turned toward a wall displaying a variety of tools and implements, each carefully arranged and gleaming under the soft light. Her fingers danced over the options before settling on a familiar favorite: a metal-tipped flogger, polished and menacing.

Veronica held it up, the leather straps swaying as she turned back to Jay, her grin widening. "Now," she said, her voice cold and deliberate, "it's time to really get started."

Without warning, she swung the flogger, the metal tips striking his chest in a sharp X motion. Mr. Jay cried out, his body jerking against the restraints. Veronica stepped back, examining the red marks forming on his skin with satisfaction.

She struck again, this time across his thighs, then his stomach, each swing precise and merciless. Jay's screams filled the room as Veronica moved methodically, her expression calm and focused.

"Every stripe," she said between swings, her voice steady, "is a reminder. A reminder of the lives you've ruined. Of the pain you've caused. And of just how powerless you really are."

Grip leaned against the wall, arms crossed, watching the scene unfold with a quiet intensity. "You've really perfected this," he muttered, half to himself.

Veronica smirked, not breaking her rhythm. "Practice makes perfect, darling."

Veronica continued to thrash Mr. Jay, each calculated strike of the flogger drawing a cry of pain from him. He squirmed against the restraints, cursing and shouting through clenched teeth, but his words held no power. Veronica took her time, ensuring every stroke landed with precision, each blow leaving angry red welts across his exposed skin.

Satisfied for the moment, she walked over to the counter, her movements calm and deliberate. She picked up a spray bottle of rubbing alcohol, turning back to him with a cold smile.

She aimed the bottle and sprayed a generous amount over his wounds. The liquid soaked into the open scratches, and Mr. Jay screamed, his body writhing in agony as the alcohol burned.

"Please!" he begged, his voice cracking under the weight of his pain. "You can just let me go! We can forget all of this happened. I'll have Penelope killed—no one will ever know what you did here."

Veronica tilted her head, her expression darkening. "So quick to throw your wife away, huh?" she said coldly, her voice sharp enough to cut. "You really are a disgusting little man."

She turned back to the wall of tools, scanning the collection until her eyes landed on something particularly sinister—a medical contraption resembling a vaginal speculum, designed to spread and hold tissue apart. She picked it up, turning it over in her hands as she inspected its mechanics.

"Well, Mr. Jay," she said with a smirk, holding up the

device for him to see. "Since you're so eager to offer up your wife, I think it's only fair we have a look inside you for a change."

Jay's eyes widened in horror, and he shook his head violently. "No, no, you can't! Don't you dare!"

Veronica ignored him, her focus now on Grip. "Grip, if you would, please. Untie him—but make sure he knows why it's in his best interest to behave."

Grip stepped forward, his movements steady and purposeful. With one hand, he drew his pistol, letting the weight of the cold steel speak for itself as he pressed it against the back of Mr. Jay's head. His other hand quickly unfastened the restraints, leaving Jay free but trembling.

"Now," Veronica said, her voice firm and commanding, "bend over the bed—the same one your wife enjoyed so much."

Jay hesitated, his body stiffening as fear overtook him. Grip cocked the pistol, the sharp click cutting through the air like a warning bell. Reluctantly, Jay shuffled forward, his head bowed in defeat as he bent over the edge of the bed.

Veronica stepped closer, the speculum gleaming in her hand. "Spread 'em," she ordered, her tone cold and unyielding.

Jay let out a shuddering breath as he reached back with trembling hands, pulling himself apart as instructed. Veronica didn't hesitate. She positioned the device and inserted it with deliberate carelessness, a smirk playing on her lips as Jay cried out in pain and humiliation.

"That's a good boy," she taunted, turning the handle to widen the device. "Let's see what you've been hiding all this time."

Mr. Jay groaned in pain, his fingers gripping the edge of the bed tightly as Veronica twisted the handle of the speculum, forcing it to spread wider. His breathing grew ragged, the discomfort etched across his face.

"Aw, don't be shy," Veronica mocked, tilting her head as she peered over his trembling body. "We're just having a little look. After all, isn't transparency important in all relationships?" Her smirk deepened, and she gave the speculum another turn.

Mr. Jay let out a guttural cry, his body instinctively jerking forward. Grip stepped closer, pressing the barrel of the pistol lightly against his back to remind him of his precarious position. "Stay still," Grip said simply, his tone void of emotion.

Veronica took her time, inspecting her handiwork as she leaned down. "Well, Mr. Jay," she began, her voice calm but dripping with malice, "it seems you've been hiding a lot more than your sins, haven't you? Not so tough now, are you?" She clicked her tongue mockingly.

Jay, his face buried in the bed's fabric, muttered through gritted teeth, "You'll burn in hell for this... You're monsters."

Veronica straightened, letting out a soft laugh as she loosened the handle, withdrawing the device with deliberate slowness. "Oh, I don't doubt I've earned a place in hell," she said casually, tossing the speculum onto the table with a clatter. "But I think we can agree, you'll be there long before me."

Stepping back, she exchanged a glance with Grip, her eyes gleaming with dark satisfaction. "I think he's ready for the final act," she said with a smirk. "Don't you?"

Grip nodded, holstering his weapon. "He's all yours."

Veronica turned her attention back to Mr. Jay, her expression calm but menacing. "Now, Mr. Jay," she said slowly, "we've been through so much together tonight. But it's time we give you a choice."

Jay lifted his head slightly, his face slick with sweat and his expression wary. "Choice?" he muttered, his voice weak.

Veronica leaned in close, her eyes locking with his. "That's right. I'll let you decide how this ends. You can cooperate with what I'm about to ask, and I'll let you leave here alive—well, mostly." She gestured toward the jar of severed appendages on the table. "Or you can resist and lose a lot more than your pride."

Jay's body stiffened, his breathing shaky. "What... what do you want?" he whispered.

Veronica's smile widened as she leaned back, folding her arms. "Oh, don't worry. I think you'll find it... poetic." She gestured to the tools behind her, and Grip stepped forward, ready to assist.

Veronica's smirk deepened as she stepped back, beginning to unbutton her blouse with deliberate slowness. "I want you to make me cum," she said, her voice calm but carrying an undeniable edge.

Mr. Jay froze, his body trembling as he processed her words.

She continued undressing behind him, letting her clothes fall to the floor one piece at a time. Once fully naked, Veronica climbed onto the bed, positioning herself on all fours, her body poised in a provocative display. She shook her hips slightly, teasing, her backside mere inches from his face.

The speculum still hung awkwardly from Jay's exposed body. He reached back instinctively to remove it, grimacing from the discomfort.

"Leave it," Veronica snapped sharply, turning her head to glare at him. Her expression was cold and commanding. "You don't get to do anything I haven't instructed."

Jay hesitated, his hand dropping to his side, his face a mix of humiliation and desperation.

"You have ten minutes," she said firmly, her voice icy and unwavering. "If you don't make me cum, you die. So I'd suggest you fuck like your life depends on it—because it does."

The room fell into an oppressive silence, broken only by the faint sounds of Veronica's slow, steady breaths as she arched her back, presenting herself fully.

Jay swallowed hard, his trembling hands reaching out hesitantly. "Please," he whispered weakly, "don't make me do this..."

Veronica turned her head slightly, her eyes narrowing as she shot him a sharp look. "Clock's ticking, Jay."

Jay moved hesitantly at first, positioning himself awkwardly behind Veronica. His trembling hands gripped her hips, and he attempted to enter her with his four-inch manhood. His movements were frantic, his pace erratic as he thrust desperately, knowing his life depended on the results.

Veronica let out an exaggerated sigh, her face blank with disinterest. She barely felt him, his size and clumsy movements doing little more than irritating her. Turning her head slightly, she smirked.

"Is that really the best you can do?" she teased, her voice playful but biting. "No wonder Penelope needed real men to satisfy her. You're barely inside me, Jay. I've had more satisfying itches."

Jay gritted his teeth, his pace becoming more frantic as sweat dripped down his face. He was visibly panicked, his movements becoming desperate as the seconds ticked away.

Veronica chuckled softly, her mocking laughter cutting through the tension in the room. "Oh, Jay," she said, reaching over to the edge of the bed, "let me show you what a real man looks like."

She grabbed Grip by the waistband of his pants and pulled him closer, unzipping him with practiced ease. His thick, throbbing cock sprang free, and Veronica's eyes gleamed with excitement.

"See this, Jay?" she taunted, wrapping her hand around Grip's length and stroking it slowly. "This is a real man's dick. Something you'll never be."

Jay's face contorted with humiliation, his thrusts faltering as his confidence crumbled.

Without hesitation, Veronica leaned forward and took Grip into her mouth, her lips moving expertly as she pleased him. Her moans of pleasure were deliberate, loud enough to emphasize the contrast between what she was doing and Jay's pitiful attempts.

Grip stood tall, his gun trained on Jay, unwavering. His expression was cold, his focus unshaken as he let Veronica continue.

Jay, now visibly shaking, stopped mid-thrust, his desperation giving way to despair. "Please …" he muttered weakly, his voice cracking.

Veronica pulled away from Grip, glancing back at Jay with a smirk. "Clock's ticking, Jay," she said coldly, before returning her attention to Grip, taking him even deeper into her mouth as she ignored Jay's pathetic efforts.

Veronica suddenly felt Jay's body tense behind her. Before she could mock him further, she felt the warm release of his climax—a surprisingly large amount, given his size.

"Really?" she sneered, pulling away from him as she flipped onto her back, reclining casually on the bed. His seed dripped from her slickened entrance, pooling onto the sheets as she eyed him with mock disgust. "You can't even last more than a few minutes. Pathetic."

She didn't let the moment linger long. Reaching for Grip's cock again, she took him eagerly into her mouth, her lips working rhythmically as she moaned softly, making a show of her pleasure. Between pauses to catch her breath, she spoke, her voice sharp and commanding.

"Use your mouth, Jay," she ordered, locking eyes with him. "You're running out of time. Do something useful for once."

Jay hesitated, trembling as he stood frozen in place.

"Now!" Veronica snapped, her tone icy.

Reluctantly, Jay fell to his knees, positioning himself between her thighs. His face flushed with humiliation as he leaned forward, his lips trembling as they met her skin.

He began, tentatively at first, his tongue flicking awkwardly as he licked up the remnants of his own release. Veronica groaned theatrically, her eyes rolling back as if to taunt him further.

"Not bad for a start," she said mockingly, her hand still stroking Grip's length while she sucked on him intermittently. "But if you want to live, Jay, you'd better make me believe you want this. Pleasing me isn't optional."

Jay's efforts grew more desperate, his tongue moving faster, trying to appease her. The room filled with the obscene sounds of his labor and her exaggerated moans, amplifying his humiliation further.

Grip stood silently above them, his gaze cold and detached, the pistol in his hand still trained on Jay.

"Better," Veronica mused, leaning her head back with a grin, savoring the power she held over him.

"But let's see if you can actually finish what you started, little man."

Veronica's body tensed, her moans muffled as she continued to please Grip, her lips wrapped around his massive, throbbing cock. The combination of his stimulation and Mr. Jay's frantic efforts finally sent her over the edge. With a sharp gasp, her body convulsed, releasing a wave of ecstasy that left her trembling.

She let out a loud, satisfied groan as her juices erupted, drenching Mr. Jay's face in a relentless torrent. He coughed and sputtered as her release overwhelmed him. Veronica leaned back, grinning as she looked down at him with a mixture of amusement and disdain.

"Well, I guess that tongue of yours isn't just for lies," she taunted, wiping a bead of sweat from her brow. "You did okay, I suppose."

Jay sat back on his knees, his face wet and flushed, desperation still etched across his features.

"So," he croaked, his voice trembling, "I get to live? You're not going to kill me?"

Veronica tilted her head, her smirk widening. "Well," she said slowly, her tone dripping with malice, "you do have one more task."

Her finger pointed toward the jar of severed appendages on the table, its grotesque contents glinting under the dim light. "You have a debt that needs to be paid," she said coolly, her eyes narrowing. Jay froze, his body trembling as she continued, "You're going to walk over there, pick whatever tool you like, and come back here." She paused, her voice turning icy and deliberate. "Then, you're going to cut off your own dick. Right in front of me. While I suck Grip's real dick."

Jay's face went pale, his lips quivering as he stammered, "You … you can't be serious…"

Veronica's smirk deepened as she leaned forward, her gaze locking on his. "Oh, I'm completely serious, Jay. You want to live, don't you? Then pay the price."

She turned her attention back to Grip, her lips parting as she took him into her mouth once more, her actions slow and deliberate. Her moans of pleasure filled the room, adding to the suffocating tension.

Jay sat frozen for a moment, his mind racing. He glanced toward the tools, his breaths shallow and erratic.

"Tick-tock, Jay," she murmured between movements, her voice teasing and cruel. "You don't have all night."

Jay shuffled toward the table of tools, his steps hesitant and shaky. His eyes darted over the horrifying array of implements before settling on a pair of large pruning shears. He picked them up with trembling hands. Turning back toward Veronica, he saw her still locked in position, her lips working expertly over Grip's cock. Her eyes, however, never left him—cold, unyielding, and full of cruel anticipation.

He swallowed hard as he returned to the center of the room, holding the shears with both hands. His breathing was ragged, his body visibly trembling as he stammered, "I-I can't… Please, don't make me do this…"

He raised the shears, positioning them around his tiny manhood, but his hands froze. Pulling back, he let out a desperate sob. "Fuck! God damn it, fuck!" he screamed, pacing in a small circle, trying to summon the courage.

Again, he raised the shears, his face contorted with fear and anguish.

Veronica, still pleasuring Grip, finally released him with an audible pop, her expression bored and impatient. "Do it," she commanded coldly, her voice devoid of empathy. "Or die. Your choice."

Jay screamed in frustration, his face red and tear-streaked. With a guttural cry, he grit his teeth and tightened the shears, enclosing his entire four-inch manhood and his testicles in their sharp grasp. With one final scream, he squeezed the handles together. The sickening snip echoed through the room, followed by Jay's agonized howl.

He stumbled backward, his hands instinctively clutching at the bloody mess between his legs. Blood poured down his thighs, pooling on the floor as he staggered before collapsing to his knees. His face was pale, his breaths shallow, and his entire body trembled uncontrollably.

Veronica stood up, wiping her lips as she looked down at him with a twisted grin. "Now," she said, her voice calm and mocking, "pick it up. Use your mouth and hand it to me."

Jay stared at her, his eyes wide with disbelief. "W-what...?" he stammered, barely able to form words through the haze of pain.

"You heard me," Veronica said. "Pick it up with your mouth and bring it to me. Show me how much you want to survive."

Shaking and barely able to move, Jay leaned over, his face inches from the bloodied floor. He gagged as he opened his mouth, struggling to pick up the severed flesh. The metallic taste and texture made him retch, but he forced himself through it, lifting his dismembered manhood with trembling lips.

He crawled on his hands and knees, the pain nearly overwhelming him as he presented the severed piece to Veronica, dropping it into her outstretched hand.

Veronica looked down at him, her grin widening. "Good boy," she said mockingly, holding the grotesque prize aloft. "See? That wasn't so hard, was it?"

As Veronica continued working on Grip's cock with her skilled lips and tongue, she suddenly felt him tense. With a deep grunt, he released, a powerful shot of seed splashing across the bed and her bare, perfect breasts. She paused, glancing down in mock surprise.

"Oh," she said with a playful pout, running her fingers over the warm mess, "I missed! I wanted that reward." She sighed dramatically, shrugging. "Oh well."

Turning her attention back to Mr. Jay, she smirked. "Now, be a good little pet and clean me up," she commanded, gesturing to her chest.

Jay, face pale and body trembling from blood loss, hesitated for a moment before reluctantly leaning forward. His lips touched her skin as he began licking the remnants of Grip's release from her breasts. Each movement was slow and labored, his body visibly weakening with every passing second as blood pooled beneath him.

Once he finished, Veronica tilted her head, examining him with a cold smile. "Well," she said casually, turning to Grip, "I think we've covered everything…" She paused, her smirk turning into a wicked grin. "Oh wait—nope! There's one last thing."

Veronica snatched Grip's gun from his hand, pressed it to Jay's temple, and pulled the trigger. The deafening shot rang out, and Jay's body went limp, collapsing onto her. Blood spattered her skin and the bed as his lifeless form slumped forward.

"Ugh," Veronica muttered, shoving him off of her with disdain. She stood up, brushing herself off as if nothing had happened. Turning to Grip, she placed a hand on his cheek, pulling him into a deep, passionate kiss. "You should've told me guns were this much fun," she said with a sly grin, handing the weapon back to him.

Walking over to the wall, she pressed a button to summon the staff. The team entered, their expressions stoic and professional. Veronica gestured to the mess with a wave of her hand.

"Clean everything up, as usual," she instructed. "Take his little dick and drop it in the collection jar. Then take his body back to the gala and display it with all the evidence tying him and Penelope as the heads of the trafficking ring. Make it clear to anyone who sees it what they've been up to."

She paused, turning back to the staff with a devilish glint in her eye. "Oh, and cuff Penelope near his body. She won't say a word now that she's had a taste of what living really feels like."

The staff nodded, efficiently beginning their cleanup. Veronica turned to Grip, her smile softening just slightly as she brushed a stray lock of hair from her face.

"Well, love," she said, her tone thoughtful, "we've ended this trafficking ring and saved countless lives. I wonder what's next for us?"

Grip chuckled, placing an arm around her as they exited the playpen together.

CHAPTER 20

EUNUCH COLLECTORS

The shrill, piercing wail of the fire alarm jolted Veronica awake. She shot up in bed, disoriented and confused to see Grip already reaching for his pants. The sound was deafening, and just as she was about to question what was happening. Monroe's voice cut through the chaos over the condo's speaker system.

"Guys, you've got company headed your way," Monroe said urgently. "I tried to reach you sooner, but it's too late—they've got the condo covered. Looks like Penelope identified you two. The FBI is swarming the building. They're coming."

Grip froze for half a second before springing into action. "Damn it," he muttered under his breath, throwing on a shirt as he moved. "Monroe, is it time for Operation Xavier?"

"Yes," Monroe confirmed, her voice tense. "Get moving. I'll see you both when it's over. Good luck."

The fire alarm abruptly silenced, leaving an eerie stillness in its wake. Veronica turned to Grip, her expression a mixture of fear and confusion.

"Operation Xavier? What's going on?" she asked, her voice trembling.

Grip finished strapping a watch onto his wrist and turned to her, his expression calm but serious. "I knew this was a possibility, doll. What we've been doing ... it was always risky. I wanted to make sure we had a plan in place, just in case."

She blinked, processing his words. "So … what now? What do we do?"

Grip stepped closer, gently cupping her face in his hands, his gaze steady and reassuring. "The police are already on their way up. I wish I had more time to explain everything, but we don't. Listen to me carefully—just go with them. Don't talk. Don't say anything. They'll separate us, but don't worry. Everything is under control."

Veronica's breathing slowed as she stared into his eyes. "You promise?"

Grip leaned in, pressing a soft, lingering kiss to her lips. "You trust me, don't you?"

She nodded, her resolve hardening as she took a deep breath. "I trust you."

The soft chime of the elevator bell echoed through the condo, snapping them both back to the moment. The doors slid open, and within seconds, eight armed SWAT officers swarmed the room, their weapons drawn and voices shouting commands.

"On the ground! Hands where we can see them!"

Grip and Veronica complied without resistance, moving to their knees as the SWAT officers secured them in handcuffs. The room buzzed with tension, and as the agents pulled them to their feet, Grip turned his head slightly, catching Veronica's eye one last time.

"Remember," he said softly, his voice steady despite the chaos. "Don't say a word."

Veronica nodded as the officers led them toward the elevator, her heart pounding as she clung to Grip's final reassurance.

Veronica sat calmly in the back of the mobile police transport, her wrists cuffed tightly in front of her. The vehicle hummed steadily along the highway, but the silence was broken by the crackle of the radio coming through the speakers.

"We come to you tonight with a shocking development," the announcer began, their voice tinged with disbelief. "According to police, a raid on a remote house on the outskirts of Houston has uncovered a grisly scene—a room filled with torture tools and, most disturbingly, a jar filled with severed male genitalia. Authorities have confirmed the arrest of two suspects, Grip and Veronica Williams, the alleged perpetrators behind the infamous crimes of the Eunuch Collector. Shocking as it is, police say the Eunuch Collector wasn't a single individual—it was a couple all along."

A grin slowly spread across Veronica's face as she turned her gaze to the young police officer sitting across from her, his expression tense and uneasy. Catching his nervous glance, she puckered her lips and blew him a playful kiss.

The officer, clearly inexperienced and rattled, shifted uncomfortably in his seat, his face flushing as his hand subconsciously adjusted the front of his pants.

Veronica chuckled softly, her voice smooth and taunting. "Oh, come on, big boy," she purred, leaning forward as far as her restraints would allow. "Why don't you let me out? I'll make sure you never forget me ..."

The officer's face turned crimson, his lips parting as if to respond, but before he could, the transport came to an abrupt, jarring halt, throwing Veronica forward slightly, her grin vanishing as her head whipped toward the front of the van.

"What the hell—" the officer started, but his words were drowned out by the unmistakable sound of gunfire.

A hail of bullets peppered the exterior of the vehicle,

and then—BANG—a canister smashed through the side window, releasing a thick, choking cloud of smoke. The acrid burn of OC gas quickly filled the cabin. Veronica coughed uncontrollably as her eyes watered, blinding her.

The young officer gasped, his hands clutching his face as he fell unconscious, his body slumping forward onto the floor. Veronica's breaths came in short, shallow bursts as she struggled against the effects of the gas, her vision swimming as the world tilted.

Just as she felt herself slipping into unconsciousness, a cool rush of air hit her face. A gas mask was placed securely over her nose and mouth, and strong hands grabbed her arms, pulling her roughly out of the back of the van.

Disoriented but regaining clarity with each clean breath, Veronica's blurry vision focused on the dark, masked figure dragging her to safety. The sounds of chaos surrounded her—shouting voices, more gunfire, and the screech of tires—but the figure remained calm and efficient, moving her quickly out of harm's way.

"What—who—" Veronica started, her voice muffled by the mask, but the figure didn't respond. Instead, they shoved her into another vehicle waiting nearby, slamming the door shut behind her as the tires screeched and the vehicle sped away.

Veronica found herself in the back of a sleek black Suburban, surrounded by masked men dressed in tactical gear. The vehicle sped through the dark streets, the low hum of the engine the only sound for a moment. Looking around, she steadied her breathing and asked, "Operation Xavier?"

One of the men, who seemed to be in charge, nodded.

She exhaled deeply, allowing herself to relax into the seat. The tension in her shoulders eased as she realized she was safe, for now.

After a beat, she glanced at the leader. "I didn't want any innocent people to die," she said, her voice firm but laced with concern.

The leader turned his masked face toward her. "Our orders were clear: shock and awe, non-lethal only," he said in a measured tone. "The gunfire was a distraction. We apprehended the driver and the escort without resistance. Your guard was dragged out of the van and left in fresh air to recover. No one was harmed—well, except for their egos."

Veronica nodded. "Good," she said softly.

The Suburban descended into an underground parking garage, the headlights cutting through the dimly lit space. The team moved fluidly, transitioning Veronica into a more inconspicuous car—an unassuming sedan already waiting for them. They helped her into the back seat, ensuring everything was in order before stepping away.

One of the men leaned in through the open door. "A change of clothes and a wig are in the bag behind your seat," he said. "Safe travels."

Without hesitation, Veronica opened the bag and began changing into the new outfit. She discarded her old clothes without care, briefly exposing her naked body in the dim light. The driver, a quiet professional, kept his eyes on the road, pretending not to notice as the car started moving.

As they drove for some time, the silence was broken only by the hum of the engine. Eventually, they pulled up to a back gate at a private airport. Two men, dressed similarly to the team from earlier, unlocked the gate and swung it open. The car drove straight through, pulling right up to a waiting private jet.

Veronica stepped out of the car, smoothing the hem of her dress as the driver closed the door behind her. The jet's door opened with a mechanical hiss, and the stairs descended smoothly. From the entrance of the plane, a familiar figure emerged—Mistress Blue.

"Your chariot awaits," Mistress Blue said, a sly grin spreading across her lips as she descended the stairs.

As she reached Veronica, she grabbed her by the waist, pulling her into a long, slow, passionate kiss. Veronica melted into the moment, their lips lingering as if savoring every second.

When they finally broke apart, Mistress Blue ran a thumb over Veronica's cheek and whispered, "Not much time. Safe travels."

With that, Mistress Blue turned and climbed into the car Veronica had just left. The vehicle pulled away smoothly, leaving Veronica standing at the base of the jet's stairs.

She ascended quickly, stepping into the luxurious cabin. Her gaze immediately fell on Grip, sitting comfortably with a bottle of champagne and two glasses on the table before him. His grin widened as she entered, and he popped the cork with a flourish.

"Well, aren't you full of surprises?" Veronica said, taking the glass he handed her and settling into the plush seat across from him.

Grip leaned back. "You didn't think I'd leave us without a backup plan, did you?"

She raised her glass in a mock toast. "Where are we

headed?"

Grip sipped his champagne, his eyes sparkling with mischief. "I have a place in mind," he said, his voice smooth. "Somewhere we can either settle down and live out our days quietly…" He trailed off, a devilish smirk spreading across his face. "Or," he added, leaning forward, "we wait and find a new direction."

Veronica clinked her glass against his, a slow smile spreading across her lips. "A new direction, huh?" she mused. "Well, let's see where the wind takes us."

As the jet engines roared to life, the two leaned back in their seats, champagne in hand, ready for whatever came next.

Liked this book?
Please leave a review!

*Reviews are important to authors and publishers.
Please take a moment to leave a review on Amazon and/or Goodreads.*

They help authors sell more books.

*20-25 reviews and Amazon includes the book in the "Also Bought" and "You Might Like" lists.
50-70 reviews and Amazon highlights the book in spotlight positions and in its newsletter.*

Thank you!

www.ingramcontent.com/pod-product-compliance
Ingram Content Group UK Ltd.
Pitfield, Milton Keynes, MK11 3LW, UK
UKHW020737200325
456518UK00005B/234

9 798992 117233